AN *ORANGE* FROM PORTUGAL

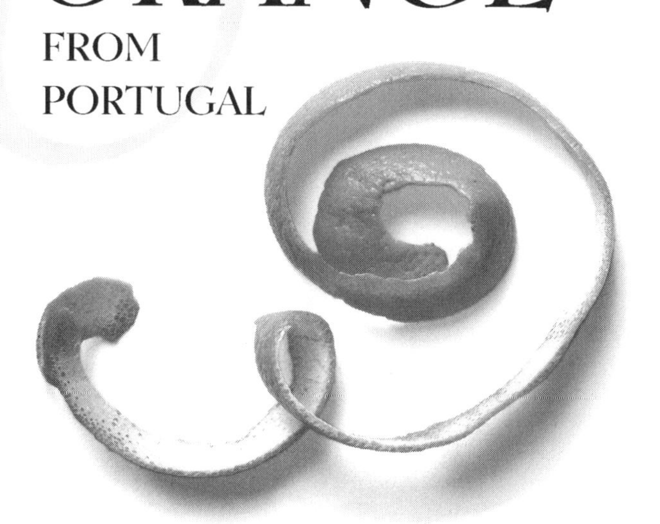

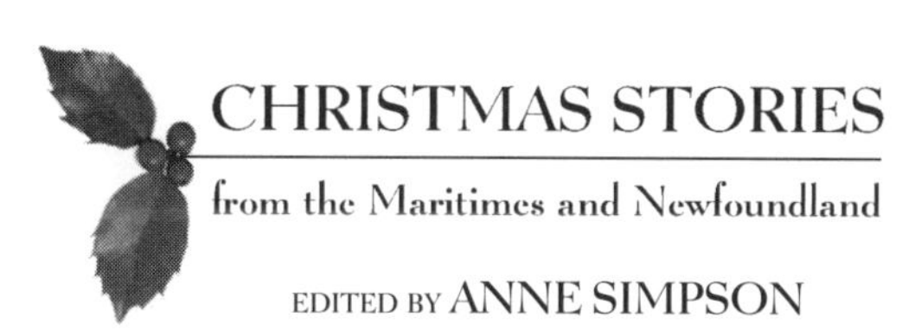

CHRISTMAS STORIES

from the Maritimes and Newfoundland

EDITED BY ANNE SIMPSON

Cover of orange peel by Noel Chenier.
Cover design by Paul Vienneau.
Book design by Julie Scriver.
Printed in Canada by Transcontinental.
10 9 8 7 6 5 4 3 2

National Library of Canada Cataloguing in Publication

An orange from Portugal:
Christmas stories from the Maritimes and Newfoundland / Anne Simpson, editor.

ISBN 0-86492-345-7

1. Christmas — Atlantic Provinces — Literary collections.
2. Canadian literature (English) — Atlantic Provinces.
I. Simpson, Anne, 1956-

PS8237.C57O7 2003 C810.8'0334 C2003-904737-7

Published with the financial support of the Canada Council for the Arts, the Government of Canada through the Book Publishing Industry Development Program, and the New Brunswick Culture and Sports Secretariat.

Goose Lane Editions
469 King Street
Fredericton, New Brunswick
CANADA E3B 1E5
www.gooselane.com

An Orange from Portugal

Contents

A Gift of Oranges

On Christmas Eve, from New Brunswick to Labrador, people sit in comfortable armchairs, drinks of eggnog or whisky in hand, admiring the lights gleaming on their Christmas trees. In the kitchen, someone takes out the last batch of cookies, in the shapes of reindeer, stars, and angels. She puts them on a rack to cool. Outside, snow falls gently — by morning it will lie on the bare branches of trees, atop the cenotaph in the middle of town, and on the roof of Our Lady of the Sacred Heart — but now it's merely a feathery lightness in the air. This could be Christmas in Petit-de-Grat, Nova Scotia, or Summerside, Prince Edward Island, or Heart's Delight, Newfoundland.

An Orange from Portugal: Christmas Stories from the Maritimes and Newfoundland is a collection of tales, short fiction, memoirs, and poems that take us to the warm hearth of Atlantic Canada. Christmas is a time when such tales should be told; it's the bright flame in the winter night. And these tales *are* like flames. Alden Nowlan recounts how his grandmother told him that, on Christmas Eve, anyone spying on the cattle — which, she firmly believed, could kneel in adoration of the Christ Child — would be struck blind by God Himself, no questions asked. Paired with this is a similar tale by Harry Bruce. He offers a slight twist: cattle acquired powers of speech at midnight, and anyone overhearing them would not live to see morning. To keep evil spirits at bay, men fired their guns and afterwards "drank toasts to cows, corn and apple trees." Maybe they drank to their houses and barns, too, just for good measure.

Christmas was a time of hope and magic and danger. It was a sacred festival, but it was not one for the faint of heart. Some of the stories included here bear witness to this fact. They were written long ago, by authors long since dead, and they take us back to times when Christmas was lived out on the edge of existence. Wilfred Grenfell's "How Santa Claus Came to Cape St. Anthony" records a country doctor's journey to save a boy who accidentally shot himself in the leg. Charles G.D. Roberts tells the story of a boy and his father in their horse-drawn sledge as they make their way home — followed by wolves — on Christmas Eve. Grace Ladd, who married Captain Frederick A. Ladd in 1885, spent much of her married life at sea with her husband. Her account of a seafaring Christmas in 1897 describes the feast on board, for which a pig was killed, as the ship headed into the storm squalls off South America.

Hugh MacLennan depicts Halifax in "An Orange from Portugal," a place, he says, where Dickens would have gone, "given a choice of a Canadian town in which to spend Christmas." It's not difficult to imagine Dickens wandering the streets of Halifax in the midst of the rough and tumble of wartime life. And Ronald F. Hawkins presents Leslie Williams's recollection of what it was like to be in a trench near the Rhine during the Second World War. On Christmas Eve, he heard — for three or four minutes in which the shelling ceased — the melodious notes of "Silent Night" as a musician played the bugle in the cold December night under a sky full of stars.

Contemporary writers show us just as clearly that Christmas, that time of celebration, may be shadowed with ominous possibilities. Mark Jarman tells of a man who leaves his house to get a Christmas tree during a holiday season which he finds about as much fun as "an annual root canal"; instead, he finds himself outside town, wrestling for his life with a cougar. Michael Crummey's "What Possessed Him" portrays a good man who is trying to deal gracefully with bad news. In Mary Pratt's "The Far-Away Present," the power goes out on Christmas Eve. It comes back on, goes out again. In the midst of the power failure, a man and a woman open a gift together. It is this simplest of gestures that brings them back to the grace of the present moment.

Yet the festive season is also, fundamentally, a time of joy and humour. Herb Curtis regales us with his story of a boy who desperately wants, not just *any* present, but a very particular present. He is willing to go to great lengths to ensure that he gets it. Wayne Johnston — in "Draper Doyle's Debut," an excerpt from *The Divine Ryans* — provides us with the hilarious scene of a singer who cannot sing but manfully tries to fake it.

Every story and poem in this collection is a gift that is unexpected, simple and delightful: an orange in the hand of a streetwise boy in Halifax. Each one can be lingered over and savoured individually. Together they make a Christmas feast.

ANNE SIMPSON

Draper Doyle's Debut

WAYNE JOHNSTON

The weeks leading up to Christmas seemed to be an endless succession of corny movies, most of them, as luck would have it, featuring priests and nuns and orphans. We were forced to sit through *Boys Town*, *Going My Way*, and *The Bells of St. Mary's*, all of which moved Aunt Phil to tears and even made Sister Louise and Father Seymour look a little wistful. Uncle Reginald observed that Father Seymour was a cross between Spencer Tracy and Bing Crosby, which pleased Aunt Phil until he pointed out that what he meant was that Father Seymour sang like Spencer Tracy and acted like Bing Crosby.

We spent half our time lampooning Aunt Phil's favourites. "He ain't heavy, Fadder, he's my brudder," Mary kept saying as, with eyes bulging and face beet red, she strained to lift me from the chesterfield. The day after we watched yet another version of *A Christmas Carol*, Uncle Reginald devoted a full session of oralysis to it. He invented something called the Tiny Timometer, an instrument which measured cuteness, and said that we should take readings from it throughout Christmas, especially when corny movies were playing. Every night after that, as we sat watching the likes of Hayley Mills and Julie Andrews succumbing to the call of the convent while angels sang and light came breaking through the clouds, Uncle Reginald would consult the Tiny Timometer, take readings, and announce them to the living room.

The lowest reading on the Tiny Timometer, "the least nauseating," as Uncle Reginald put it, was "God bless us, everyone," which he would have me say in the most puny, pathetic voice whenever some corny movie was about to start. Next nauseating on the Tiny Timometer, warranted by any scene in which Bing Crosby broke into song, was "Oh Mother, will there be no plum pudding this year?" The highest reading, that of supremely nauseating, came from the mouth of, as Uncle Reginald called him, "The Bobsequious Cratchett," who, shortly after being fired by Ebenezer Scrooge, said "He's not such a bad man, Mother." "He's not such a bad man, Mother," Uncle Reginald would say, whenever our heroes forgave their enemies some heinous crime.

I often played Tiny Tim to Uncle Reginald's Scrooge, or Uncle Scrooginald, as he called himself. "Please, Mr. Scrooge," I'd say, "something to eat for my little sister."

"I will give you," Uncle Scrooginald would say, "in exchange for your wheelchair and your sister's crutch and all the clothes that you and your sister have on your backs, one cup of lukewarm water."

"Oh, God bless you, Mr. Scrooge," I'd say, "God bless you, you're a saint."

Other times, I played Scrooge's nephew, blurting out, "I say, Uncle, make merry," whenever Uncle Reginald was looking glum. Uncle Reginald would respond, "I say, nephew, if you persist in this nauseating cheerfulness, I shall make pudding of your plums."

The relevance of *A Christmas Carol* to the visitations I was having was not lost on Uncle Reginald. Perhaps, he said, I should do like Scrooge, and the next time my father's ghost appeared dismiss him as a bit of undigested beef.

"You wouldn't think," Aunt Phil said, "that a man would make jokes about a brother not six months in the grave."

In the days leading up to Christmas Day, Mary kept giving me looks that told me that her annual solemn declaration of love was in the offing. Every year, Mary for some reason felt the need and somehow worked up the nerve to say she loved me. This year, she did it in a Christmas card. "Merry Christmas, Draper Doyle," the card said, "I love you," the word love underlined three times.

Nor was this year any different for what happened afterwards. As always, Mary regretted telling me she loved me the minute she did it. "Oh my God," she said, "I can't believe I said 'I love you' on that card." Mortified to the point of speechlessness by the card, I now had to reassure her that it had seemed entirely appropriate. "No, no," I said, in a tone that begged her not to pursue the matter any further, "it was nice."

"*Nice?*" Mary said. "*Nice?* Nice if we were married maybe. Nice if we had about fifty kids. My God, why do I do these things, why?"

Father Seymour gave my mother a necklace, a gesture seen by most of the adults as being both charming and proper from a priest to a sister-in-law who had recently been widowed, who, for the first time in years, had no husband to give her gifts at Christmas. Aunt Phil seemed to think that the necklace would cinch my mother's membership in Father Seymour's Other Number. As it turned out, it had just the opposite effect. There was an awkward moment, or more like an awkward ten minutes, when, on Aunt Phil's insistence, Father Seymour tried to put the necklace around my mother's neck. He was tall enough but unfortunately tried to put it on from the front and stood for an embarrassing amount of time more or less face to face with my mother's bosom, more or less embracing her, while she tried to smile and he struggled to join the clasp of a necklace for perhaps the first time in his life. No one wanted to acknowledge the awkwardness of what was happening by telling him to put it on from behind.

There they were, my mother and Father Seymour in the middle of the room, my mother leaning as far forward in her high heels as she dared, her arms limp at her sides, as if she was terrified of somehow, inadvertently, throwing them around him, Father Seymour standing on tiptoe, trying both to get closer to the necklace and further from my mother, his whole body showing the strain of this impossibility. How precariously balanced each of them was. It looked as if, at any moment, one of them might topple forwards, straight into the arms of the other, as if this great show they were making of not touching one another would end with them falling to the floor in a kind of mad, we'll-both-be-damned embrace right in the middle of Aunt Phil's living room.

So we all sat there watching them, Sister Louise and Aunt Phil trying hard to seem charmed by their predicament, smiling at them. Aunt Phil kept glancing towards the front door, as if she was worried that someone who might misunderstand the situation would suddenly barge in. It seemed it would never end, this strange embrace. There were shouts of what was meant to sound like mock encouragement, as if we were all so relaxed with what was happening that we really didn't care how long it took. "Come on, Father," said Aunt Phil, using her best not-in-the-least-distressed tone of voice. "You can tell he hasn't had much experience," Sister Louise said, which brought a great roar of laughter that trailed off badly and made everyone feel even worse. Finally, his face bursting red, Father Seymour somehow managed it, then raised his arms slowly from our mother's shoulders as if, at the slightest touch, the necklace might come undone. "Ta-dah," someone said, and everyone applauded.

Once each year, at Christmas, after some drinks and much encouragement, Father Seymour agreed to dance, and this year was no different. He took off his jacket, removed his collar, and went out into the hall, where the floor was hardwood and where he could be seen from all parts of the living room. I was relieved to see that he did not wear the eager-to-please expression which he coached the hundred orphan boys to wear in his dancing, singing, boxing club, Father Seymour's Number. Instead, he stared at his feet most of the time, only now and then looking up with what might have been an expression of humility on his face, as if he was saying either that what he was doing was no big deal, or that he himself could not, perhaps absolutely would not, take any personal credit for it. How seriously they watched him, the grownups, their expressions betraying only the faintest trace of irony.

It was tap-dancing at its best that we were seeing, their faces seemed to say, a master practitioner of an ancient, now declining art. What I felt, more than anything, was sheer astonishment. It was somehow off-putting to know that the man who forgave your sins was fond of tap-dancing. Here was Father Seymour, his white socks and black shoes a blur as he went through his routine, Father Seymour without his collar, his shirt two buttons open, his chest hair showing.

There was much applause when he was finished, by which time he was sweating quite a bit, mopping his brow with his handkerchief, smiling quite boyishly, as if he was some child who each year was coaxed into dancing for his relatives. For how many years before I came along had he been doing it? I wondered. How old was this command performance?

For a moment, I could see the boy he must have been on that first occasion, grinning sheepishly when praised, looking about the room to see the effect that he was having. Now, it was as though there was a kind of sacrifice in it, a sacrifice on his part, as though, for some reason that none of them could quite have put their fingers on, it was important that once a year he indulge in this display that even to them seemed faintly absurd. How they gathered about him afterwards, shaking his hand, slapping him on the shoulder, again with only the faintest trace of irony in their smiles, as if he had suffered some humiliation on their behalf, as if they were congratulating him, not so much on his performance as on the fact that it was over for another year, on his having endured it, somehow for their sake. The Divine Ryans. Uncle Reginald said they had first been called that almost two hundred years ago.

The Christmas recital came just after Christmas, early in the New Year. Father Seymour, still unwilling to own up to my mother and Aunt Phil about his failure, or rather his refusal, to make me part of the chorus, told me that I would appear on stage with the choir, not singing, of course, but pretending to sing, "lip-synching," he said. "Just move your mouth like you're singing the words," he said. When I looked doubtful, he put his hands on my shoulders. "Now you'll do it, Draper Doyle," he said. "And it will be our secret, won't it? You don't want to disappoint your mother, do you?" I shook my head.

***

In the days leading up to the recital my mother kept asking me to sing my part.

"C'mon, Draper Doyle," she said. "Let's hear it."

"I'm in the chorus," I said, trying to sound casually dismissive, "I can't sing by myself."

I was at least relieved that I would not be among the dancers, there being no known way to fake tap-dancing — tap-synching, perhaps? Moving to the sound of someone else's feet?

The day before the concert, Aunt Phil took me to Parker's barbershop where, for some reason, there were pictures on the wall of boys my age with various hairstyles. I say "for some reason" because the only haircut Mr. Parker knew was the brush-cut, which he promptly gave me. ("Men have hair there, too," my mother had said. Imagine if, like the hair on your head, it just kept growing. I could see myself choosing, from pictures on Mr. Parker's wall, what style I wanted.)

I spent most of that night in front of the mirror, begging my hair to grow, pulling on it, one hair at a time. I might have used my mother's eyebrow tweezers except I was worried that instead of making the hairs longer, I might just pull them out altogether, leaving my head completely bald, not to mention covered with red dots. I got my mother's mirror and had a mock consultation with Methuselah.

"Oh Great Hairless One," I said, "oh Great Wrinkled One, oh Oracle of Oracles, oh Prune of Prunes, oh Wisest of the Wise, tell me all."

"What is your question?" said Methuselah.

"Will my mother notice that I'm not singing?" I said. That sage of sages, that centre of the world's wisdom, just sat there, looking back at me.

The only full-length mirror in the house was in the hall, and, while they were getting ready for the recital, Aunt Phil and my mother took turns using it, going back and forth without speaking to each other. Once, they shared it, Aunt Phil standing just behind my mother. For a moment their eyes met in the mirror. My mother seemed surprised, but Aunt Phil, as if she believed she was looking at herself, stood as my mother was standing and, in perfect imitation of her, touched her throat softly with her fingers. Then my mother smiled, and, as if to conform to what she still thought was her own reflection, Aunt Phil smiled back. Finally, something broke the spell. Aunt Phil, addressing what she now realized was my mother's image in the mirror, said, "Don't you smile at me." When my mother, her face protesting her innocence, gestured to the mirror, as if to accuse it of having played a trick on both of them, Aunt Phil turned away.

My mother belonged to a family even older than the Ryans, a once-great family whose fortune was long since spent and whose members had begun to scatter even before some of them came across from Ireland in the nineteenth century. Her parents had died before I was born, and her two sisters, her only close relatives, were living on the mainland. Delaney, my mother's maiden name, was a good name, according to Aunt Phil, who spoke not of good and bad families but of good and bad names. All Protestant names were bad, of course, but so were most Catholic names as far as she was concerned. A family had a bad name if it had a bad history or, even worse, no history at all. Delaney was still a good name when our mother joined the family. "No money but good blood" was how Aunt Phil put it, and since the Ryans' own fortune was declining, it must have seemed there were no real grounds for complaint. Besides all this, there was our mother herself, who, within the circle of church families in the city, was thought to have been something of a catch. People had talked about how Donald Ryan was soon to marry "that tall Delaney girl." Do you, Donald Ryan, take that tall Delaney girl to be your wife? was how I had often imagined their wedding.

We walked into St. Martin's Hall together, all the Divine Ryans, made the kind of entrance we knew people were expecting, first Father Seymour pushing Sister Louise, then Aunt Phil leading me by the hand, then my mother walking side by side with Mary, and finally Uncle Reginald, not dressed in his uniform, of course, but looking impressive nonetheless, walking with that mournful grace he had and looking about as if he really was head of the family, as if the train in front of him was his creation. Everyone turned to look at us, and a wave of whispering went down the hall. How many of them, I wondered, could have imagined my mother and Aunt Phil working at Reg Ryan's, vacuuming beneath the caskets, polishing the brass and silver handles?

For there was Aunt Phil, the famous Philomena, and there was our mother, a fixture at her side, "the Young Widow," as she was called: "the Young Widow," people whispered, as if this was her official title, bestowed upon her by the Ryans, as if she was the latest in a long and distinguished line of Young Widows. It was mostly at our mother people stared, mostly about her they whispered. "She's lovely," people said, nodding their heads, as if that was exactly the right word. Opinion was unanimous that she was "lovely," not "beautiful" or "pretty," but "lovely," implying, it now seems to me, a kind of untouched, even untouchable attractiveness.

They stared because we were still the Divine Ryans, because it was only our fortune that was declining, and not, as people put it, "the family itself." It was as if people believed that our privilege, our status, had nothing to do with money. It was as if they believed that these things were God-given, as if we were simply blessed with them the way that other people were blessed with good looks or intelligence. You could think of the Ryan house, Uncle Reginald had once said, as a kind of giant headstone for which all the Catholics of the city had chipped in, a monument to all the people who had ever read the *Chronicle* or been waked at Reg Ryan's. An audience of customers is what they were, happy customers, I hoped, given that Father Seymour's Number was about to perform for them.

As the others took their seats in front, Father Seymour and I went backstage. He began to see to the dancers, who would go on first, while I put on my choir uniform. Before the recital got underway, I peeked out through the curtain. Most of the Catholic dignitaries of the city were in the front row. My mother and Uncle Reginald were sitting together. Mary beside Uncle Reginald, nodding solemnly as he whispered God knows what sort of nonsense to her. Aunt Phil and Sister Louise sat on either side of the archbishop, who would nod his head on the rare occasions when they spoke to him, but did not speak so much as one word in return, only continued to stare with apparent fascination at the empty stage. It was clearly the umpteenth such event that he had attended, and I suspected that he had mastered the art of seeming to watch and listen when in fact he neither had nor wanted to have the faintest idea of what was going on. I had seen him sit in just this fashion at every other performance of Father Seymour's Number, staring straight ahead of him. Everyone acted as if the point was not to impress the archbishop, but to refrain from doing anything which would startle him into an awareness of his surroundings.

I watched from the wings as the dance recital got underway. Out came the dancers, all wearing the same look of ingenuous enthusiasm, all smiling at the archbishop as if to watch a group of orphans tap-dancing was known to be the highlight of his year, his favourite pastime. He sat there, still staring straight ahead, wearing that same look of intense concentration, as if he did not want to miss a single click of their shoes. One row came forward as the other went backward, and it went like that as the tempo gradually increased, the dancers tapping faster and faster, the rows interchanging more and more rapidly, coming closer and closer together until, the clicking of their shoes at its height, the dancers formed one row and came to the very edge of the stage, all of them smiling with wide-eyed enthusiasm at His Grace, whose head was still at the same angle, so that he now appeared to be staring at their feet, or more accurately at the feet of Young Leonard, who was in the middle. There they were, Father Seymour's dancers, at the very edge of the stage, doing their much-loved running-on-the-spot dance, in which they appeared to be fighting for balance, waving their arms, trying desperately, it seemed, not to fall forwards, though still smiling. Somehow, they moved even closer to the edge, leaned even further forward, smiling more broadly as oohs and aahs came from the audience, smiling as if to say "We're terribly close to falling, aren't we, we're terrible close to falling." (How many boys had been lost, Uncle Reginald asked me later, in practising this manoeuvre?)

The dancers were a huge success. As they left the stage, tap-dancing one by one into the wings, there was great ovation, the largest for Young Leonard, who was the last to leave, tap-dancing sideways while twirling his green Swiss hat above his head.

Then, after a short intermission during which many of the dancers changed into fresh uniforms, came Father Seymour's choir. I, feeling every bit the fraud and pretender that I was, stood among them, dressed like them, looking just like a real member of the junior choir, even when Father Seymour tapped his baton and the singing began. I stood there, lip-synching "Greensleeves," "Ave Maria," "Barbara Allen," "Sad are the Men of Nottingham."

"Which one is Father Seymour's nephew?" I imagined people in the crowd were asking one another. "Oh he's the one whose mouth is wide open when the rest of them are closed." There was my mother, in the front row, beaming with pride. Looking at her, I was so ashamed that I forgot to move my mouth, but she didn't seem to notice.

I suppose it wouldn't have been so bad if there hadn't been so much talk about my being in Father Seymour's Number. "His own nephew?" I imagined people saying.

"Yes, Draper Doyle is his name. Six months ago, he couldn't carry a note and now look at him."

And there was my mother, to whom the supposed miracle had been meant as a gift, a special favour. Father Seymour takes widow's little boy and makes a special case of him, teaches him to sing in record time. Widow is fairly lifted from her misery by the sight of her boy singing in the chorus of Father Seymour's choir. How guilty I felt! There was my mother, husband-less, sick with worry about me and Mary. Why *couldn't* I be the sort of boy who charmed his mother by singing "Ave Maria"? Why couldn't that pride beaming on my mother's face be justified? What on earth was wrong with me? I was feeling so sorry for myself, I had a sudden urge to burst out bawling, yes, even to confess, right there on the stage, own up to the whole world that I was faking it. Draper Doyle, impostor. I could see the headlines in tomorrow's *Daily Chronicle*, my own family's newspaper. PRIEST'S NEPHEW PRETENDS TO SING WHILE MOTHER BEAMS WITH PRIDE.

Instead of breaking down and confessing, I tried to comfort myself by lip-synching with all my might, belting out the words of "Ave Maria" in my mind, giving what was perhaps the greatest bogus rendition ever given of that song. My mouth was wide open, my shoulders rose and fell with every word. Never had "Ave Maria" been faked more sincerely, more convincingly. I put everything I had into it, straining, straining, sweat breaking out on my forehead, all the while trying desperately not to break down in a fit of shameful weeping on the stage.

It was then, through a glaze of tears, that I saw him. My father was sitting near the back of the hall, at the end of one of the rows. He was dressed as he might have dressed in life for this occasion, wearing his best suit, across the vest of which the gold chain of his watch was visible. He was sitting there, smiling like everyone else, looking not in the least out of place, except that once again he held a hockey puck in his hands. He was turning it over and over as if he was either admiring it or wondering what on earth it was. It might have been something that had fallen from the sky for the way that he was looking at it, now and then tapping it as if to see what it was made of. "Cryptic," his expression seemed to say; "inscrutable," as if the mystery of its origin was as dark and densely opaque as the puck itself.

I looked at the people beside him. Would he show the puck to one of them? He had never appeared this close to other people before. Surely they could see him. Surely, it seemed to me, everyone could see him. He had been as well known among this crowd as any of the Divine Ryans, so why was his presence not causing a commotion? Why was the person sitting next to him ignoring him as if he wasn't there?

I was determined not to let him get away this time. I knew that with his tendency to disappear in an instant, I had better waste no time in getting to him. He seemed to know what I had in mind, for he looked up from the puck and a mischievous, almost encouraging smile came on his face. To reach the part of the hall in which my father was sitting, I would have to break ranks with the back row of the choir, run clear across the stage, right in front of Father Seymour, then pass within a few feet of Aunt Phil and the archbishop at the bottom of the stairs — after which I would still have to run the length of the hall. Looking once again at my father, whose mischievous expression had become more pronounced, I jumped down from the bleachers we were standing on and, so fast that I didn't notice anyone's reaction, ran across the stage. I was just descending the stairs, just about to reach the floor of the hall, when I glanced up to find that the chair in which my father had been sitting was now empty.

I should simply have kept on going, I suppose, down through the audience and out the door. It wouldn't have been any more difficult to explain. Instead, I came to a skidding halt in front of the archbishop. It was quite a while before the audience realized that what was happening was unplanned. Everyone seemed to think that it was part of the act, some daring innovation of Father Seymour's perhaps, having one of his choirboys run across the stage, descend the stairs and stop in front of the archbishop, there to burst into some spectacular solo for his benefit.

Even Aunt Phil seemed to be hoping desperately that this was the case, hoping the whole thing would suddenly resolve itself into a scene from *Boys Town*, hoping that somehow I, her nephew, whom she knew to be the newest, least practised member of Father Seymour's Number, would suddenly burst into song, and what had seemed to be a catastrophe would turn out to be one of the great moments in the history of Father Seymour's Number — perhaps it would be remembered as the time that Father Seymour's nephew, on the ingenious instructions of Father Seymour, had fooled everyone into thinking that some horrible embarrassment was taking place, and then had burst into song, his mouth as roundly and as sweetly open as that of some Vienna choirboy, his head gesturing for emphasis, his whole body caught up in serenading the archbishop. For surely, surely, her face seemed to say, I had not simply taken it into my head to flee from the stage and come to a screeching halt in front of His Grace.

Not the least of those who must have been expecting some such face-saving performance was the archbishop himself, who had been more or less woken up, not by me so much as by the sudden silence, to find that, inexplicably, one of Father Seymour's choirboys was standing right in front of him, staring at him with an expression of simple horror on his face. The archbishop was the first to recover, the first to admit to himself that no serenade, no unprecedented solo would be forthcoming. Smiling at me, he extended his hand, not to shake mine, I was fairly certain, since he did so palm down, but for what reason I had no idea.

Out of the corner of my eye, I saw Sister Louise motioning frantically for me to do something. I saw her rubbing one of her fingers, and making a frantic downward motion with her hands. What this meant, I could not begin to guess. I stared at her in panic, wondering what on earth she wanted me to do.

I dearly wished I understood her, for her expression seemed to assure me that what she had in mind would not only save the moment, but was quite easy to do. When I shrugged, she knitted her forehead, and the motion of her hands became so ferociously concentrated, that her whole body began to shake as if with sheer spite. She was rubbing her finger so vigorously she appeared to be trying to erase her knuckle, all the while staring at me with ever increasing exasperation. What by this time was obvious to everyone but me was that Sister Louise and the archbishop wanted me to kiss his ring. When it became apparent that I would not, the archbishop lowered his hand, looked away from me, and went back to staring at the stage.

I could think of nothing else to do but turn around and go back onstage, which I began to do, every step of my black buckled shoes resounding throughout the hall. Suddenly, I was acutely aware of my outfit, my elf's hat, my green suspenders, my short pants, the six inches or so of absurdly skinny leg that showed between the pants and my knee-high yellow socks. And finally, the shoes, the famous shoes of Father Seymour's Number in which, one day, if Father Seymour changed his mind about my dancing potential, I might be tap-dancing, footing it about the stage with the same pointless expertise as Young Leonard.

Somehow, Father Seymour got the choir going again and the recital went on as planned, with the audience giving us a kind of bemused, sympathetic ovation at the end. My mother was backstage waiting for me when we went off. Perhaps she had meant to head off the chewing out that I was sure to get from Father Seymour. She needn't have worried. Father Seymour was quite clearly enraged, but he was not about to say anything, for he knew that I might very well blurt out our secret, tell her that, on his instructions, I had only been pretending to sing.

The dressing room was silent as my mother led me out by the hand. When we got to the car, Aunt Phil and Sister Louise had already gone home, so disgusted had they been by my performance. I climbed into the back seat with Mary, and my mother got in front with Uncle Reginald, who, saying it might be best if we gave Aunt Phil time to cool off, took us for a drive. For a while, no one but Uncle Reginald spoke. He made the inevitable joke about how, with only three months' training, I had stopped the show. Then my mother turned around.

"I don't suppose," she said, "that you would like to explain yourself." I considered telling the truth, but, remembering my promise to Mary, decided I better not.

"I thought I had to use the bathroom," I said.

"You thought you had to use the bathroom," my mother said. "And then, once you had interrupted everything and spoiled the concert, you discovered that you didn't have to use the bathroom?"

Trying not to mimic her look of incredulity, I nodded.

Mary and my mother looked at one another, rolled their eyes, shook their heads. And then everyone, me included, burst out laughing.

The Kneeling of the Cattle

ALDEN NOWLAN

At midnight on Christmas Eve, so my grandmother told me when I was a small boy, the cattle kneel in their stalls in adoration of the Christ Child, who was born in a stable. When I got to be about eight years old I asked her if she had ever seen them kneel. "Of course not," she said. It was not a sight that God permitted human beings to see. She had heard of a man who hid in his barn, hoping to spy on the cattle. In punishment, God struck him blind.

She lived in Nova Scotia, but she might as easily have been an old peasant woman in Galicia or Moldavia.

Years later I learned from a poem by Thomas Hardy that the legend of the kneeling cattle flourished among the peasantry of the old pre-industrial England. For all I know, it may have originated in the Middle Ages, or earlier.

The North Atlantic wind hurled itself against the house, roaring like a demented bear. The snow was piled in great Himalayan drifts between barn and house, so that there was a howling white valley between. Beyond the whiteness of the snow and the blackness of the night, the cattle sank to their knees in a barn warmed by the heat of their own bodies. There, to borrow a phrase from Robert Graves, is the iconotrophic instant, the sacred picture, that best represents the Christmas of my earliest childhood.

We were poor. So poor that my memories of that poverty sometimes seem to me to be less private recollections than dark glimpses of the collective unconscious, dreams from another country and another century . . . yet I don't recall a year when there wasn't a Christmas.

If the three wise men had been wiser they'd have known they needn't bring gold, frankincense, and myrrh to the Christ Child. He'd have been equally happy with a shiny button, a little sugared milk, and a single flower.

I can't recall that any new decorations were ever bought for our tree. There were two stands of crepe paper rope, one red and one green, a box of hollow, coloured glass balls, a tinsel star for the top, and some odds and ends of things. Every Christmas the ropes were a bit shorter, and there were one or two fewer glass balls. But there always seemed to be enough.

If new decorations had appeared, I think we children would have been vastly pleased — but only at first; then we'd have begun to worry. It would have been a superstitious kind of worry. I think we'd have knocked on wood or performed some similar rite of exorcism if we'd been confronted with a third strand of paper rope or another box of glass balls. For the old decorations weren't simply pretty things we hung on a tree; they were Christmas. We were even a little uncomfortable, just for an instant, if we happened to see them at any other time of year. To a small child they looked so dead, thrown together in a heap in their cardboard box in a closet.

There were foods we ate only at Christmas, never at any other time. In retrospect, I suppose it was poverty that caused us to eat grapes, oranges, and nuts only at Christmas. But we didn't think of it that way at the time; we no more expected grapes in July than we expected snow. Those delicacies were sacramental to the season. At least that's what we children felt. It was as though Christ had ordained that they should be eaten in honour of his birth.

Consider the grapes. They were always red grapes, incidentally, never purple or green. The texture of the grapes was like a kiss. And they offered a trinity of tastes — the hot roughness of the skin, the cool secret inner pulp, so full of juice that you both drank and ate of it, and crisp nutty seeds you broke between your teeth. Occasionally, when we were almost satiated, we separated skin, pulp, and seeds and ate them one after the other, so that the flavour of each was distinct. It was a religious rite, the eating of those grapes, although we didn't need to call it religious.

Oranges. We ate peel and seeds as well as pulp, and it was like swallowing a piece of summer that had been rolled into a ball and preserved in honey. The pulp was a sweet as sunlight, the skin as acidulous as sunburn.

And nuts. The strange, almost sinister crab-shaped hearts of the walnuts, the meaty, slight woody texture and taste of them. The white meat of the Brazil nuts that tasted like cake frosting. The rubbery bittersweet hazel nuts. The protracted spiciness of the almonds. The peanuts, so salty and oily that they tasted almost fishy. We opened them with a claw hammer or a piece of stove wood, never having heard of nutcrackers.

There was ribbon candy, a corkscrew-shaped rainbow of colours and flavours: mint, banana, wintergreen, lemon, orange, cherry, and strawberry. Cinnamon sticks: tiny cherry-pink walking sticks, the cinnamon encased in molasses candy. And barley toys, which we always ate last because they were shaped like little animals, tigers, horses, and camels, which we hesitated to destroy — and, besides, they tasted like nothing except sugary water.

Dinner was chicken and roast pork. But after eating fruit, nuts, and candy all morning, we children were never very excited about dinner.

The gifts were mostly homemade, except for the occasional doll or box of crayons. Once there was a team of wooden horses, hand-carved with a jackknife and complete with harness and wagon. Another time, a miniature ship, a tern schooner, made with the same jackknife, and with every sail in working order. Still another time, a homemade bow and arrows, accurate and powerful enough to kill a rabbit or a partridge, although I never used them for that. And if there was no new doll, there was a handmade wardrobe for the old one.

But the gifts were never so important as the feasting.

All the great holy days down through history have been feasts. That was true in ancient Greece and Rome. It was true in Middle Ages and during the Renaissance. It is true to a certain extent even today. In fact I suspect that the very conception of the holiday originated in prehistoric times when the hunters came home with meat and the people prepared a great feast, a festival. The adults in that grim time and place must have felt about their chicken and pork much as we children felt about our fruit, nuts, and candy.

Often there was music. Sometimes the only instrument was a fiddle. Sometimes there was an improvised orchestra whose members, if they chose, came or went in the middle of a tune. There might be a violin, a mandolin, a guitar, a banjo, a mouth organ, and autoharp. Somebody might play the spoons or the comb and tissue, both of which are precisely what their names suggest. And there would be step-dancing. The first black man I ever knew was a farmhand who vied with my grandmother for the distinction of being the best step-dancer in the parish. Some of the most spirited competitions took place in our kitchen at Christmas, the two of them facing one another less as dancers than as choreographers. The trick was to improvise new and increasingly complicated movements involving, towards the end, almost every part of the body.

When I come to think about it, it was all very religious. Religious in the subconscious and mystical rather than in the liturgical and public sense. The Christmas of my childhood belonged to the great tradition, as old as the human race, of holy days and festivals. Everyone sensed that, I think, although hardly anyone ever referred to the formalities of Christianity, its rituals and theologies. Historically, in a sense, it was pre-Christian, the music and dancing, but in a curious way it was holy. It was the human spirit finding joy in an all but intolerable environment. Even the gods envy man's gift of laughter.

The Far-Away Present

MARY PRATT

When Christopher and I went to Salmonier to live, we did so with visions of a life in the country — in the forests, beside a salmon river, away from the demands of society and the internal politics of jobs within Memorial's extension service. For Christopher it would be an opportunity to paint. For me it would be an adventure.

When we moved from St. John's in May, we didn't think at all about Christmas. And, if we had, we would have imagined a frozen river for skating, real Christmas trees — or a whole forest of them — covered in real snow and, at night, stars brilliant in a sky innocent of city lights. We did not foresee a power failure that was to black us out and freeze us all from December eighteenth until the afternoon of December twenty-fourth.

It might have been fun if we'd known how to deal with it, if we hadn't been raised in cities where electricity was taken for granted, or if the oil stove hadn't blown up, or if the Christmas baking had been finished, or if the baby had not had infected ears, or if the cats hadn't continuously sought warmth in the attic and just as frequently fallen through the makeshift insulation we'd tacked onto the ceiling.

Finally, on the afternoon of December twenty-fourth, the electricity flowed through the wires again, and we began to string lights on the Christmas tree and vacuum up soot. Civilization and its comforts returned. The children sent their letters to Santa up the chimney and snuggled down to dreams of magic, while Christopher and I, now warm, confident and delighted with the prospect of the great celebration of Christmas tomorrow, prepared to snuggle down ourselves. Then, just as we were about to turn out the lights — like magic — they turned themselves out. The electricity was gone again.

I began to light candles, as we had done all week, putting one in the bathroom to safely light the bathroom all night, one in the kitchen sink and one to get me back to bed. I think I was crying.

Christopher said, "Why don't we open a present?"

"Before tomorrow?" I was shocked. We had never allowed such an indulgence.

"Why not? I think we deserve a treat."

A treat! What an exotic notion! "Which one?" I was an easy convert.

"The one from furthest away — from the English cousins."

We took our candle and found the small flat parcel under the tree. It was wrapped in the thin red tissue and decorated with stickers — Santa Clauses, angels, and candles. We shook it solemnly to draw out the magic, to guess.

"It rattles," I said. "And there are bits that feel like metal."

We pulled away the wrapping to discover a set of angel chimes. A circle of cherubs, carefully suspended by hooks from a small canopy, were set turning slowly, persuaded into action by the heat of the flames of six little red candles lit beneath them. We put the delicate ornament on the window sill, where it was reflected against the black glass, and watched with delight as the little angels rotated slowly, striking small chimes at appropriate intervals, twinkling, tinkling, the perfect time, the perfect gift. Suddenly — and with such unexpected sweetness — it was Christmas.

The Tale of a Tree

DAVID ADAMS RICHARDS

By December 23, 1972, we did not have a tree. And it had been storming a week, with the intermittent snowfall that starts in November and ends sometime in April. And there were two days left. But who was counting? My brothers and I, in our early twenties and back in New Brunswick for Christmas, did not think hurrying was necessary. Even though our mother did.

"Everyone seems to have their tree up now," she said to us. She was right. Still, we reassured her that it would be easy to go into the woods and get a tree. The woods in New Brunswick are never far away. And the trees are — you guessed it — in the woods.

Oh, there were a few "tree lots," but what were they for? I mean, these were the days (long ago) when no New Brunswicker would ever actually think of buying a tree. Buying a tree was tantamount to admitting failure as a man. That was the way it was.

In fact, until I was in my mid-twenties — being a slow learner in my formative years — I did not know anyone in New Brunswick would ever stoop so low. We had heard that once somebody sold an artificial tree to someone in a *mall*.

"I hear they sold one of those silver trees at the *mall*!"

"Made in New York!"

"Prob-ly!"

What more could be said?

Still, we could not put it off. So on a blustery and freezing December

23, after our game of road hockey, we set out to get the tree, my brothers and I and a little neighbourhood child about six years of age I did not know. Perhaps a cousin of someone, who decided to come along just as the hockey game broke up.

But in those more innocent days, not knowing a child, or even who he or she belonged to, did not mean you could not drive about with them in your car all day. The last thing on anyone's mind, good men and women naively thought, was injury to a child.

The only problem was the sub-zero temperature and the rising wind. I sat behind the wheel of my sky-blue 1961 Chevy, with pins at the front so the hood would stay on (though it flapped continually), and away we went. At the top of the lane, I made my decision. We could have gone anyplace, even a few miles down river — but I thought of someplace special. I decided that we would go to *the North Pole*.

The North Pole Stream is north of Newcastle. It is near where Christmas Mountain is, surrounded by little bitty mountains, like Dasher, Rudolf, and Blitzen. It would be no trouble to get a tree there, I said.

"Isn't that a little far?" my younger brother said.

It was an eighty- or ninety-mile round trip, but worth it, if you brought a smile to the gob of a child. So off we went, the valves in the old Chevy ticking a mile a minute and a huge plastic-carton-top cover on my gas tank.

The roads were ice and snow, and by the time we got to the Renous the wind had risen to gale force, and visibility was almost zero. In fact it took everything I had to keep the car on the road. The wind under the hood gave the car an element of lift, so going downhill we were airborne.

Our radio did not work, the thermostat was stuck, and the going was getting rougher. Then the carton cap came off my gas tank, and I had to stop and search for it. Not able to find it, I stuffed a pair of white socks I had bought for my brother-in-law into the tank.

In retrospect, I remember that the youngster did not seem troubled by any of this. Finally I decided, halfway to Christmas Mountain, that we were in a good enough place. "This looks like a fine place for a tree to be hiding."

My brothers grunted agreement.

"This is wonderful," the little boy finally exclaimed. "I've never seen anyone get a tree before!"

My brothers and I looked at him. It became evident that none of us knew who he was. I studied him carefully for some sign of recognition. He looked like a Foley, I decided. He could pass for a Foley on a bad day. But then couldn't he be a Matheson — or a Casey? Yes! Perhaps a Casey! His hands were folded on his lap, mittens pinned with big silver pins, winter coat buttoned to his chin.

"Where you from?" my younger brother asked.

He answered with grave and solemn earnestness. "I'm afraid from Dublin, sir," he said.

"Afraid from Doob-lun?" my brother said. "Where in heck is Doob-lun?"

"He means Dublin," I whispered. "*Ireland*."

"*Dublin!*"

"Yes — from Doob-lun. I'm here visiting — me grandmum. I'm Owen," he said, "and I've never seen anyone get a Christmas tree."

"Well, you're in luck," I said. "We're all like Paul Bunyan here — you ever hear of Big Joe Mufferah?"

I tucked Owen's mittens over his hands, repinned them, and out we got, my brothers leading the way, plowing over the now-frozen snowbanks and into the by now dark, frozen woods, looking for a tree. We found one, fifty yards off the road, a fir tree about six feet tall. A perfect tree, except for a slight crookedness at the base and an overlapping bough — but these were minor flaws. And not flaws, really, for one might appreciate them as defects that heightened beauty. In fact, I could already see it sitting in our living room. I could see it trimmed, lights glowing. "It will bring you great happiness and peace," the Dubliner said suddenly.

What a fine little boy I thought; all the way from Dublin, standing in the middle of godforsaken nowhere, up to his bum in snow, and still thinking of peace. His uncle was probably a priest, a melancholy man who drank a bit. Perhaps his mother had died, or something, of — tuberculosis — and he had come here to be with his grandmother, I thought.

Everyone was silent, thinking about peace. Or thinking we would take the tree home and, duty done, get back to drinking eggnog and playing another game of road hockey.

"How are you going to cut it down?" the Dubliner asked.

We were silent. All of us kept staring at the tree.

"Don't you need an axe?" he asked.

So I went back to the car. I searched the back seat, the trunk, and solemnly walked into the woods again.

"Don't look at me," I shrugged guiltily, when I saw them looking at me. After the road hockey, we had all jumped into the car without thinking that the axe was leaning against the garage.

I watched my younger brother as he tried to break the tree in two with his hands. But it proved fruitless; the tree still stood.

"It's getting late," my younger brother said. "Mom expects to have some kind of a tree for Christmas; I think she'd be disappointed if we came back without one."

That was true enough.

"Put a ribbon on this one, to show we found it, and we will come back," I said.

But no one wanted to drive another forty miles just to come back to this spot. Besides, no one had a ribbon.

It was decided that we would take a jaunt back to town to get an axe and cut the very first tree in the very first yard we came to. We might even cut a tree in our yard.

"What about the pine in the back yard?" my younger brother said. "It's useless where it is — it just keeps getting in the way when I mow the lawn."

"It'd look far better in the living room." I agreed. "That's the place for it."

"But how would we keep Mom from knowing?"

She would soon find out, if she looked out her kitchen window, that her favourite pine tree was in the living room.

Then we wondered if we couldn't buy one on the sly. In fact, it might be considered conservation-minded if we did. There were far too many trees being cut, and that would be our out. There were some for sale at the Irving station on the Boom Road.

But, we asked each other, how could we keep it quiet? What a time they would have! Three grown men off to get a tree, and having to buy one.

It might be possible to steal one, already decorated. But we did not entertain that thought for long.

Owen listened to all of this with great serenity as we drove back out along the highway. Having no radio, we asked him if he knew a Christmas song. I was waiting for "Jingle Bells." But Owen, mittens folded, eyes closed, broke out singing "O Tannenbaum" in a voice that seemed straight from the Vienna Boys' Choir.

After that we were a little dumbfounded. And we remained silent until ten miles from home, when I slammed on the brakes and yelled, "There's my plastic carton cap!!!"

I jumped out and ran, with the car still sliding behind me. It proved a difficult carton cap to catch. The wind had given it life, and five or six times I missed it. But finally I was able to grab it. I went back to the car, took my brother-in-law's present out of the gas tank (I would rewrap them) and placed the cap back on.

Turning, I saw Owen staring past me. "There's a tree over there," he said.

"There are many trees, son," I said. "The woods is a veritable cornucopia of trees —"

"However, this one just fell out of the sky," he said simply.

I turned and saw a pine-top blowdown rolling back and forth in the centre of the road. It had not been there ten seconds before.

"It just fell from heaven and landed there — a second ago," the child said, amazed. Anyone who has ever heard an Irish child say "it just fell from heaven" will know how I felt at that moment.

Owen and I walked over to inspect it. It was a beautiful tree, about seven-and-a-half feet tall. It had sustained no damage; all its boughs were still fluffy and intact. In fact, it had just broken from the top of a large pine. The only thing we would have to do was to saw the butt even.

Delighted at our good fortune, I tied it to the trunk of the car. "Thank God for the wind," I muttered.

"Yes." Owen said. And off we went.

Now it was night. The stars came out and the wind died down. The town was lit up top to bottom, front to back, all the houses decorated, and soon ours would be, too.

"Thank you for letting me help get the tree," Owen said. "I've never seen anyone get a tree before." Then our little Dubliner fell fast asleep. We took him home, to where he'd said his grandmother lived. My brother carried him to the door.

We went back home. With some sleight of hand about where we had found it, we put up the tree. My mother loved it. My father spent the night trimming it.

All that was long ago; both my parents now are gone. The house is no longer ours, and most of the people I grew up with I no longer know. My brothers and I get together when we can. There is still road hockey on our lane, though the city council tried to forbid it and almost started a war, and kids still gather in droves to play there near Christmastime.

We still speak about a child we didn't know, who came with us to find a tree the wind blew from the sky when we had no axe — of the carton cap stopping the car, so the child, himself, could light the way. And we have come to the conclusion, over many rum and beer, that at the very least he was a kind and wonderful child from Dublin, named Owen, visiting his grandmom who lived two lanes from us.

Unfortunately, I have never seen him again, and I expect now I never will.

Midnight Gossip

HARRY BRUCE

Merchants so eager to exploit the jolly Yuletide season that they tart up their shops with Christmas decorations right after Halloween are asking for a whole lot of trouble. Folks once knew something we've all forgotten: if you deck your halls with boughs of holly too early, you goad friends into punishing you in horrible ways.

Of course, country people also knew that, to prosper in the coming year, they'd better visit their orchards and barns on Christmas Eve, shoot guns to ward off evil spirits, and drink toasts to their cows, corn, and apple trees. At midnight, however, it was best not to be within earshot of cattle. That's when they got down on their knees, found the power of speech, and prayed to Jesus. If you overheard them, you wouldn't be around in the morning to open your gifts.

A variation of this belief, which folklorist Helen Creighton recorded in Nova Scotia, has the oxen not only praying, but chatting with one another. A farmer sneaked into his stable to eavesdrop, heard one oxen telling another, "Tomorrow we'll be hauling our master to his grave," and dropped dead out of sheer fright.

Such stories crossed the Atlantic with settlers from Britain and continental Europe. Thomas Hardy's "The Oxen," written in 1915, is about praying livestock. In Cornwall, people long believed that, at midnight on Christmas Eve, sheep bowed their heads in memory of the sheep at Bethlehem on that long-gone silent night, holy night.

The descendants of the pioneers doubtless put their own spin on these ancient beliefs. In Lunenburg County, for instance, Creighton learned about a man so enraged by what he overheard an ox say about him that he tried to kill the creature with an axe. The axe rebounded and killed the farmer. But what in the world had the ox called him? A smelly, two-legged scumbag, or just a pig?

"The injunction against listening, which will result in death, is strong in Nova Scotia," Creighton wrote, "and Newbolt Niles Puckett also has it from Southern Negro sources." Heaven knows how black slaves in the American South and Lunenburg fishermen came to share the identical Christmas Eve superstition.

In the hillbilly country of the Ozark Mountains, a press release from the University of Arkansas says, settlers celebrated Christmas "by talking to farm animals and blowing things up." Children were encouraged not to avoid cattle on Christmas Eve, but to turn their attention "toward the cow pasture, where it was believed the livestock would kneel and pray with human voices."

"The idea of talking animals is a devotional gesture," said Bob Cochran, director of the University's centre for regional studies. "It was believed the advent of the Christ child was marked even in nature. Stars shone more brightly, and even the animals had an impulse to worship."

The odd thing is that much of what we love about Christmas predates Christ. Long before He arrived on earth, the Roman, Scandinavian, and Germanic peoples had joyful celebrations at what's now Christmastime. It's from those orgies of feasting and carousing that we inherited the hanging of mistletoe, the decorating with holly and evergreen boughs, the lighting-up of trees, the burning of Yule logs, the traipsing from house to house with gifts of fruit, cake, dolls, candles, perfume, and jewellery, and the exchanging of best wishes for the coming year.

The festivities were expressions of sun worship. People believed that winter ended the sun's reign and ushered into power the horrible forces of darkness. But right after the Winter Solstice, the shortest day of the year, daytime grew longer and sunlight stronger. Yahoo! The big, golden guy in the sky is making his comeback. Help him out. Light up the streets. Let's party! A highlight of the Roman festival in honour of their god of agriculture, Saturn, was not the birthday of the Son of God, but "the birthday of the unconquered sun."

The Church eventually decided that, since it could not beat these beloved celebrations, it should join them. It took some doing over some time, but it injected into the happiest seasonal traditions of European pagans the story of His birth. So wherever you are in the Maritimes and Newfoundland, just remember that when you drape a pine bough over a mirror or deliver a plum pudding to your neighbour, you're only doing what some heathen did one day in December thousands of years ago. Have a very Merry Christmas, but please stay out of the barn.

Silver Bells

CAROL BRUNEAU

On Christmas Eve the cold snap breaks. There's not a stitch of snow. Instead, it rains and rains. A couple of people come in to buy pop — mixer, I suppose, though I wouldn't know for sure. Ruby and I close up at the usual time and eat supper as always. Potatoes, a couple of pork chops, peas, carrots cut like boards, not coins. Sawing into my meat, I can't help thinking of work — the after-Christmas chore of taking down the store decorations, packing all the red and green stuff that never sells and sticking it upstairs till next year. Over my carrots and peas I make a resolution to move the Christmas stock out of there by New Year's, and maybe get a jump on Valentine's. I have to make way for the red candy hearts, the frilly heart-shaped boxes of Ganong's I ordered at Halloween.

Maybe I seem distracted. At one point, cutting through her chop, lifting the bone like a teacup to gnaw off the last morsel of gristle, Ruby meets my eyes and asks, "Whatever's the matter, Lucinda — cat got your tongue?" She sets the bone down daintily and wipes her mouth on her serviette, a Christmasy one recycled from last year. She looks at me with beseeching concern, like a news anchor saying, "Talk to me!" or some prim and proper Fido begging for food.

"Don't mind me," I say and she nods, befuddled. For the next little while we sit in silence finishing supper, listening to the rain pounding the back steps.

"You stay put now." She rises first, laying a hand on my wrist. "I'll tidy up." She goes to the ironing board folded beside the fridge, where she's gotten into the habit of hanging things, and yanks down her apron. It's a pink-flowered print that looks faded and shabby against her good wool dress. She'll have that dress threadbare, the way she's wearing it lately. I get up to help but she says, "No, sit," and for once I'm just as happy to do her bidding. She's awfully spry tonight, unusually spry. Which is how she gets when there's something up her sleeve.

I realize she has something planned, some little surprise or treat in mind. For a while I'm content to sit and watch her, those three-quarter-length sleeves shoved up, elbows see-sawing in and out of the suds. The plates clink gently, clots of bubbles sliding off them into the drainer. She's forgotten to rinse — oh heck, her heart's in the right place. But as I think this, panic leaps in — what was it I got her for a present? Will she like it, will it be enough?

It's one of those Magic Bags advertised on TV — hope she won't be insulted. "Zap in the microwave; presto! an instant heating pad; clap it on your neck." Except we don't have a microwave, but I figured the oven would do the trick; it's not as if she's pressed for time.

"Go on now, Lucinda — go see what's on the news, why don't you?"

Oh, she's up to something all right. Wouldn't want to ruin her surprise. So I go and sit in the parlour, one eye on *Live at Five*, the other on the *Herald*, waiting. I listen to her out in the kitchen, the squeal and thud of drawers and cupboard doors shutting, the wire dish rack being shoved under the sink. She slips into her bedroom and I hear her riffling round. There's the rustling of plastic bags, soft at first, then suddenly frantic.

"Ruby?" I yell. "Anything I can do?"

No answer, but the rustling's turned to ripping now, loud and frenzied as a pit bull rooting for something.

The TV, meanwhile, blares a feature on Christmas lights, and I feel a twinge of guilt for not bothering with a tree this year. Too much trouble. Just as easy, I convinced myself, to shut your eyes and imagine last year's or the year before's, propped in the corner, the same gold balls hung the same old . . . at least this way there'll be no needles to vacuum, no fire hazard.

What in *tarnation* is keeping her in there?

The rustling's stopped; I have to check.

Ruby's sitting on the bed, arms folded, her feet together on the carpet. But her hands are shaking, her knees too, and the room looks like a hurricane hit; the entire closet has been emptied onto the floor. There are clothes and shoeboxes spilling ancient receipts; a crusty-looking ledger, the black leather binding cracked and frayed. Grocery bags overflow with old nylons, bits of yarn, fabric scraps, magazines — I recognize the covers of some I've cut recipes from: gals on the front with beehives and white-frosted lips. Everything's spilled and tangled, one unholy mess. Before I can open my mouth, she makes a jagged lunge off the bed, her knees buckling as she swoops down after the ledger.

"Aunt Ruby," I cry, "what the devil —?"

Ruby glares at me, scuffling slowly to her feet, all the while clasping that ledger like a Madonna hugging the Holy Infant. Reeling backwards, she flumps onto the bed, then sits smoothing her dress over her knees, staring at the dresser.

"I can't find it."

I suck in a long, deep breath.

"What is it you're looking for?"

"A surprise — for you, for both of us, you know, to brighten things up. I know it's here someplace. I had it made specially — well, since you didn't have time to get a tree. I thought it would be lovely, just lovely. But now . . . I've misplaced it. I'm sure it was here, why, just the other day —"

Shoving the ledger under the pillow, she shoots me this accusing look.

"You peeked, that's it. I'll bet. Why, Lucinda — you didn't like it? Well. Perhaps you didn't appreciate the craftsmanship, or it wasn't quite to your taste — but that's no reason to dispose of something, is it? To throw it out! The nerve, dear. When all I wanted was to surprise you. If you didn't *like* it, Lucinda, you just had to say."

"Aunt Ruby, I don't know what in God's earth you're on about!"

"Please don't swear."

I throw up my hands. Her eyes jackrabbit around the room, like somebody gauging a quick exit. She wrings her hands, then, fixes her gaze on me, madder than a hatter's — ticked off, I mean. As if I've played some dreadful trick, and all this is my fault.

When she speaks, her tone would ice up antifreeze.

"Well, it's a tree, of course. A little ceramic one. I thought it would look nice on the TV set. It plugs in, you know — it's one of those pretty things with the bulbs set in. Oh, I ordered it weeks ago — that lady who makes them, she comes in sometimes? I don't know where you were. She makes them from a mould. Very smart, not at all cheap or homemade-looking. I thought it was something we could have — save you the bother of a real one each year."

I'm on my knees now, stuffing things into bags. Lining up shoes, putting back clothes ripped helter-skelter from their hangers. Pushing everything neatly as possible back into the closet, I notice a square white box on a shelf. Not something I've seen before, it's large enough to fit a good-sized hat. But sliding it down to take a peek, I find it's heavier that I expected — the weight, say, of a cookie jar or the dishes that use to come in detergent.

Sure enough, the tree is inside, its neat white cord wrapped around the base. Some green paint has flaked off the pointy branches, but no matter; the clay underneath looks like snow.

Ruby's eyes light, then glaze with the funny guilt I've seen so often, of little kids unwrapping Dubble Bubbles without slapping down their nickels first.

"Oh Lucinda" — she tugs on the pearl stud in her soft, creased earlobe — "I don't know what's eating me lately. 'Jimmy crack corn an' I don't care!'" she tries to quip, rolling her eyes, a spurt of gaiety. "You're going to think I'm cuckoo. The way one gets, being old. Not too glamorous, I must say — is it, dear?"

She laughs, twisting the little gold band round and round on her finger.

"If Leonard were alive, heaven knows what he'd do with me." Then she clasps her hands together tight; her dark grey eyes cloud with a stubborn, wistful look.

"Well, I'm not fit for the boneyard yet, am I? Now don't just stare — give me a hand, would you? Let's get this thing plugged in and see if it works. I'm dying to see how it looks, especially in the dark."

In the parlour I lift the tree from the box and set it beside the rabbit ears. The bulbs embedded in the little branches blink red, blue, green. Quite pretty, especially with the boob tube off and just the light from the kitchen. For a while we sit side by side on the couch admiring it, Ruby's crazy quilt over our laps. When I squint, the lights wink like stars, and I can almost imagine a real fir, like one in *Tom Thumb* or *Gulliver's Travels*, with midgets scrambling around it. Anyhow, the sight pleases Ruby and she smiles and nods, and presently asks if I'll be a pet and go and get some eggnog.

In the kitchen I fill two mugs from a carton from the store, the stuff glugging out like yellow Pepto-Bismal. Sneaking a taste, for fun I dash in a capful of brandy flavouring. It's old as the hills, heaven knows how long it's been in the cupboard; the tiny glass flask is a type they don't even make anymore.

Ruby cradles her mug in her lap and takes a couple of tiny gulps, wincing as if it's scalding. "Lovely, dear."

The drink hasn't an ounce of kick, I know; still, it gives me a cozy, holed-up feeling, and I put on *Fresh Prince of Bel Air*. We pass the rest of the evening watching TV, muting the ads to listen to the rain. Without let-up, it hammers the eaves all night.

"I hope we don't wash away!" Ruby jibes, rising stiffly when it's time for bed. She takes her cup out to the kitchen while I stay put, eyes on the screen but not really watching. After a bit, she shuffles in in her housecoat, props a box wrapped in silver-bell paper against the TV stand.

"G'night, dear," she says as always, turning her cheek to get a kiss.

She smells of toothpowder and Dippity-Do, the crusty blue setting-gel she's kept in the medicine cabinet for as long as we've lived together, it seems.

"Don't let the bedbugs bite, Aunt Ruby."

For the briefest second I touch my lips to her soft withered face, that skin that feels like crinkled velvet, and give her arm a quick little squeeze. I feel her flinch, the brittle bones beneath her loose, warm flesh.

Oh my.

Next morning I open her present to me, a cardigan the colour of mushroom soup, with a jar of solid Avon perfume tucked inside. It smells like aftershave, but I do as she says and swipe out a fingertipful and apply it to my wrist.

"Your neck too," she urges, "all the different pulse points." She shakes her head, as much as to say: A woman your age, Lucinda — how on earth did you get this far and miss such basic training?

Don't worry, I could sauce back but don't. Between you and the *World News*, I've gotten all the education I need.

I hand her a box done up in identical paper.

"This is for you, Aunt Ruby, go on, open it. Don't mind the wrapping." All the same, she peels off the tape as if performing surgery. Sliding the box out, she folds the paper, laying it carefully aside for inspecting the contents. There's the Magic Bag, some bath salts, and a needlepoint kit complete with a plastic frame, pink to match her bedspread. The scene is of kittens curled in a basket, a rather complicated pattern. Idle hands make for idle minds, was my reasoning when I ordered it from *Canadian Living*.

"You've gone overboard," is her reaction. "But everything's lovely, Lucinda. Beauteeful." And I believe she means it, too.

So Christmas passes quiet as usual, so much foofaraw for one piddling day. We cook a chicken instead of a turkey — why not, with just us two old crows? The only hitch is when Ruby adds sugar instead of salt to the gravy.

A honest mistake, I tell her, heck, something anybody could do. But I decide then and there — like my New Year's resolution about packing away stuff in the store — to make her go for a checkup.

How Santa Claus Came to Cape St. Anthony

WILFRED GRENFELL

A universal robe of white had long covered our countryside, hiding every vestige of our rocky soil, and every trace of the great summer fishery. The mail steamer had paid its last visit for six months; and thus the last link with civilization was broken. Even the loitering sea-ducks and lesser auks had left us. The iron grip of winter lay on sea and shore.

At its best the land here scarcely suggests the word *country* to a southerner — scarcely even the word *moors*. For the rock is everywhere close to the surface, and mosses and lichens are its chief products. The larger part of the country we call *barrens*. Few of the houses deserve even to be called cottages, for all are of light, rough wood. Most are of only one story, and contain but two rooms. The word *huts* would convey a more accurate idea of these humble abodes. The settlements themselves are small and scattered, and at this time the empty tilts of the summer fishermen give a still more desolate aspect to these lonely habitations.

Early in December we had been dumped from the little mail steamer on the harbour ice about half a mile from shore, and hauled up to the little Mission hospital, where we were to make our head-quarters for the winter. The name of our harbour was St. Anthony. Christmas was close upon us. The prospect of enjoying the conventional pleasures of the season was not bright. Not unnaturally our thoughts went over the sea to the family gathering at home, at which our places would be vacant. We should miss the holly and mistletoe, the roast beef and plum-pudding, the inevitable crackers, and the giving and receiving of presents, which had always seemed essential to a full enjoyment of the Christmas holiday.

We soon found that few of the children here had ever possessed a toy, and that there was scarcely a single girl that owned a doll. Now and again one would see, nailed high up on the wall, well out of reach of the children, a flimsy, cheaply painted doll, and the mother would explain that her "Pa had got un from a trader, sir, for thirty cents. No, us don't allow Nellie to have it, 'feared lest she might spoil un" — a fear I found to be only too well grounded when I came to examine its anatomy more closely.

Christmas trees in plenty grew near the hospital; and we could easily arrange for a "Father Christmas." The only question was, whether our stock of toys would justify us in inviting so many children as would want to come. It is easy to satisfy children like these, however, and so we announced that we expected Santa Claus on a certain day. There was great talk about the affair. Whispers reached us that Aunt Mary thought her Joe weren't too big to come; sure he'd be only sixteen. May White was only going eighteen, and she would so like to come. Old Daddy Gilliam would like to sit in a corner. He'd never seen a Christmas tree, and he was nigh on eighty. We were obliged to yield, and with guilty consciences expected twice as many as the room would hold. All through the day before the event the Sister was busy making buns; and it was even whispered that a barrel of apples had been carried over to the "room."

In the evening a sick call carried me north to a tiny place on the Straits of Belle Isle, where a woman lay in great pain, and by all accounts dying. The dogs were in great form, and travelling was fair enough till we came to a great arm of the sea, which lay right in our path, and was only recently caught over with young ice. To reach the other shore we had to make a wide detour, bumping our way along the rough edge of the old standing ice. Even here the salt water came up through the snow, and the dogs sank to their shoulders in a cold mush that made each mile into a half a dozen. We began to think that our chance of getting back in time on the morrow was small indeed. We were also wondering that it seemed to be a real disappointment to ourselves that we should miss the humble attempt at Christmas keeping.

One thing went a long way toward reconciling us to the disappointment. The case we had come to see proved to be one in which skilled help was a real service. So we were contented company round the log fire in the little hut, as we sat listening to stories from one and another of the neighbours, who, according to custom, had dropped in to see the stranger. Before long my sleeping bag was loudly calling to me after the exercise of the day. "We must be off by dawn, Uncle Phil, for there's no counting on these short days, and we have promised to see that Santa Claus is in time for the Christmas tree tomorrow night at St. Anthony." Soon, stretched out on the floor, we slept as soundly as in a feather bed.

Only a few minutes seemed to have passed when, "'Twill be dawning shortly, Doctor," in the familiar tones of my driver's voice, came filtering into my bag. "Right you are, Rube; put the kettle on and call the dogs; I will be ready in a couple of shakes."

Oh, what a glorious morning! An absolute stillness, and the air as sweet as sugar. Everywhere a mantle of perfect white below, a fathomless depth of cloudless blue overhead — and the first radiance of the coming day blending one into the other with a rich, transparent red. The bracing cold made one feel twenty years younger. We found it a hard job to tackle up the dogs, they were so mad to be off. As we topped the first hill, the great bay that had caused us so much trouble lay below us, and my driver gave a joyous shout. "Hurrah, Doctor! there's a lead for us." Far out on the ice he had spied a black speck moving toward the opposite shore. A *komatik* had ventured over the young ice, and to follow it would mean a saving of five miles to us.

We had made a good landing and scaled the opposite hill, and were galloping over the high barrens, when the dogs began to give tongue, loudly announcing that a team was coming from the opposite direction. As we drew near, a muffled figure jumped off, and hauling his dogs to one side, shouted the customary, "What cheer?'

Then a surprised, "The Doctor, as I live! You're the very man I'm after. Why, there's *komatiks* gone all over the country after you. A lad has shot hisself down at St. Ronald's, and he's bleeding shocking."

"All right, Jake, old friend. The turn for the path is off the big pond, is it not?"

"That's it, Doctor, but I'm coming along anyhow, 'feared I *might* be wanted."

My little leader must have overheard this conversation, for she simply flew over the hills. Yet it was already dusk when at length we shot down the semi-precipice on the side of which the little house clings like a barnacle. The anxious crowd, gathered to await our arrival, disappeared before the avalanche, like a morning mist when the sun rises. Following directions, I found myself in a tiny, naked room, already filled with well-meaning visitors, though they were able to do nothing but look on and defile what little air made its way in through the fixed windows. Fortunately, for want of putty, air leaked in around the glass.

Stretched on the floor behind the stove lay a pale-faced boy of about ten years. His clothes had been taken off, and an old patchwork quilt covered his body. His right thigh was covered with a heterogeneous mass of bloody rags. Sitting by him was his mother, her forehead resting in her hands as if she were wrestling with some inscrutable problem. She rose as I entered with: "'Tis Clem, Doctor. He got Dick here to give him the gun to try and shoot a gull, and there were a high ballicater of ice in the way, and he were trying to climb up over it, and he pushed the gun before him with the bar'l turned t'wards hisself, and she went off and shot him, and us doesn't know what to do next — next, and —"

While she ran on with her story I cleared the room of visitors, and kneeling down by the boy, removed the dirty mass of rags that had been used to staunch the blood. The charge had entered the thigh at close quarters above the knee and passed downwards, blowing the kneecap to pieces. Most of it had passed out again. The loose fragments of bone still adhering to the ragged flesh, the fragments of clothing blown into it, and the foul smell and discoloration added by the gunpowder made the outlook a very ugly one. Moreover, there rose to my mind the memory of a similar case in which we had come too late, blood poisoning having set in, and the child having died after much suffering.

The mother had by this time quieted down and was simply repeating, "What shall us do?"

"There's only one thing to be done. We must pack Clem up and carry him to the hospital right away."

"Iss, Doctor, that's the only way, I'm thinking," she replied. "An' I suppose you'll cut off his leg, and he'll never walk no more, and Oh, dear! what —"

"Come tear up this calico into strips and bring me some boiling water — mind, it must be well boiled; and get me that board over there — 'twill serve to make a splint; and then go and tell Dick to get the dogs ready at once; for we've a Christmas tree at St. Anthony tonight, and I must be back at all costs."

In this way we kept her too busy to worry or hesitate about letting the child go; for we well knew it was his only chance, and she had never seen a hospital, and the idea of one was as terrifying as a morgue.

"Home, home, home!" to the dogs — and once again our steel runners are humming over the crisp snow. Now in the darkness we are clinging tightly to our hand-ropes as we shoot over the hills. Now the hospital lights are coming up, and now the lights in the windows of the "room." As we get near they look so numerous and so cheerful that we seem to be approaching a town. Now we can hear the merry ring of children's voices, and can make out a crowd of figures gathered around the doorway. They are waiting for the tardy arrival of "Sandy Claws." Of course, we are at once recognized, and there is a general hush of disappointment as if they had thought at last "Sandy" himself was come.

"He is only a little way behind us," we shouted. "He is coming like a whirlwind. Look out, everybody, when he gets here. Don't get too close to his dogs."

Only a little while later, and the barking of dogs announces the approach of the other *komatik*. But we alone are in the secret of its real mission. Some one is calling from the darkness, and a long sleigh with a double-banked team of dogs has drawn up opposite the doorway. Two fur-clad figures standing by it steady a huge box which is lashed upon it. The light shining on the near one reveals of his muffled face only two sparkling eyes and large icicles bristling over the muffler from heavy moustache and whiskers, like the ivory tusks of some old bull walrus. Both figures are panting with exertion, and blowing out great clouds of steam like galloping horses on a frosty morning. There could be no doubt about it, this time. Here was the real Sandy Claws at last, come mysteriously over the snows with his dogs and *komatik* and big box and all!

The excitement of the crowd, already intense from anxiety over our own delay, now knew no bounds. Where had they come from? What could be in that big box? How large it looked in the darkness! Could it have really been dragged all the way from the North Pole? Luckily, no one had the courage left to go near enough to discover the truth.

The hospital door was swung open, and a loud voice cried out: "Welcome, welcome, Sandy Claws! We're all so glad you've come; we thought you'd forgotten us. Come right in. Come right in! Oh, no! don't think of undoing the box outside; why, you'll freeze all those toys out there! Just unlash it and bring it right in as it is. Come in; there's a cup of tea waiting for you before you go over to start your tree growing fruit."

There had been rumours all the week that Sandy Claws would bring his wife this year. There had been whispers even of a baby. So we could explain the second man; for the Eskimo men and women all dress alike in Labrador, which would account for Mrs. Claws's strange taste in clothes. A discreet silence was observed about her frozen whiskers.

A few minutes later another large box was carried over to the "room." It was full of emptiness, for the toys were on the tree long ago. But two strange masked and bewigged figures stumbled over the snow with it, to carry the little drama to its close. So complete was the faith in the unearthly origin of these our guests, that when the curtain went up more than one voice was heard to be calling out for Ma and

Dad, while a lad of several summers was found hidden under the seat when it came his turn to go up and get his "prize."

And so Santa Claus came to St. Anthony and brought a gift for us as well as presents for the children. Indeed, the best was the one he had kept for us, who had so unworthily thought that the outlook for a happy Christmas was but a poor one. Sleeping overhead, in a clean, white cot, free of pain, and with a good fighting chance for his life, lay our bright-faced lad — Clem. The gift to us this Christmas Day was the chance to save his life. We would not have exchanged it for any gift we had ever heard of. At the old home, where doctors are plentiful, such a gift were impossible.

The great life-giving gift to the world, that Christmas stands for, was to be *ours* to thus faintly re-echo on this needy, far-off shore.

Katherine Brooke Comes to Green Gables

L.M. MONTGOMERY

Anne was already tasting Christmas happiness. She fairly sparkled as the train left the station. The ugly streets slipped past her . . . she was going home . . . home to Green Gables. Out in the open country the world was all golden-white and pale violet, woven here and there with the dark magic of spruces and the leafless delicacy of birches. The low sun behind the bare woods seemed rushing through the trees like a splendid god, as the train sped on. Katherine was silent but did not seem ungracious.

"Don't expect me to talk," she had warned Anne curtly.

"I won't. I hope you don't think I'm one of those terrible people who make you feel that you have to talk to them all the time. We'll just talk when we feel like it. I admit I'm likely to feel like it a good part of the time, but you're under no obligation to take any notice of what I'm saying."

Davy met them at Bright River with a big two-seated sleigh full of furry robes . . . and a bear hug for Anne. The two girls snuggled down in the back seat. The drive from the station to Green Gables had always been a very pleasant part of Anne's week-ends home. She always recalled her first drive home from Bright River with Matthew. That had been in spring and this was December, but everything along the road kept saying to her, "Do you remember?" The snow crisped under the runners; the music of the bells tinkled through the ranks of tall pointed firs, snow-laden. The White Way of Delight had little festoons of stars tangled in the trees. And on the last hill but one they saw the great gulf, white and mystical under the moon but not yet ice-bound.

"There's just one spot on this road where I always feel suddenly . . . 'I'm home,'" said Anne. "It's the top of the next hill, where we'll see the lights of Green Gables. I'm just thinking of the supper Marilla will have ready for us. I believe I can smell it here. Oh, it's good . . . good . . . good to be home again!"

At Green Gables every tree in the yard seemed to welcome her back . . . every lighted window was beckoning. And how good Marilla's kitchen smelled as they opened the door. There were hugs and exclamations and laughter. Even Katherine seemed somehow no outsider, but one of them. Mrs. Rachel Lynde had set her cherished parlor lamp on the supper-table and lighted it. It was really a hideous thing with a hideous red globe, but what a warm rosy becoming light it cast over everything! How warm and friendly were the shadows! How pretty Dora was growing! And Davy really seemed almost a man.

There was news to tell. Diana had a small daughter . . . Josie Pye actually had a young man . . . and Charlie Sloane was said to be engaged. It was all just as exciting as news of empire could have been. Mrs. Lynde's new patchwork quilt, just completed, containing five thousand pieces, was on display and received its meed of praise.

"When you come home, Anne," said Davy, "everything seems to come alive."

"Ah, this is how life should be," purred Dora's kitten.

"I've always found it hard to resist the lure of a moonlight night," said Anne after supper. "How about a snow-shoe tramp, Miss Brooke? I think that I've heard that you snowshoe."

"Yes . . . it's the only thing I can do . . . but I haven't done it for six years," said Katherine with a shrug.

Anne rooted out her snow-shoes from the garret and Davy shot over to Orchard Slope to borrow an old pair of Diana's for Katherine. They went through Lover's Lane, full of lovely tree shadows, and across fields where little fir trees fringed the fences and through woods which were full of secrets they seemed always on the point of whispering to you but never did . . . and through open glades that were like pools of silver.

They did not talk or want to talk. It was as if they were afraid to talk for fear of spoiling something beautiful. But Anne had never felt so near Katherine Brooke before. By some magic of its own the winter night had brought them together . . . almost together but not quite.

When they came out to the main road and a sleigh flashed by, bells ringing, laughter tinkling, both girls gave an involuntary sigh. It seemed to both that they were leaving behind a world that had nothing in common with the one to which they were returning . . . a world where time was not . . . which was young with immortal youth . . . where souls communed with each other in some medium that needed nothing so crude as words.

"It's been wonderful," said Katherine so obviously to herself that Anne made no response.

They went down the road and up the long Green Gables lane but just before they reached the yard gate, they both paused as by a common impulse and stood in silence, leaning against the old mossy fence and looked at the brooding, motherly old house seen dimly through its veil of trees. How beautiful Green Gables was on a winter night!

Below it the Lake of Shining Waters was locked in ice, patterned around its edges with tree shadows. Silence was everywhere, save for the staccato clip of a horse trotting over the bridge. Anne smiled to recall how often she had heard that sound as she lay in her gable room and pretended to herself that it was the gallop of fairy horses passing in the night.

Suddenly another sound broke the stillness.

"Katherine . . . you're . . . why, you're not crying!"

Somehow, it seemed impossible to think of Katherine crying. But she was. And her tears suddenly humanized her. Anne no longer felt afraid of her.

"Katherine . . . dear Katherine . . . what is the matter? Can I help?"

"Oh . . . you can't understand!" gasped Katherine. "Things have always been made easy for you. You . . . you seem to live in a little enchanted circle of beauty and romance. 'I wonder what delightful discovery I'll make today' . . . that seems to be your attitude to life, Anne. As for me, I've forgotten how to live . . . no, I never knew how. I'm . . . I'm like a creature caught in a trap. I can never get out . . . and it seems to me that somebody is always poking sticks at me through the bars. And you . . . you have more happiness than you know what to do with . . . friends everywhere, a lover! Not that I want a lover . . . I hate men . . . but if I died tonight, not one living soul would miss me. How would you like to be absolutely friendless in the world?"

Katherine's voice broke in another sob.

"Katherine, you say you like frankness. I'm going to be frank. If you are as friendless as you say, it is your own fault. I've wanted to be friends with you. But you've been all prickles and stings."

"Oh, I know . . . I know. How I hated you when you came first! Flaunting your circlet of pearls . . ."

"Katherine, I didn't 'flaunt' it!"

"Oh, I suppose not. That's just my natural hatefulness. But it seemed to flaunt itself . . . not that I envied you your beau . . . I've never wanted to be married . . . I saw enough of that with father and mother . . . but I hated your being over me when you were younger than I . . . I was glad when the Pringles made trouble for you. You seemed to have everything I hadn't . . . charm . . . friendship . . . youth. Youth! I never had anything but starved youth. You know nothing about it. You don't know . . . you haven't the least idea what it is like not to be wanted by any one . . . any one!"

"Oh, haven't I?" cried Anne.

In a few poignant sentences she sketched her childhood before coming to Green Gables.

"I wish I'd known that," said Katherine. "It would have made a difference. To me you seemed one of the favorites of fortune. I've been eating my heart out with envy of you. You got the position I wanted . . . oh, I know you're better qualified than I am, but there it was. You're pretty . . . at least you make people believe you're pretty. My earliest recollection is of some one saying, 'What an ugly child!' You come into a room delightfully . . . oh, I remember how you came into school that first morning. But I think the real reason I've hated you so is that you always seemed to have some secret delight . . . as if every day of life was an adventure. In spite of my hatred there were times when I acknowledged to myself that you might just have come from some far-off star."

"Really, Katherine, you take my breath with all these compliments. But you don't hate me any longer, do you? We can be friends now."

"I don't know . . . I've never had a friend of any kind, much less one of anything like my own age. I don't belong anywhere . . . never have belonged. I don't think I know how to be a friend. No, I don't hate you any longer . . . I don't know how I feel about you . . . oh, I suppose it's your noted charm beginning to work on me. I only know that I feel I'd like to tell you what my life has been like. I could never have told you if you hadn't told me about your life before you came to Green Gables. I want you to understand what has made me as I am. I don't know why I should want you to understand . . . but I do."

"Tell me, Katherine dear. I do want to understand you."

"You do know what it is like not to be wanted, I admit . . . but not what it is like to know that your father and mother don't want you. Mine didn't. They hated me from the moment I was born . . . and before . . . and they hated each other. Yes, they did. They quarreled continually . . . just mean, nagging, petty quarrels. My childhood was a nightmare. They died when I was seven and I went to live with Uncle Henry's family. They didn't want me either. They all looked down on me because I was 'living on their charity.' I remember all the snubs I got . . . every one. I can't remember a single kind word. I had to wear my cousins' castoff clothes. I remember one hat in particular . . . it made me look like a mushroom. And they made fun of me whenever I put it on. One day I tore it off and threw it on the fire. I had to wear the most awful old tam to church all the rest of the winter. I never even had a dog . . . and I wanted one so. I had some brains . . . I longed so for a B.A. course . . . but naturally I might just as well have yearned for the moon. However, Uncle Henry agreed to put me through

Queen's if I would pay him back when I got a school. He paid my board in a miserable third-rate boarding-house where I had a room over the kitchen that was ice cold in winter and boiling hot in summer, and full of stale cooking smells in all seasons. And the clothes I had to wear to Queen's! But I got my license and I got the second room in Summerside High . . . the only bit of luck I've ever had. Even since then I've been pinching and scrimping to pay Uncle Henry not only what he spent putting me through Queen's, but what my board through all the years I lived there cost him. I was determined I would not owe him one cent. That is why I've boarded with Mrs. Dennis and dressed shabbily. And I've just finished paying him. For the first time in my life I feel free. But meanwhile I've developed the wrong way. I know I'm unsocial . . . I know I can never think of the right thing to say. I know it's my own fault that I'm always neglected and overlooked at social functions. I know I've made being disagreeable into a fine art. I know I'm sarcastic. I know I'm regarded as a tyrant by my pupils. I know they hate me. Do you think it doesn't hurt me to know it? They always look afraid of me . . . I hate people who look as if they were afraid of me. Oh, Anne . . . hate's got to be a disease with me. I do want to be like other people . . . and I never can now. That is what makes me so bitter."

"Oh, but you can!" Anne put her arm about Katherine. "You can put hate out of your mind . . . cure yourself of it. Life is only beginning for you now . . . since at last you're quite free and independent. And you never know what may be around the next bend in the road."

"I've heard you say that before . . . I've laughed at your 'bend in the road.' But the trouble is there aren't any bends in my road. I can see it stretching straight out before me to the sky-line . . . endless monotony. Oh, does life ever frighten you, Anne, with its blankness . . . its swarms of cold, uninteresting people? No, of course it doesn't. You don't have to go on teaching all the rest of your life. And you seem to find everybody interesting, even that little round red being you call Rebecca Dew. The truth is, I hate teaching . . . and there's nothing else I can do. A school-teacher is simply a slave of time. Oh, I know you like it . . . I don't see how you can. Anne, I want to travel. It's the one thing

I've always longed for. I remember the one and only picture that hung on the wall of my attic room at Uncle Henry's . . . a faded old print that had been discarded from the other rooms with scorn. It was a picture of palms around a spring in the desert, with a string of camels marching away in the distance. It literally fascinated me. I've always wanted to go and find it . . . I want to see the Southern Cross and the Taj Mahal and the pillars of Karnak. I want to know . . . not just believe . . . that the world is round. And I can never do it on a teacher's salary. I'll just have to go on forever, prating of King Henry the Eighth's wives and the inexhaustible resources of the Dominion."

Anne laughed. It was safe to laugh now, for the bitterness had gone out of Katherine's voice. It sounded merely rueful and impatient.

"Anyhow, we're going to be friends . . . and we're going to have a jolly ten days here to begin our friendship. I've always wanted to be friends with you, Katherine . . . spelled with a K! I've always felt that underneath all your prickles was something that would make you worth while as a friend."

"So that is what you've really thought of me? I've often wondered. Well, the leopard will have a go at changing its spots if it's at all possible. Perhaps it is. I can believe almost anything at this Green Gables of yours. It's the first place I've ever been in that felt like a home. I should like to be more like other people . . . if it isn't too late. I'll even practice a sunny smile for that Gilbert of yours when he arrives tomorrow night. Of course I've forgotten how to talk to young men . . . if I ever knew. He'll just think me an old-maid gooseberry. I wonder if, when I go to bed tonight, I'll feel furious with myself for pulling off my mask and letting you see into my shivering soul like this."

"No, you won't. You'll think, 'I'm glad she's found out I'm human.' We're going to snuggle down among the warm fluffy blankets, probably with two hot-water bottles, for likely Marilla and Mrs. Lynde will each put one in for us for fear the other has forgotten it. And you'll feel deliciously sleepy after this walk in the frosty moonshine . . . and first thing you'll know, it will be morning and you'll feel as if you were the first person to discover that the sky is blue. And you'll grow learned in lore of plum puddings because you're going to help me make one for Tuesday . . . a great big plummy one."

Anne was amazed at Katherine's good looks when they went in. Her complexion was radiant after her long walk in the keen air and color made all the difference in the world to her.

"Why, Katherine would be handsome if she wore the right kind of hats and dresses," reflected Anne, trying to imagine Katherine with a certain dark, richly red velvet hat she had seen in a Summerside shop, on her black hair and pulled over her amber eyes. "I've simply got to see what can be done about it."

Saturday and Monday were full of gay doings at Green Gables. The plum pudding was concocted and the Christmas tree brought home. Katherine and Anne and Davy and Dora went to the woods for it . . . a beautiful little fir to whose cutting down Anne was only reconciled by the fact that it was in a little clearing of Mr. Harrison's which was going to be stumped and plowed in the spring anyhow.

They wandered about, gathering creeping spruce and ground pine for wreaths . . . even some ferns that kept green in a certain deep hollow of the woods all winter . . . until day smiled back at night over white-bosomed hills and they came back to Green Gables in triumph . . . to meet a tall young man with hazel eyes and the beginnings of a mustache which made him look so much older and maturer that Anne had one awful moment of wondering if it were really Gilbert or a stranger.

Katherine, with a little smile that tried to be sarcastic but couldn't quite succeed, left them in the parlor and played games with the twins in the kitchen all the evening. To her amazement she found she was enjoying it. And what fun it was to go down cellar with Davy and find that there were really such things as sweet apples still left in the world.

Katherine had never been in a country cellar before and had no idea what a delightful, spooky, shadowy place it could be by candle-light. Life already seemed warmer. For the first time it came home to Katherine that life might be beautiful, even for her.

Davy made enough noise to wake the Seven Sleepers, at an unearthly hour Christmas morning, ringing an old cowbell up and down the stairs. Marilla was horrified at his doing such a thing when there was a guest in the house, but Katherine came down laughing. Somehow, an odd camaraderie had sprung up between her and Davy. She told Anne candidly that she had no use for the impeccable Dora but that Davy was somehow tarred with her own brush.

They opened the parlor and distributed the gifts before breakfast because the twins, even Dora, couldn't have eaten anything if they hadn't. Katherine, who had not expected anything except, perhaps, a duty gift from Anne, found herself getting presents from every one. A gay, crocheted afghan from Mrs. Lynde . . . a sachet of orris root from Dora . . . a paper-knife from Davy . . . a basketful of tiny jars of jam and jelly from Marilla . . . even a little bronze chessy cat for a paper-weight from Gilbert.

And, tied under the tree, curled up on a bit of warm and woolly blanket, a dear little brown-eyed puppy, with alert, silken ears and an ingratiating tail. A card tied to his neck bore the legend, "From Anne, who dares, after all, to wish you a Merry Christmas."

Katherine gathered his wriggling little body up in her arms and spoke shakily.

"Anne . . . he's a darling! But Mrs. Dennis won't let me keep him. I asked her if I might get a dog and she refused."

"I've arranged it all with Mrs. Dennis. You'll find she won't object. And, anyway, Katherine, you're not going to be there long. You must find a decent place to live, now that you've paid off what you thought were your obligations. Look at the lovely box of stationery Diana sent me. Isn't it fascinating to look at the blank pages and wonder what will be written on them?"

Mrs. Lynde was thankful it was a white Christmas . . . there would be no fat graveyards when Christmas was white . . . but to Katherine it seemed a purple and crimson and golden Christmas. And the week that followed was just as beautiful. Katherine had often wondered bitterly just what it would be like to be happy and now she found out.

She bloomed out in the most astonishing way. Anne found herself enjoying their companionship.

"To think I was afraid she would spoil my Christmas holiday!" she reflected in amazement.

"To think," said Katherine to herself, "that I was on the verge of refusing to come here when Anne invited me!"

They went for long walks . . . through Lover's Lane and the Haunted Wood, where the very silence seemed friendly . . . over hills where the light snow whirled in a winter dance of goblins . . . through old orchards full of violet shadows . . . through the glory of sunset woods. There were no birds to chirp or sing, no brooks to gurgle, no squirrels to gossip. But the wind made occasional music that had in quality what it lacked in quantity.

"One can always find something lovely to look at or listen to," said Anne.

They talked of "cabbages and kings," and hitched their wagons to stars, and came home with appetites that taxed even the Green Gables pantry. One day it stormed and they couldn't go out. The east wind was beating around the eaves and the gray gulf was roaring. But even a storm at Green Gables had charms of its own. It was cozy to sit by the stove and dreamily watch the firelight flickering over the ceiling while you munched apples and candy. How jolly supper was with the storm wailing outside!

One night Gilbert took them to see Diana and her new baby daughter.

"I never held a baby in my life before," said Katherine as they drove home. "For one thing, I didn't want to, and for another I'd have been afraid of it going to pieces in my grasp. You can't imagine how I felt . . . so big and clumsy with that tiny, exquisite thing in my arms. I know Mrs. Wright thought I was going to drop it every minute. I could see her striving heroically to conceal her terror. But it did something to me . . . the baby I mean . . . I haven't decided just what."

"Babies are such fascinating creatures," said Anne dreamily. "They are what I heard somebody at Redmond call 'terrific bundles of potentialities.' Think of it, Katherine . . . Homer must have been a baby once . . . a baby with dimples and great eyes full of light . . . he couldn't have been blind then, of course."

"What a pity his mother didn't know he was to be Homer," said Katherine.

"But I think I'm glad Judas' mother didn't know he was to be Judas," said Anne softly. "I hope she never did know."

There was a concert in the hall one night, with a party at Abner Sloane's after it, and Anne persuaded Katherine to go to both.

"I want you to give us a reading for our program, Katherine. I've heard you read beautifully."

"I used to recite . . . I think I rather liked doing it. But the summer before last I recited at a shore concert which a party of summer resorters got up . . . and I heard them laughing at me afterwards."

"How do you know they were laughing at you?"

"They must have been. There wasn't anything else to laugh at."

Anne hid a smile and persisted in asking for the reading.

"Give Genevra for an encore. I'm told you do that splendidly. Mrs. Stephen Pringle told me she never slept a wink the night after she heard you give it."

"No; I've never liked Genevra. It's in the reading, so I try occasionally to show the class how to read it. I really have no patience with Genevra. Why didn't she scream when she found herself locked in? When they were hunting everywhere for her, surely somebody would have heard her."

Katherine finally promised the reading but was dubious about the party. "I'll go, of course. But nobody will ask me to dance and I'll feel sarcastic and prejudiced and ashamed. I'm always miserable at parties . . . the few I've ever gone to. Nobody seems to think I can dance . . . and you know I can fairly well, Anne. I picked it up at Uncle Henry's, because a poor bit of a maid they had wanted to learn, too, and she and I used to dance together in the kitchen at night to the music that went on in the parlor. I think I'd like it . . . with the right kind of partner."

"You won't be miserable at this party, Katherine. You won't be outside looking in. There's all the difference in the world, you know, between being inside looking out and outside looking in. You have such lovely hair, Katherine. Do you mind if I try a new way of doing it?"

Katherine shrugged.

"Oh, go ahead. I suppose my hair does look dreadful . . . but I've no time to be always primping. I haven't a party dress. Will my green taffeta do?"

"It will have to do . . . though green is the one color above all others that you should never wear, my Katherine. But you're going to wear a red, pin-tucked chiffon collar I've made for you. Yes, you are. You ought to have a red dress, Katherine."

"I've always hated red. When I went to live with Uncle Henry, Aunt Gertrude always made me wear aprons of bright Turkey-red. The other children in school used to call out 'Fire,' when I came in with one of those aprons on. Anyway, I can't be bothered with clothes."

"Heaven grant me patience! Clothes are very important," said Anne severely, as she braided and coiled. Then she looked at her work and saw that it was good. She put her arm about Katherine's shoulders and turned her to the mirror.

"Don't you truly think we are a pair of quite good-looking girls?" she laughed. "And isn't it really nice to think people will find some pleasure in looking at us? There are so many homely people who would actually look quite attractive if they took a little pains with themselves. Three Sundays ago in church . . . you remember the day poor old Mr. Milvain preached and had such a terrible cold in his head that nobody could make out what he was saying? . . . well, I passed the time making the people around me beautiful. I gave Mrs. Brent a new nose, I waved Mary Addison's hair and gave Jane Marden's a lemon rinse . . . I dressed Emma Dill in blue instead of brown . . . I dressed Charlotte Blair in stripes instead of checks . . . I removed several moles . . . and I shaved off Thomas Anderson's long, sandy Piccadilly weepers. You couldn't have known them when I got through with them. And, except perhaps for Mrs. Brent's nose, they could have done everything I did, themselves. Why, Katherine, your eyes are just the color of tea . . . amber tea. Now, live up to your name this evening . . . a brook should be sparkling . . . limpid . . . merry."

"Everything I'm not."

"Everything you've been this past week. So you can be it."

"That's only the magic of Green Gables. When I go back to Summerside, twelve o'clock will have struck for Cinderella."

"You'll take the magic back with you. Look at yourself . . . looking for once as you ought to look all the time."

Katherine gazed at her reflection in the mirror as if rather doubting her identity.

"I do look years younger," she admitted. "You were right . . . clothes do do things to you. Oh, I know I've been looking older than my age. I didn't care. Why should I? Nobody else cared. And I'm not like you, Anne. Apparently you were born knowing how to live. And I don't know anything about it . . . not even the A B C. I wonder if it's too late to learn. I've been sarcastic so long, I don't know if I can be anything else. Sarcasm seemed to me to be the only way I could make any impression on people. And it seems to me, too, that I've always been afraid when I was in the company of other people . . . afraid of saying something stupid . . . afraid of being laughed at."

"Katherine Brooke, look at yourself in that mirror; carry that picture of yourself with you . . . magnificent hair framing your face instead of trying to pull it backward . . . eyes sparkling like dark stars . . . a little flush of excitement on your cheeks . . . and you won't feel afraid. Come, now. We're going to be late, but fortunately all the performers have what I heard Dora referring to as 'preserved' seats."

Gilbert drove them to the hall. How like old times it was . . . only Katherine was with her in place of Diana. Anne sighed. Diana had so many other interests now. No more running round to concerts and parties for her.

But what an evening it was! What silvery satin roads with a pale green sky in the west after a light snowfall! Orion was treading his stately march across the heavens, and hills and fields and woods lay around them in a pearly silence.

Katherine's reading captured her audience from the first line, and at the party she could not find dances for all her would-be partners. She suddenly found herself laughing without bitterness. Then home to Green Gables, warming their toes at the sitting-room fire by the light of two friendly candles on the mantel; and Mrs. Lynde tiptoeing into their room, late as it was, to ask them if they'd like another blanket and assure Katherine that her little dog was snug and warm in a basket behind the kitchen stove.

"I've got a new outlook on life," thought Katherine as she drifted off to slumber. "I didn't know there were people like this."

"Come again," said Marilla when she left.

Marilla never said that to any one unless she meant it.

"Of course she's coming again," said Anne. "For weekends . . . and for weeks in the summer. We'll build bonfires and hoe in the garden . . . and pick apples and go for the cows . . . and row on the pond and get lost in the woods. I want to show you Little Hester Gray's garden, Katherine, and Echo Lodge, and Violet Vale when it's full of violets."

Noseworthy (Est. 1929)

PAUL BOWDRING

I was clearing my head in front of the display window of Noseworthy's, a confectionary cum deli cum second-hand furniture store on Water Street, a minimalist convenience or a maximum inconvenience, depending on how you looked at it. A "found gallery" was the way Kate once described it. You never knew what you might find in the place.

Mr. Noseworthy was minimizing even further, if that was possible. The store had been painted long ago and was now a weary shade of red — the colour of one of those ancient sheds on long-abandoned fishing stages. Above the windows a homemade sign had been repainted and no longer said "Noseworthy's Store," or even "Noseworthy's." He had dispensed with the possessive altogether, underlining his obvious desire to own or sell little or nothing. His shop was the mercantile equivalent of a monastery, and on its way to becoming just a thought in his head. Soon he would run the whole business — what there was of it — at home, lying on his back. It was a great place to rest your head and turn your back on the Christmas rush.

I examined this season's Christmas display cum exhibit, though there was little that could be called Christmasy about it. In fact, it was the same one that he had year round, but with subtle variations that only the regular observant window shopper or gallery hopper would notice. Sundry items of second-hand furniture appeared and disappeared, and were replaced by others of the same timeless vintage. Sometimes things reappeared weeks or months later. Whether they had been through the hands and houses of shoppers, it was impossible to tell. Perhaps all the items were from Mr. Noseworthy's own house, and he simply liked to shuffle them back and forth.

In one window were what I had come to think of as his perennials: three tall chrome poles with signs on top, a grouping that, from a distance, looked like a miniature Crucifixion. The two shorter poles had terraced rectangular bases; the base of the middle one was sloped and circular. Atop this pole a backlit plastic Pepsi sign sometimes flashed on and off, depending on whether or not he had bothered to plug it in. The other two held rough-cut cardboard signs with very heavy black hand-printing, one advertising hot dogs, the other, coffee and cigarettes. But something new had been added. The central pole was now encircled with empty soft drink cans, like an ancient Stone Circle, adding to the religious — or pagan — aspect. This was Mr. Noseworthy's Christmas message perhaps — an anti-Nativity scene, or the Nativity fast-forwarded to its inevitable and foretold conclusion.

Tacked to a side wall was an unseasonable soft drink sign — "Pepsi Beats the Others Cold," a beach scene with a frosted border. The back wall had a small grey door, or hatch, which was surrounded by red-brick wallpaper. On the floor was a black patent leather and chrome swivel chair with matching footstool. It was the sort of chair I imagined Mr. Noseworthy sitting in, gazing into the gloom somewhere at the back of his shop as far away as possible from the Christmas rush. He would be humming some old standard perhaps and swivelling a semiquaver every now and then, his feet set into the soft footstool.

On a display shelf in the other window were a pair of ice tongs, a bar jigger, an empty Hostess chip rack that looked like a spinal column, and a modest-looking chandelier, circa 1955. Behind these, on a square of parquet tiles, were a grey Arborite chrome table and a pilled and faded red sofa chair. Inside the shop itself there seemed to be nothing at all.

Though I had been observing what I had come to think of as Mr. Noseworthy's spiritual project for years, I still could not decide whether his business ethic was merely an eccentric personal statement, an unconscious asceticism rooted in some profound whim of his private nature (someone once told me that he used to be a tailor), or a deliberate avant-garde mercantile metaphysics that some member of the corporate elite might soon spot and develop into a franchise operation with Mr. Noseworthy at the helm. Minimalist inconveniences from St. John's to Saint John, then on to Toronto, Calgary, and Victoria by the sea.

I would not have been surprised, however, to come down here some day and find the place closed, the windows caged, and Mr. Noseworthy himself on display behind them — like Kafka's hunger artist, a professional faster, performing for passers-by, wasting away in his cage.

Standing there on the sidewalk of the oldest street in the oldest city of the oldest colony, et cetera, looking into the display window of what was now, perhaps, the oldest store on the street — established, appropriately enough, in 1929; standing there with cold wet snowflakes falling on my head, with the ghostly reflections of centuries of shoppers, their arms full of bags and boxes, rushing east and west behind me, the bells of forgotten streetcars echoing in my ears; standing there in the cold I warmed to the thought that Mr. Noseworthy was single-handedly and single-mindedly shepherding us all in the right direction.

Clear out, pare down, jettison, minimize. The past was a sad and wearisome weight. There was just too much history here to think about. Layers and layers, centuries of salt and sediment, had settled upon us, weighing us down. And no rusty rhetoric or golden arrows on bunting pointing toward the bright mirage of a future were ever going to get us out from under it. But it helped to stand in front of Noseworthy's and inhabit for a few pure and peaceful moments the uncluttered space that hung like a magnetic field around his shop. Headroom, to borrow a term from the audiophiles.

And as I stared into the empty shadowy space beyond the display windows and, for the hundredth time, only *imagined* myself going in and actually buying something (somehow that seemed what he would prefer me to do), I had two not uncomplimentary thoughts. One: John

Cabot and his maggoty crew may have started all this by bringing up fish in hand baskets, and the rapacious fishmongers with their deep sea draggers may have inadvertently put a temporary stop to it, but it was Mr. Noseworthy who was finally going to put the Flemish Cap on the whole sorry misbegotten enterprise, exorcise its greedy wasteful consumptive spirit, jettison the cod merchants and Cabot, and perhaps very soon set sail in a handbasket. Two: If Kate and I could only come here for a Pepsi and a hot dog (sans condiments, to be sure), or a black coffee and a cigarette, our own burdensome history might be lifted from our shoulders, and our too sullied flesh that had once been one might resolve itself anew. *O flesh, flesh, how art thou fishified!*

But the bare truth was, I had never spoken to, or even seen, Mr. Noseworthy. I had never been inside his shop, and neither had anyone I knew. He was even more retiring than his merchandise. Perhaps there was no Noseworthy at all.

I turned and stood on the edge of the sidewalk looking through the falling snow at the "The" building across the street — a three-storey structure with a clothing shop at street level and the definite article above the windows on the second floor. It was followed by the indefinite impressions of two words that I had never been able to figure out. All of a sudden a bus — I would have been less startled by a streetcar — pulled up at the stop I hadn't noticed I was standing at, and its front and rear doors *hissed* open. The driver gave me a businessy and expectant look, and I got on without a moment's hesitation, as if I actually had been waiting for it.

The bus was even emptier than Noseworthy's store. As I tend to do when being driven around in buses or cars, I drifted into a drowsy reverie as it proceeded on its route west along Water Street. The shabby storefronts beneath the new cross-town arterial overpass drifted by, then the old train station, the barber shop where I had once lost my shoulder-length hair, and the sign pointing to the road to Cape Spear. At some point along this route — though I had no recollection at all of the bus stopping or the doors opening — a woman with longer than shoulder-length hair had got on and sat down directly in front of me and thrown her tangled locks over the back of her seat almost into my lap.

Though the bus was warm, large unmelted snowflakes hung like stars from her long black hair — mesmerizing in their intricacy and seemingly imperishable. Perfect hexagrams and hexagons; hexagrams inside hexagons; hexagrams with other stars at their centres; mandala-like hexagons within hexagons, receding into infinity. It was as if I had awoken with lidless eyes under a low-domed planetarium. After the restful emptiness of Noseworthy's store, my head was filling up too fast.

At the Crossroads we left Water Street and began the long climb up Old Topsail Road. I felt the hollow nostalgic ache as we passed the old house, gentrified now almost beyond recognition, where Kate and I had once lived, where we had first made love, in a bedsitting room with a view of the Waterford River. And as the house fell from sight and my eyes fastened once again on the glittering tangled fall of hair inches from my face, burning with regret and desire I had an overwhelming urge to touch it, to kiss it, to bury my face in it. Surely it was being offered to me — a gift of balm. Had she not chosen this seat over all the others in this empty bus, where she could have kept a safe distance from needy lovelorn strangers?

"Man on bus sobs into woman's hair," said the next day's *Daily News*.

"Pathetic," flashed the *Daily Mirror*.

And as I entertained these thoughts, the hair was drawn up, it disappeared through an open door, which closed with a *hiss* and a rubbery *clunk*. And the bus with its driver and his lone companion laboured up the steady incline of Old Topsail Road.

"Kate!" I shouted at the back of his head, and he instinctively hunched his shoulders and let up on the gas. He looked at me in his oversized rearview mirror. I got up and stood facing the rear exit with both hands clasping the chrome pole that ran from ceiling to floor. It felt colder than metal had ever felt before.

He let me off at the next stop. I looked up and down the street, but there was no sign of anyone. Large snowflakes were still falling, drifting down through the bare branches of the elms and maples, but melting almost as soon as they touched the sidewalk. Though it was only four-thirty, it was getting dark, and the street lights were beginning to flicker on. I began to walk back down the hill, but I didn't meet a soul until I reached Water Street. A woman was waiting at a bus stop beneath a streetlight, holding a black umbrella studded with stars.

Christmas Aboard the *Belmont*

GRACE LADD

One of the treasures of the Yarmouth County Museum Archives is a collection of letters written by Grace F. Ladd to her father. Grace Ladd was married to Captain Frederick A. Ladd, a master of several Yarmouth sailing vessels. Following their marriage in 1886, the couple went on a "honeymoon voyage" to Hong Kong in the ship Morning Light. *For the next thirty years or so, Grace Ladd spent a great deal of time at sea with her husband. The couple had two children: Forrest was born in 1890, and Kathryn was born in 1901. Both children were raised at sea. They were among the last Yarmouthians to go to sea in sailing vessels. This particular voyage began in 1897 in Tacoma, Washington, and ended in Buenos Aires. — Eric Ruff, Yarmouth County Museum*

Sunday 28th [November, 1897] Lat. S. 45° 30' Long. W. 188°. Fine weather all the week. Today has been beautiful. Tuesday we sighted the ship *Erby* of Liverpool from Victoria BC with a load of salmon for London. Yesterday we killed our pig, dressed it. [It] weighed 180 lbs. the largest one we have ever had. Today had a fine spare rib for dinner. We had apple sauce, but squash had to take the place of turnips. The squash have kept well; we still have three. Tomorrow I am going to make sausage meat and head cheese. We are sugar-curing one 15 lb. ham, more to experiment than anything else. If it is good we will cook it for Christmas. We were all weighed yesterday while the scales were aft. Fred, 207 lbs.; Mr. Durkee, 176½; Ron, 178½; Forrest, 60; and myself, 138. I think we are all in good condition to go around the Horn. There is a new moon. This is a perfect night.

Thursday 2nd Dec. Lat. S 50° 1' Long. W. 97°. Today is my 33rd birthday. I cannot realize it. The weather is still fine. Ron said tonight, "If this is Cape Horn I would like to be down here all the time." I told him he had better say it easy, a gale can come up so quickly, but the sky looks fine and the barometer is high. I had good luck with my sausage meat and head cheese — have also made mincemeat and prepared the fruit for the Christmas pudding. I use tinned apple and steak for mincemeat, and when I make the pies put little pieces of butter in to take the place of suet, so you see I have been busy this week. Forrest has his lessons regularly, is getting on pretty well. He likes to talk about when we go home again, just as he used to about meeting Fred at the boat. He has written a letter to Santa Claus. When Santa came to get the letter he dropped his mitten in the grate.

Sunday 5th. Lat. S. 54° 30' Long. W. 84°. Weather still fine with a strong westerly breeze, quite a sea running. Forrest thought he would commence a letter to Grace today but it was too rough for him. Yesterday I had to read all of his letters over to him. He can almost read them himself. We have two fires going. The grate keeps the after cabin very comfortable in this weather, but in NY last winter Fred had to get a stove. Forrest is getting ready to go to bed. He does not see much fun in going to bed in broad daylight. Last night there was daylight in the sky all night long. The sun rises in the morning at 3:30, sets at 8:30.

11th Dec. Fred's birthday, 39 years old. We feel such a change in the climate, so much warmer. We are now in Lat. 53° S. and Long. 59° 5' W. Can see plainly a small island called Beauchêne 30 miles south of the Falklands. Thursday at 2 AM (broad daylight), passed 8 miles south Cape Horn. Spoke the English ship *Travancore* from San Francisco for Queenstown, out 60 days. On the 9th we had 6 ships in sight, all coming east. Yesterday, the 10th, at 3 AM, Mr. Durkee called Fred saying, "4 masted ship astern showing flags." We knew he wanted something, or a friend, to signalize at that time. It was the ship *Corinnea*, sailed from Tacoma 5 days after we. He asked us if we would take letters for him. Of course we were pleased to do so. It was a lovely morning. We were just 30 miles South Staten Island. Almost calm, 9 ships in sight, 2 going west. At 6 AM, Captain MacMillan and his passenger, Mr. McGrady, were alongside. It was pleasant meeting them again. They stayed with us about an hour, would not wait for breakfast, so we gave them some hot chocolate. They brought us a piece of spare rib and were so disappointed when they found we had just killed a pig. Their steward has not made any sausage meat so I gave them about 2 lbs., also some mincemeat and books. Capt. MacMillan said they had spoken a great many ships: the *Pendeere*, one of the ships in sight, 70 days from Frisco; and one ship, 80 day[s] from Frisco. Three weeks ago sighted the *Brodick Castle* too far off to signalize. She was sailing very slowly he said. Soon after he left us we got a breeze and separated as we wanted to go west of Falkland, but the wind headed us so we had to come east. I am glad we are bound to the river as we would make a very long passage home. Forrest has written a letter to Grace today.

Christmas evening. Lat. S. 40° 30' Long. W. 55°.20' We have thought of you all at home today, and hoped you were having a very happy Christmas. Notwithstanding head winds and rain squalls, we have all enjoyed ourselves although we have almost given up ever getting in. We are in a trap here, we have a strong current against us running 3 miles an hour, as that is all the *Belmont* can sail now, she is so dirty. The outlook is poor. This last week have only neared our port 94 miles. I just heard the man at the wheel say she would not steer so probably before tomorrow we will lose some of that. Last evening Ron represented Santa Claus (Forrest's faith in him is as great as ever). The makeup was splendid. A sailor had made a fine large tam, with a long new manila rope wig and beard which was combed out. We were afraid Forrest would recognize Ron by his eyes, but we kept the light turned down on account of it hurting them. He changed his voice and acted it out splendidly. It was really fun for us all. We had ginger and sandwiches for him and again Santa was delighted with the tree we had ready for him to trim later. We had already put on the popcorn, tinsel, and bags of nuts. Forrest awaked early this morning and was not disappointed in any of his wishes. Everybody was remembered. We invited all the sailors in to see the tree and gave them a cigar. The steward gave who wanted it a strong drink, and for the others ginger beer. They had a good dinner. They were supposed to have a holiday instead of which have been hauling yards since 7 AM. Ron had dinner with us, which we all decided could not have been better had we been in port. A beef steak pie took the place of turkey, but we had squash, mashed potatoes, boiled ham, jelly, etc. Forrest is just going to bed, tired out, wishing next Christmas was not so far off — Good night.

Thirsts of the Soul

HERB CURTIS

A fast gun for hire, a soldier of fortune, a champion, a paragon of knighthood; his symbol the horse's head, the chess piece; a gentleman living in a swank hotel in San Francisco; a hard hitter with an expensive pistol and a hidden derringer — Paladin, of *Have Gun Will Travel*. In the early sixties, when I was a little boy, Paladin the bounty hunter, the vigilante dressed in black, was my hero.

Cowboy was our favourite game back then, and our barn was where we played it. There were cows and horses in our barn, so we actually did smell like cowboys, not that I remember our odour ever being an issue. We didn't ride the big old draft horses and we didn't rope and hog-tie the cattle, but we were all under the same roof, and somehow they were as much a part of the game as us boys were. I suppose they supplied the sound effects. It was all imagination anyway. If I, with a piece of board sawn to look like a gun on my hip, could be Paladin, our old mares with the dung balls on their hips were as good as the sleekest, blackest alpha stallions that ever galloped upon the western plains.

In 1960, my favourite line was, "Okay, boys, I'm about to introduce you to the rough and tumble." I don't know where I got the line. Picked it up in a comic book, on TV, from Paladin maybe. In the barn, while watering and feeding the cows and horses, my father must have heard me say that line just about every day we played there. He would have heard "Bang! Bang! Bang! Ping! You missed!" a good many times as well.

Yelling out "Ping! You missed!" was how my friend George managed never to get hit. You could be ten feet away from him, aim a cap gun straight at him, and yell "Bang!" Even if there was no boulder or door hinge or anything else handy to him for the bullet to hit and ricochet from, George would immediately yell "Ping! You missed!" I suppose he figured that if your gun fired make-believe bullets, he could conjure up a make-believe object for your bullets to glance from. Sometimes even at point blank range, with the muzzle of your cap gun pointed directly into his back or belly, he'd yell, "Ping!"

"How'd that happen?" you'd ask.

"You hit my belt buckle" — or silver dollar, or gold watch — he'd say. There was no way you could gun him down.

In 1960, all I wanted for Christmas was a toy derringer like the little one that Paladin of *Have Gun Will Travel* always kept hidden somewhere on his person. Putting it into perspective, it wasn't much to ask for. Other kids wanted dolls and skates, skis and trucks, wagons, hockey sticks, chemistry sets, microscopes, bicycles, books, and clothes. But me? A derringer. The one I wanted was displayed in the toy section, page thirty-one of the Eaton's Christmas Catalogue.

I wrote a note much like the following:

Dear Santa,

I've been a good boy all year. All I want for Christmas is a derringer. You'll see it at the bottom of page 31 of the Eaton's Christmas Catalogue, number 29038-62, $3.95.

Yours truly and thank you very much,
Luther Corhern

I gave the note to my mother. My mother always put our notes to Santa in the oven of our kitchen range. Santa or one of his elves would find them there sometime during the night after everyone was in beddy-bye land. We didn't have a fire-place at our house, so Santa always had to come down our stovepipe and out through the oven in order to pick up our notes and deliver our gifts.

Santa Claus dealt directly with the T. Eaton Company and the Post Office Department in those days. We'd write our letters to Santa, and a few weeks before Christmas, my father would go to the post office and return with a box, always from Eaton's, but somehow, too, everything within was always from Santa. Mail, including our box from Eaton's, was delivered to the post office by train. In this way, according to my father, Santa didn't have to carry so much in his sack, saved wear and tear on the reindeer.

About two weeks before Christmas, 1960, a box the size of a refrigerator arrived at our house. I assumed a derringer was in it.

I was ten years old in 1960, a thin, scrawny, spoiled kid with a whole bunch of imagination and a curiosity great enough, almost, to be harmful and dangerous. I'm still curious. I can never leave well enough alone. But in 1960, what can I say? I was a boy.

Now, the box the size of a refrigerator had many gifts in it. Hopefully the derringer was in it, too. I wasn't sure. I had seen the little thing in the catalogue, and I'd written to Santa about it. But I couldn't help but wonder if it really came or not. I also felt a burning need to see what it looked like, to hold it in my hand. It was two weeks before Christmas, and two weeks was a very long time. My mother had placed the box in her bedroom, right there in the corner where I could see it every time I just happened to go in. And it was funny how many times I felt I needed to enter my mother's bedroom during those days. I'd come home from school and select my mother's room to do my homework in. "The lighting's better there," I told my mother. "And it's so private."

"But it's not private," she reasoned. "You can hear every noise in the house from up there."

"I like to hear the radio while I work," I told her. "You play the radio while you prepare supper, right?"

"Yes, but . . ."

"I like to listen to the Christmas songs while I work in your room, in your well-lighted and private room. Just yesterday I heard "O Come All Ye Faithful" while I was up there doing a math problem, and it all worked out so much easier for me. I felt kind of like Einstein. There's nothing like a good background choir to bring out the genius in a person."

"Yeah, well, stay away from the big box."

"Oh, sure, Mom. Sure."

"If I see that you've been tampering with the box, I'll send whatever it is you want for Christmas back to Santa," she warned. "So leave it alone."

I remember the box was surprisingly light for the size of it. One day, while graphically analyzing a paragraph from my English text, with Gene Autry's voice singing "Up on the House Top" coming from the radio in the kitchen, I learned, quite by accident, that I was able to tip the box over so that it rested on its side. I also learned that there was a little crack in the bottom of the box right where the flaps joined. I was curious about that. Another curious thing about the box was that it was very dark inside. You couldn't see a thing in there without a flashlight. Even with a flashlight, I found I couldn't see much. What I really needed, I learned, was a bigger crack.

Now, a derringer is such a tiny thing. And it did not seem to be at the bottom of the box. I could see other things, a sweater, a tie, a big pair of gloves, a scarf, what could have been a lamp . . . but no derringer.

The crack where the flaps joined at the top of the box was covered with strips of tape. Nice tape, but too much of it, I thought. I removed some of it. Just a bit. Just enough so that I could see with the aid of a flashlight that my sister was going to get the doll she wanted. I could see another box big enough to accommodate a pair of boots or skates, but nothing that looked like it might have a derringer in it.

On another day, while I was studying for a geography exam and listening to Bing Crosby singing "Jingle Bells," I noticed that the corner of the big box had somehow gotten damaged. Not a big tear, but big enough to peep through, if you were so inclined. You could see right in . . . with a flashlight.

But you couldn't see a tiny derringer, of course.

Through other damaged parts of the box, through other holes in other corners, I learned what everyone in the family was getting for Christmas, but never did I accidentally stumble upon a little *Have Gun Will Travel* derringer.

A couple of days later, while I was into some serious studying, my mother came into her room and seemed amazed to find that the box had been damaged a bit here and there.

"Did you do that?" she asked pointing at a hole in one of its corners.

"Me? Now, you know me better than that, Mom!"

"Then how did it get torn?"

"Mice, I suppose."

She hid the big box, put it in the closet and locked the door. She put the key next to her bosom. I told her it wasn't necessary, that I would trap the mice, but Mother insisted, locked it away.

"Well, I tried," I said to myself. "Now what?"

The next day I said to my mother, "Know what, Mom? Donald Keenan is getting a derringer for Christmas, too. I think it's the same as the one I asked for."

"What in the world is a derringer?" she asked.

"You know, the little gun I want for Christmas."

"My goodness, Luther! Why didn't you tell us you wanted a little gun for Christmas?"

"I did, Mom! I did! I told you three weeks ago! I wrote it in my note to Santa!" Her insinuation crushed me. Had I forgotten to tell them? Had they forgotten? Had Santa received my note? It seemed to me that I had given the big box a thorough examination.

"So what am I getting for Christmas?" I tried in a casual, conversational way.

"I can't tell you that, dear. You want to be surprised on Christmas morning, don't you?"

"Yeah, yeah, I forgot what I was asking. A good thing you didn't slip it out. To know would spoil everything."

Then Mother said something that threw me off the scent. She said, "We got you something, dear, and I know you're really going to like them."

Them.

Them?

A derringer could not be referred to as a *them*. A derringer was a single item. *Them* is plural. Did this mean they really hadn't purchased a derringer? Did they maybe get me a bag of marbles instead? Could I expect to awaken on Christmas morning and open a gift to find perhaps a bag of plastic toys that no kid in his right mind would be caught dead playing with?

Them. I tried to picture what *them* could be. A pair of something, perhaps. Mitts? Socks? *Them* sounded like clothing. *Them* suggested sunglasses, coloured pencils, ear muffs, skates, two or more books, a box of chocolates, a lunch box and thermos, things, plural, two front teeth, not a derringer.

Sleepless nights is what her reference to *them* caused me. I didn't want a *them*. I wanted one, singular, a derringer that I could hide in my sneaker or pocket or just about anywhere at all, and someday, when Donald or George or Franky or whoever least expected it, just when he thought he had the jump on me, I'd pull the tiny gun, and — "Bang! Bang! Bang!" — the whole lot would be vanquished by none other than Luther Corhern. Luther *Have Gun Will Travel* Corhern and his single-unit, not-a-*them* derringer. I envisioned George shooting me at point blank range and me yelling, "Ping! You hit my derringer!"

My mother was a very smart woman, a superior intellect. She was always smarter than me. Still is. She knew all about me, knew what I was up to. She knew I'd been on the trail like a bloodhound on a still day, and she knew I would not give it up. My mother knew more about me, my imagination and curiosity, the hungers and thirsts of my soul, than I did. She had deliberately used the word *them* to throw me off, and it had worked magnificently. Not only that, she had used the word *them* and hadn't lied.

On Christmas morning, I opened a box big enough to accommodate a pair of skates. Fumbling with the ribbon and the paper, I thought, "Too big for a derringer." I had a lump in my throat because I distinctly remembered emphasizing that a derringer was what I wanted. I did not feel greedy or selfish in any way for my humble request. I did not think it unreasonable for a boy ten years old to expect one tiny, inexpensive little toy gun for Christmas. I had tossed the concept around to the point of preoccupation and couldn't understand the principle behind not getting it, behind getting something she referred to as *them* instead. I knew that my sister was getting pretty much what she wanted. I knew this from accidentally peeping into the big box the size of a refrigerator. Why not me? Had I been a bad boy? Was I not loved? And there I was opening a box big enough to put a pair of skates in, a box big enough to house a *them*, a box big enough to house twenty-five derringers.

The moment it took me to open that gift was an important one, maybe one of the most important moments of my life. I say this because it was nearly forty years ago and I remember it as if it had occurred yesterday. I remember the tree with its shabby decorations, the gentle snowstorm beyond the window, the ribbons and wrapping paper strewn about the room, the sudden lull of activity, all eyes on me.

In the box was a black leather gun belt with two holsters, two beautiful cap guns with white plastic handles, and just above the right holster was a tiny pocket. A derringer exactly like the one I wanted was in the little pocket. Also in the box was a little wallet with about twenty-five calling cards that read, "Have Gun Will Travel."

Yes, it was an important moment. To weep with joy is not something that often occurs in a person's life.

Merry Christmas, Nancy Rose

JOAN CLARK

Cape Race, November 15

Dear Nancy,

Enclosed is a money order for $15 to buy Christmas books for Tom and Stanley. For your father I want a good book, with clear maps, of the constellations. For Stanley I would like a book with illustrations, preferably colour, of the underwater world. I'm early with this request because I know you are busy with your studies and won't have a lot of time to shop. Don't bother mailing them, just bring them down when you come for Christmas.

Please give my regards to Maggie and Wilfred.

Love, Mom

Nancy bought the books and mailed them to the Cape along with the pressed flowers; she had already made up her mind that if she could arrange to stay in the city, she wouldn't go home for Christmas. She hadn't yet asked the Hunts if she could stay, but she thought they might be glad of the company. Philip had already mentioned that he would be spending Christmas in St. John's and had asked the class to his flat at the end of term for an evening of wassail, whatever that was. Not only did Nancy plan to be there, but she intended to invite Philip to Christmas dinner at Hunts'.

Cape Race, December 7

Dear Nancy,

Of course we're disappointed that you won't be here for Christmas but we certainly understand your wish to stay in St. John's with your cousin and friends. It will be a boon for Maggie and Wilfred who find Christmas particularly hard since Peter's plane went down on December 22nd. We'll send our presents to town with John when he sees the eye doctor next week.

There's about a foot of snow on the ground here which means your brother more or less lives outside where he and Kenny Halleran have built an igloo. They want to sleep in it tonight but I've said No to that but have agreed to let them have their supper out there, your mother having spoiled them with a basket of food. I must say it looks spectacular in the dark seeing the ice lit up from inside with a flashlight.

Good luck with your exams. Don't stay up all night studying.

Love, Dad

Philip Palmer's flat in Rawlin's Cross was three rooms on the third floor of a wedge-shaped building overlooking the harbour. The living room was furnished with shelves made from apple crates and boards, and a chesterfield stinking of cat piss. The students sat on cushions scattered on the floor; there were nine of them; the rest of the class was either too shy to come or had left for home. Nancy had never drunk mulled wine and was wooed by the headiness of its warmth and by the shadows flickering on the walls from candles burning in jar tops set on shelves and sills. Acutely aware of her attraction for Philip, she staked out a cushion by the window where he could plainly see her as someone separate from the others. She was wearing one of her aunt's hand-me-downs, a red wool dress with a black cinch belt that gave her breasts a voluptuous swell, and had reddened her lips with Scarlet Poppy. Gazing out the window at the buoy light marking the harbour entrance, with the nipple of Signal Hill on one side and the South Side hills on the other, she ignored the conversation of her male classmates, who were little more than boys — from their banter and lack of seriousness you could tell that they weren't really men — but she listened closely to Philip, who was lying cross-legged on the floor, his head on a cushion. She hadn't yet asked him for Christmas dinner, though her aunt had said yes, by all means, invite Mr. Palmer to join us. If only he would get up and go into the kitchen, then she would follow him in and ask — she would never hear the end of it if she invited him in front of the others. And she didn't want to wait until the others had left. That would be setting herself up as someone who was an *easy lay*. That was the way these boys spoke to each other, using words like *broad* and *chick*, *loose* and *pushover*. She also had her aunt's curfew to keep and didn't want to get on the bad side of her by staying out past midnight. Nancy had a fountain pen in her purse but no paper; before it was time to leave she went into the bathroom and, after locking the door, printed the invitation in large blurry letters on a length of toilet paper. When she went into the bedroom to fetch her coat, she put the invitation beneath Philip's pillow. He slept on the floor, on a mattress where they had piled their jackets and coats, which surprised her; she would have thought that someone of his position could afford a bed.

Christmas dinner at Circular Road was a jolly affair. There were Christmas crackers, tissue-paper hats, toy horns and whistles, hard candy, salted nuts and roasted chestnuts. Doorways and windows were trimmed with holly. The twelve-foot tree in the dining room was decorated with candle lights, each one having a tiny rotating shade. Maggie had cooked the turkey herself, the maid having gone home to Harbour Grace. Ruth had brought pease pudding, Granny Mulloy figgy duff pudding with brown sugar sauce, and Aurora had sent her version of Merla's cake. There were eight of them around the table, nine after Cheryl's boyfriend arrived. She and Reg sat opposite each other at Wilfred's end of the table while Nancy and Philip occupied the same position at Maggie's end. Nancy felt festive and light-headed, more from being paired with Philip than from drinking pink champagne. Surrounded by laughter and talk, she drifted along with the current of merriment and laughter, bumping into bits of conversation, content to half listen, to float in a reverie of conviviality and good will. But she snapped to attention when Maggie began questioning Philip, drawing him out in a way that Nancy, as his student, was unable to do. He wasn't difficult to draw out and said he was enjoying St. John's "hugely" — another of his words. What a stroke of luck that he was sitting beside Maggie, since she asked the questions Nancy wanted to ask.

His father was the rector in the village of Corfe Castle in Dorset, where Philip and his sister Elaine had grown up. He had read history at Cambridge and intended to return to England someday to complete his doctorate, but first he was eager to try his wings. What better place than Newfoundland, which until recently had been Britain's oldest colony. Added to this was the fact that his mother's family had an early connection to Newfoundland. In 1883, his mother's uncle, Edward Webb, left Poole for Trinity, where he served as curate in St. Paul's for three years, and would have served longer had he not perished on the *Clara Jillian* when she was caught in an April gale on her return from England, where Edward had gone for a holiday. Although his uncle's tenure in Newfoundland had been brief, it had affected Philip profoundly; as a boy reading his uncle's letters, he had longed to come to Newfoundland, a place that sounded as rugged and unspoilt as any of the wild places described in the *Boy's Own Annual*. Though he hadn't the slightest desire to become a man of the cloth like his father and uncle — perhaps not wanting to appear maudlin or sentimental, Philip paused and stared into his wineglass — the fact was that, in a curious way, he grew up thinking he had to carry on Edward's adventure. Not duplicate it, that was an impossible feat and he was an entirely different bloke from his uncle and this was, after all, the twentieth century. Nevertheless, he felt honour bound to connect in some way with Edward, whose life had been tragically severed in the flush of youth. Did that sound impossibly romantic and boyish? Not at all, said Maggie.

"Honour bound" was a phrase that would catch up with Nancy later on; for now, she was busy trying to pin down the kind of man Philip Palmer was. She already knew he was unselfconscious and animated, forthcoming, without the reputed English reserve. When he was speaking full tilt, he smacked his lips, oblivious to tiny particles of saliva spraying from his mouth, landing, where were they landing? On his dinner plate, she supposed. When he settled down to his food, he ate with the same smacking sound. A noisy eater — in spite of his Englishness and his height. Nancy was reducing him to a more manageable size. She could see that his boyish earnestness charmed her aunt. Somehow he knew that she expected guests to wear their best caps — in Maggie's view, there was nothing false or wrong in trying to impress, in putting the best foot forward.

They were drinking brandy when the telephone rang. Maggie looked pointedly at Nancy, and she felt a guilty jolt as she realized that her aunt knew right away who was calling. Nancy went into the hall and picked up the receiver.

"Merry Christmas, Nancy Rose." Her father was the only one who got away with using her shipwreck name.

"Merry Christmas, Dad. I was waiting until we finished eating to call," she said, though in Philip's presence she had scarcely given the Cape a thought.

He ignored the apology. Being Dad, he sounded unruffled and unperturbed, but so far away. "I forgot that townies dine late." Was he teasing or was that a trace of sarcasm in his voice? "Are you enjoying yourself?"

"Yes, we're having a lot of fun. Guess what. I've been drinking pink champagne!"

"No wonder you're having fun. We've been drinking Beatty's blueberry wine. The Newhooks are there I suppose?"

"Yes."

"I'll talk to Ruth and Maggie later, but first your mother wants a turn. She's been standing at my elbow trying to wrench the receiver from my hand."

"Merry Christmas, Nancy."

"Merry Christmas, Mom."

"We just got in from Beatty and John's. We had dinner with them." Her mother sounded breathless and excited. "We enjoyed ourselves, but it wasn't the same without you. I miss you, Nancy."

Could this be her mother talking?

"Stanley wants a word."

Her brother's voice was so faint Nancy had to strain to hear. "Would you believe Dad put hoofprints on the roof last night?" he whispered plaintively. "I'm twelve years old and I still have to pretend there's a Santa. Mom says I'll hurt his feelings if I don't go along with it."

"Did you get the telegram?"

"Yeah."

Their father was a believer in family traditions: the telegram from the North Pole, the lump of coal in the toe of the stocking, the carol-sing Christmas Eve, the scrawny spruce in the living room corner, the boughs on the door and window sills, the partridgeberry garlands, the hoof marks on the roof. The hoof marks were a mystery; ever since Nancy could remember, when there was snow on Christmas morning, their father would take Stan and her up the ladder to see the prints on the roof.

When Maggie came to the phone, Nancy fled upstairs to the bathroom, turned on the tap and splashed cold water on her face in an effort to pull herself together. If she went downstairs with a red nose and bloodshot eyes, Philip would know she was missing home. To banish homesickness, she imagined a procession of choristers in a Dorset church and a collection of maiden aunts and widowers sitting down to the Palmer's Christmas goose. There was so much more for Philip to miss, and if he could overcome homesickness, so could she.

The Still of Christmas

ERNEST BUCKLER

There were the three days: the day before Christmas, the day of Christmas, and the day after. Those three days lamplight spread with a different softness over the blue-cold snow. Faces were all unlocked; thought and feeling were open and warm to the touch. Even inanimate things came close, as if they had a blood of their own running through them.

On the afternoon of the first day the cold relaxed suddenly, like a frozen rag dipped in water. Distances seemed to shrink. The dark spruce mountain moved nearer, with the bodies of the trees dark as before rain.

Martha had done up all her housework before noon, and the afternoon had the feel of Saturday. It was a parenthesis in time — before the sharp expectancy began to build with the dusk and spark to its full brightness when the lamp was lit. There were so many places it was wonderful to be that afternoon that David was scarcely still a minute.

He went outside and made a snowman. The snow was so packy it left a track right down to the grass roots. It was a perfect day to be alone with, the only confidant of its mysteries. Yet it was equally nice to be with people. The claim of their ordinary work was suspended today, no one's busyness was any kind of pushing aside.

He went inside and sat close to his grandmother. He asked her a string of questions; not for information, but because he was young and she was old. To let her feel that she was helping him get things straight was the only way he knew to give her some of the splendid feeling he had so guiltily more of.

He went out again where Chris was sawing wood. How could Chris *stand* there like that, today . . . his shoulders moved so patiently, the saw sank with such maddening slowness. Yet because he did, he was somehow wonderful. When a block fell, David would thrust the stick ahead on the saw-horse with such a prodigal surge of helpfulness beyond what the weight of the wood asked for that Chris would have to push it back a little before he made the next cut.

He went back into the house and stood at the table where his mother was mixing doughnuts.

Everything was clean as sunshine. The yellow-shining mixing bowl in the centre of the smooth hardwood bread board; the circles of pure white where the sieve had stood; the measuring cup with the flour-white stain of milk and soda on its sides; and the flat yellow-white rings of the doughnuts themselves lying beside the open-mouthed jug that held the lard, drift-smooth at the centre and crinkled like pie crust along the sides. His mother carried the doughnuts to the stove, flat on her palm, and dropped them one by one into the hot fat. He followed her, watching. They'd sink to the bottom. Then, after a fascinating second of total disappearance, they'd loom dark below the surface, then float all at once, brown and hissing all over. It had never been like this, watching her make doughnuts before.

He went into the pantry and smelled the fruitcakes that lay on the inverted pans they'd been cooked in. He opened the bag of nuts and rolled one in his palm, then put it back. He put his hand deep down into the bag and rolled all the nuts through his fingers: the smooth hazelnuts that the hammer would split so precisely; the crinkled walnuts with the lung-shaped kernels so fragile that if he got one out all in one piece he'd give it to Anna; the flat black butternuts whose meat clove so tightly to the shell that if you ever got one out whole you saved it to the very last.

Then he leaned over and smelled the bag of oranges. He didn't touch it. He closed his eyes and smelled it only. The sharp, sweet, reminding, fulfilling smell of the oranges was so incarnate of tomorrow it was delight almost to sinfulness.

He went out and sat beside Anna. She was on her knees before the lounge, turning the pages of the catalogue. They played "Which Do You Like the Best?" with the coloured pages. Anna would point to the incredibly beaded silk dress that the girl wore, standing in a great archway with the sunlight streaming across it, as her choice. He'd say, "Oh, I do, too." And as his hand touched Anna's small reaching hand and as he looked at her small reaching face, he almost cried with the knowing that some Christmas Day, when he had all that money he was going to have, he'd remember every single thing that Anna had liked the best. She'd find every one of them beneath the tree when she got up in the morning.

He went out where his father was preparing the base for the tree. All the work-distraction was gone from his father today, and David knew that even if so few pieces of board were to be found as to defeat anyone else, his father would still be able to fix something that was perfect.

Joseph lay one crosspiece in the groove of the other. He said to David, "Think you could hold her just like that, son, till I drive the nails?"

"Oh yes," David said, "yes." He strove with such intense willingness to hold them so exactly that every bit of his strength and mind was soaked up. He touched the axe that would cut the tree. The bright cold touch of it shone straight through him.

He ran in to tell Anna it was almost time. He waited for her to button her gaiters. He was taut almost to pallor when Joseph stepped from the shop door, crooked the axe handle under one arm, and spat on the blade for one final touch of the whetstone.

"Chris," he called, "we're *goin!*"

"All right," Chris said. "You go on. I guess I'll finish the wood."

How *could* Chris stay here? How could anyone *wait* anywhere today?

It was almost impossible to be still even in the place where the thing was going on.

Joseph walked straight toward the dark spruce mountain. David and Anna would fall behind, as they made imprints of their supine bodies in the snow; then run to catch up. They would rush ahead, to simulate rabbit tracks with their mittens — the palms for the parallel prints of the two back feet, the thumb the single print where the front feet struck together; then stand and wait. Their thoughts orbited the thought of the tree in the same way their bodies orbited Joseph's.

"Anna, if anyone walked right through the mountain, weeks and weeks, I wonder where he'd come out . . ."

"Dave, hold your eyes almost shut, it looks like water . . ."

"There's one, there's one . . ." But when they came to it the branches on the far side were uneven.

Joseph himself stopped to examine a tree.

"Father, the best ones are way back, ain't they?" David said quickly. This *was* a good tree, but it wouldn't be any fun if they found the perfect tree almost at once.

"There's one . . ." But it was a cat spruce.

"There's one . . ." But the spike at the top was crooked.

"There's one, Father . . ." But a squirrel's nest of brown growth spoiled the middle limbs.

Joseph found the perfect fir, just short of the mountain. The children had missed it, though their tracks were all about. He went to it from the road, straight as a die. The bottom limbs were ragged, but those could be cut off; and above them, the circlets of the upward-angling branches were perfect. The trunk was straight and round. The green of the needles was dark and rich, right to the soft-breathing tip.

"How about this one?" Joseph said.

The children said nothing, looking at the lower limbs.

"From here up," Joseph said.

The children said nothing, looking at the lower limbs.

"From here up," Joseph said. He nicked the bark with his axe.

"Yes, oh yes," they cried then. "That's the best tree anyone could find, ain't it, Father?" The ridiculous momentary doubt of their father's judgement made them more joyous than ever.

They fell silent as Joseph tramped the snow about the base of the tree to chop it. David made out he was shaking snow from his mitten. He took off Anna's mitten, too, pretending to see if there was any snow in hers. He stood there holding her mitten-warmed hand, not saying anything, and watched his father strike the first shivering blow.

The tree made a sort of sigh as it swept through the soft air and touched the soft snow. Then the moment broke. The children came close and touched the green limbs. They thrust their faces between them — into the dark green silence. They smelled the dark green, cozy, exciting smell of the whole day in the balsam blisters on the trunk.

Joseph stood and waited: the good kind of waiting, with no older-hurry in him. Then he lifted the tree to his shoulders, both arms spread out to steady it at either end.

The twins walked close behind him. They let the swaying branches touch their faces. They walked straight now, because the first cast of dusk had begun to spread from the mountain. The first dusk-stiffening of the snow and a shadow of the first night-wonder were beginning. Now the things of the day fell behind them; because of all that part of the day which could be kept warm and near was in the tree, and they were taking the tree home, into the house, where all the warm things of after dark belonged.

Anna whispered to David, "I got somethin for you, Dave."

And he whispered, "I got somethin for you, too."

"What?"

"Oh, I can't tell."

Then they guessed. Each guess was made deliberately small, so there'd be no chance that the other would be hurt by knowing that his present was less than the vision of it. Each of them felt that, whatever they had for each other, all their lives would have something of the magic, close binding smell of the fir boughs somewhere in it, like the presents for each other of no other two people in the world.

***

Martha had huddled the furniture in the dining room together, to clear a corner for the tree.

"Aw, Mother," David said, "you said you'd wait!"

His mother laughed. "I just moved the sofa and mats a little," she said. "I didn't touch the trimmings. Do you think it's too late to put them up before supper?"

"No," David cried, "no. I'm not a bit hungry."

"I suppose if supper's late it'll make you late with your chores, won't it?" she said to Joseph.

"Well," Joseph said, "I suppose I *could* do 'em before supper." He hesitated. "Or do you want me to help you with the trimmin?"

"Oh, yes," David said. "Help us."

He wanted everyone to be in on it. Especially his father. It was wonderful when his father helped them with something that wasn't work, *inside* the house.

David fanned open the great accordion-folding bell (because of one little flaw his mother had got it — it didn't seem possible — for only a quarter). He tied the two smaller bells on the hooks of the blinds. Then he and his father and Chris took off their boots. They stood on chairs in their stocking feet and hung the hemlock garlands Ellen had made: around the casings and from the four ceiling corners of the room to a juncture at its centre, where the great bell was to be suspended.

Someone would say, "Pass the scissors?" and David would say, "*Sure*" beating with gladness to do them any small favours. Martha would stand back and say, "A little lower on that side," and they'd say, "Like that? Like that? More still?" all full of that wonderful patience to make it perfect. Everyone would laugh when someone slipped off a chair. His father would say, "Why wouldn't some red berries look good in there?" and to hear his *father* say a thing like that filled the room with something really splendid. Sometimes he'd step on Anna's toe as they busied back and forth. He'd say, "Oh, Anna, did that hurt?" and she'd laugh and say, "No, it didn't hurt." He'd say, "Are you *sure*?" and just that would be wonderful.

The dusk thickened and the smell of the hemlock grew soft as lamplight in the room. The trimming was done and the pieces swept up and put into the stove.

Then Joseph brought in the tree, backward through the door so the limbs wouldn't break. No one spoke as he stood it in the space in the corner. It just came to the ceiling. It was perfect. Suddenly the room was whole. Its heart began to beat.

They ate in the dining room that night. David smelled the roast spare ribs that had been kept frozen in the shop. He felt now how hungry he'd been all the time.

The room was snug with the bunching of the furniture and the little splendour of eating there on a weekday. And when Martha held the match to the lamp wick, all at once the yellow lamplight soft-shadowed their faces (with the blood running warm in them after being out in the cold) like a flood and gathered the room all in from outside the windows. It touched the tree and the hemlock and the great red bell with the flaw no one could ever notice, like a soft breath added to the beating of the room's heart: went out and came back with a kind of smile. The smell of the tree grew suddenly and the memory of the smell of the oranges and the feel of the nuts. In that instant suddenly, ecstatically, burstingly, buoyantly, enclosingly, sharply, safely, stingingly, watchfully, batedly, mountingly, softly, ever so softly, it was Christmas Eve.

The special Christmas Eve food lit their flesh like the lamplight lit the room. Even Christopher talked fast. Even the older ones spoke as if their thoughts had come down from the place where they circled, half-attentive, other nights.

David glanced out of the window. He saw Old Herb Hennessey walking down the road. When Herb went into his house tonight there'd be no fire in the stove, and after supper he'd sit and read the paper and it would be just like any other night.

David watched the blur of his heavy body move down the road in the almost-dark. It seemed as if no sound was coming from him anywhere, even if you were there where his feet were falling. He felt the funniest, scariest kind of pity for Herb. He felt the sweetest, safest sort of exaltation: that such a thing could be, however incredibly, but not ever for him. (He was to wonder, years later, if this now were some sort of justice of the unconscious cruelty in that thought.)

When he went to help his father with the chores, great-flaked Christmas snow began to fall against the sides of the yellow lantern. The barn smelled warm and cozy. He secretly poked in extra hay to the cows, because it was Christmas Eve. The torture of being outside the house was an exquisite one, because the tree was there to go back to.

All evening long, some things (the faces, the conversation) were open as never before. Other things (the packages somewhere in the closet, the sound of nuts tumbled into a bowl behind the closed pantry door) were bewitchingly secret. There were the last desperate entreaties of him and Anna on the stairs: to call each other in the morning and *please* not to go down first. His prayers were over so quickly they might have been read at a glance from some bright sheet in his mind. Then the blanket warmth and the tiredness in him stole out to meet each other.

He lay beside Chris and listened to the voices downstairs behind the closed doors, the footsteps, the rustlings. He tried to identify them at first: Would that be hanging oranges on the boughs? Would that be a sled for Chris? That sound of paper, were they unwrapping a doll for Anna? Would that be some swift gleaming thing, like skates, for him?

Then the sounds began to wave and flicker through the candlelight of drowsiness and warmth.

He whispered to Chris, "Chris, when you learn to skate fast, is it the best fun of anything?" "Kind of," Chris said. He whispered, "Chris, someday let's go way back to the top of the mountain," and Chris said, "Maybe." He whispered, "Chris, how old is Herb Hennessey? Is he four times as old as us?" and Chris said, "I guess." The pauses between questions and reply got longer. He said, "Chris, are you asleep?" There was no answer at all. He thought, "How *could* Chris go to sleep?"

Then the sounds downstairs started to flow along a stream, and he floated alongside them. Then they drifted ahead of him and he began to sink. But the stream was of wool, so foldingly deep and closingly warm that he didn't try any more to reach out for the surface.

Ellen slept dreamlessly when the house was still.

Joseph dreamed that as he lifted the log onto the sled bench, Martha and the children came running to help him, but suddenly he was powerless because the snow had disappeared. And Martha dreamed that it was morning and the children were all laughing as they opened their things, but she couldn't find Joseph anywhere in the house, and suddenly all the needles of the tree began to fall. And Chris sighed in his sleep because he and Charlotte were on the bank of a moving stream, but as they knelt together to drink they couldn't seem to draw any water up into their mouths. And Anna dreamed that it was morning and some voice kept calling her to come see the tree. She said she had to wait for David, but she couldn't resist this voice; and when David came to the head of the stairs, there was water across the step, and she couldn't quite reach his hand across it.

David slept and he dreamed that they were all walking back the road that led to the top of the mountain. All the trees along the road were Christmas trees. They were shining with presents, but as he reached for something (for himself or for Anna) the thing would disappear, and Herb Hennessey would be there, cutting down the tree.

A train whistle carried through the soft air all the way from town. As the tree fell the sound of the train whistle crept into the dream, into the sound of the falling tree.

David awoke at five o'clock. The morning was Christmas-still. He thought it must be night yet until he heard the crackle of kindling in the stove, and the voices of his father and mother in the kitchen. They were day voices. Suddenly sleep past put a sharp edge of clarity on everything. This was the morning that had had Tuesday and Wednesday before it, and then only Wednesday, and now this was the morning itself.

He shook Chris. "Chris, Chris, it's morning!" He leaped out of bed. "Anna, Anna," he called, "it's morning, the fire's made."

He and Anna waited, shivering in the hall, for Chris ("Chris, Chris, hurry up"). They went down the stairs, shivering more than cold had ever made them shiver. They went past the dining room where the wonder waited, into the kitchen. Chris glanced into the dining room as he passed, but David whispered to Anna, "Don't look." Neither of them turned a head.

They stood by the kitchen stove. They said, "Merry Christmas"; but their voices were like voices they recited with when they'd forgotten the next line. They tried to stop shivering; but they couldn't, even by the stove. These were like moments out of time altogether, because they were up and going to do something splendid, but the lamp was still lit, the day hadn't really begun.

Martha had warmed their clothes on the oven door. David pulled his on in the porch. Anna took hers into the pantry. Joseph came in from the barn with the milk, and Martha strained the milk while he washed his hands. Not till then did she pick up the lamp and say, "Come, Joseph." She led them all through the dining room door.

The tree was there. So still. So Christmas-still. So proudly, evenly full of its own mysterious bearing that even when Martha turned up the wick of the lamp, no one rushed to touch it. For a minute no one moved. This was the tree of hope: the yellow globes of oranges hanging on the boughs, the perfectly scalloped garlands of popcorn, the white tents of handkerchiefs on the green limbs, and secretly between the branches, nearer the trunk, the mesmeric presents themselves. They knew so surely that everything they wanted would be there, they could wait.

"Joseph," Ellen said, "do you remember the first little fir we . . .?" Then the children swarmed about the tree.

Joseph and Martha guided their explorations. They passed down what was beyond the reach of young arms, pointing at something that still remained for one or the other if that one had decided his allotment must be exhausted, holding one thing back for each of them, so that no one would run out of gifts first.

Chris's sled and larrigans were on the floor. But David's skates and Anna's doll were at the top of the tree. When Joseph reached for them they held their breath, as if somewhere on the way down the miracle might disappear before they had touched it once. David put one bright blade against his face. The cool touch of the bright, swift steel and the smell of the new leather mingled with the smell of the oranges and the tree. Anna touched gently the soft, fragile doll's face. There were scribblers and pencils and the jackets and the dress.

Then almost at the last, David found what Anna had got for him. It was a book. *Robinson Crusoe*. He opened it and saw the wonderful waiting words running over the starch-clean pages. He said, "Oh, Anna."

Then he told her, no higher, a little higher, this side, *there*, until at last she saw the ring he'd got for her with soap-wrapper coupons. And when she laid down the doll itself and held the ring in her hand (forgetting to finish the smile she'd started, because the ring was so beautiful), that was better even than any of the things he had found for himself.

They thought it was all finished. But it wasn't.

"You didn't look *behind* the tree," Martha said.

There they found the miniature house, perfect right down to the tiny covers on the stove, for Anna; and the kaleidoscope for David.

"Chris got them out of his rabbit money," Joseph said.

They could hardly believe it. They'd never thought of Chris getting *anything* for them, and here he (Chris!) had thought of getting them things like that.

They had the funniest feeling. It was hurtful but sweet for feeling it together: the shame that neither of them had thought of getting anything for Chris at all. He'd seemed like the older ones, who watched *their* having as if that were a gift itself. He'd seemed to have no special separate place in him that a special gift could match.

They exclaimed more about his presents, then, than about their own. They said, "Chris, ain't that sled a beauty! It's the best thing of all, ain't it!" — because, though Chris's things did add up to more than theirs in a way, there was nothing amongst them just like the kaleidoscope or the little stove with the perfect covers.

The tree was delivered now of its mysteries and the plain having began. The lamp grew pale in the beginning sunlight. Martha remembered breakfast, and Joseph remembered the rest of his chores. David got a hammer and broke the first nut. He broke the skin of the first orange and felt the first incarnate taste of its sharp juice. And suddenly it was Christmas Day.

After breakfast Chris went to his snares. "Do you wanta go with me, Dave?" he said.

"Yeah, sure." *Today?* he thought — but Chris had thought of a present for him, and he hadn't thought of Chris at all.

"Are you going to try out your new jacket?" his mother said.

"I guess not now," he said. He couldn't bear to think of putting it on just yet and maybe getting it wet and wrinkled in the snow.

There were no rabbits in the snares. When they came to the last one, David said, "I guess I gotta squirt my pickle, if it won't take all the snow off yer rabbit roads."

Chris laughed, but he turned his back to fiddle with the snare pole. David tossed his mittens quickly under a tree.

Halfway home he said, "Chris, I musta laid my mittens down back there. You go ahead. I'll run get em."

He drew up all the snares as he went. He didn't blame Chris for catching rabbits. Chris wasn't cruel. If Chris stopped to *think* about hunting, like he did, he couldn't do it at all. But David couldn't bear — not tonight, especially not when he turned the glittering kaleidoscope — to think of the rabbits strangling somewhere in the moonlight.

After dinner (the Christmas dinner food was like food to satisfy hunger developed specially for it: the Christmas Eve food had been more like something for thirst than for hunger), the tree stood still with ripeness, its wonder safely fruited. It could be left. The children went to see Effie and Charlotte.

Effie had a tree. It was a small one, but there was the same feel in her house as in theirs: of this day brought snug into the room from other days. The same touch through the window of the sun that shadowed noon lazy on the Christmas snow and on the Christmas lazy walking of anyone on the road. Yet there *was* a difference, David thought. Their Christmas was like a natural garden, with the foliage as well as the blossoms. Effie's and Bess's had only the flowers, and those were planted. They had to feed them with their own closeness.

"Our tree ain't so very pretty," Bess said. "We couldn't lug a very big one."

She always spoke like that about anything of her own. The others seemed to think that nothing pretty should rightfully *belong* to her. Somehow, if she disparaged it first, she could prevent them from taking her custody of it away.

"Why didn't you ask Father?" David said. "He'd have got you a tree."
Chris frowned at him. David didn't understand.

"We *wanted* a small tree," Effie said. "We could carry it all right, couldn't we, Mother?"

She seemed to put a fence around it. She too knew how her mother was deflected by the other women whenever their paths came close to touching. She resented beforehand any surprise that they could have special things like anyone else.

There wasn't much for Effie but the silk dress for the concert. Her silk dress and Anna's woollen one were like the plant and the flower again. They all touched the silk, Chris twice. It made David think of the play.

He whispered to Effie, "Do you know your part?'

She whispered, "Yes, do you?"

Something they shared then lifted their feet off the day. They seemed to forget for a minute where Chris and Anna were to be found. She withdrew her protectiveness from the tree. She stood looking at it *with* him; as if, if it *shouldn't* be beautiful there would be no hurt in accepting that judgement from him now. As if, if you both knew what beautiful *was*, it wouldn't matter what anything of yours looked like to the other.

"We better go," Chris said, "if we're goin to Charlotte's."

Bess slipped some candy into their pockets as they left. It wasn't a bit like the skimpy-tasting candy the women made for church socials. David wondered why his mother never said anything when he told her how wonderful Bess's candy tasted. When they came home from Bess's, she never said like she did when they came from another house: What did they have for supper? Was she cleaned up? Did she ask you what *I* was doing?

"*Dave*," Chris said, outside, "what made you say that about Father getting 'em a tree?"

"Why?"

"Why, Chris?" Anna said.

"Ohhhh, never mind."

They went to Charlotte's. Charlotte had no tree. When they went into Rachel's kitchen, it was as if they'd gone in *out* of Christmas.

Rachel rocked by the window in the cushionless chair. On no day in their house did the moments move faster or slower. Time was something captive in that room always; something she wore away, bit by slow bit, with each movement of her rocker. There was no echo of the laugh of someone who'd just gone. No lingering of a sentence spoken in the day's work, when a thing was tried one way and then another ("What do *you* think?"); or of a hum in the day's planning. There was only a kind of smell of walls, of the doily under the Bible on the centre table, the bare kerosene smell of the lamp that stood on the mirrorless bureau beside the bed when time had finally been worn away till nine o'clock.

David could hardly sit still. It was like the long dry sermon when there was only a handful at church.

"What did you get, Lottie?" Anna said.

"I got these shoes," Charlotte said. She held out one foot.

"She needed 'em, so I give 'em to her last week," Rachel said. "There wasn't any sense keeping 'em."

Wouldn't that be awful, David and Anna both thought; but Charlotte didn't seem to mind.

"And I got some scribblers."

"We didn't make much fuss," Rachel said. "We didn't feel much like Christmas this year." She sighed. "I'll be glad when it's over."

"Was you down to Effie's?" Charlotte said.

"Yes."

"I shouldn't think Bess'd feel much like Christmas, either," Rachel said. She sighed again. "I should think remorse . . ."

David whispered to Anna, "Let's go."

He took a long breath outside. He looked toward their own house. There'd be the smell of oranges in it and the cozy, personal smell of the tree. There'd be a kind of resonance lingering still of all the tea-kettle-singing words his mother and father had spoken to each other while they were away.

Chris stayed. He said he'd bring in the night's wood for Charlotte.

It's funny about Chris and Charlotte, David thought. (For a minute Charlotte seemed to like Bess, except for Bess's great free laugh and something outward-moving about Bess like the spring in their pasture that found its own force amongst the driest rocks.) When Chris went near Charlotte, something in them both seemed to reach out for touch, then recoil. They'd both stand for a second like two strangers who'd met in a path too narrow for passing.

He kept glancing down at his new jacket as he walked along the road. Little wrinkles were already showing at the crook of his elbows. He walked on, with his arms held straight at his sides. When they went into the house, he took the jacket off and folded it again the way it had been on the tree. It didn't seem to him that he could ever take it for everyday and have the sharp creases of the sleeves become round and sloppy.

He took it off now, because he and Anna were going down to the meadow with the new skates (screwed right onto the boots, like the older boys'), and he might fall. He was going to try crossing one leg over the other, to make a proper smooth turn. He could never manage that with the old spring skates. If anyone was looking when he came to a corner, he just coasted around it or stopped to make out he was tying his bootlace.

He was glad now that Chris had stayed at Charlotte's. Somehow he wouldn't want Chris to see him, if he failed. Anna was the only one he could bear to have watch him try anything in which he might fail.

But he didn't fail.

They went down the long hill behind the church, in the soft Christmas kindled air, to the meadow. Its ice shone blue and wide and smooth, so infinitely full of possible paths for the swift skates to take. The brook ran, open, through its middle. Lips of shell ice hung over the brook's edges. He stood on his skates. And Anna watched.

The skates felt stiff and strange at first. He could go fast enough on them, straight. But when he tried to turn, it was just as jerky as it had been on the old spring skates. He tried again and again. Once he almost got it, but the next time was no nearer than before.

Then just at dusk — just when there is that nice lonely feeling about the whole world as you stand below a cold hill at the edge of the trees and it is dusk in the wintertime — just when the dark spruces began to come in closer around the blue meadow ice and the blue ice seemed to stretch farther away toward the other side of the woods, hardening and booming with a far-off sound so it would bruise you if you fell on it and you were alone, but not now, because Anna was there with you, watching — just then, he did it.

He didn't know, in his head, how. But he knew the minute he felt the cool flight-smooth dip of it that it was right. Now his legs knew it, to repeat it, whenever they liked. He was so sure of it now he knew he could do it slower, or faster, or horse it up, or do it any way he liked. He was so sure of it now he knew he wouldn't even have to test it again. He knew he would be the best skater in the whole world.

"I did it!" he said to Anna.

"I know!" she said. "I saw you!" That was the best part of all.

And then his skates were off, and he was walking back up the hill in his larrigans. The funny feel of them as they touched the ground was almost as treacherous after the swift skates as the skates had been when he'd first put them on.

He was tired. The little lonely feel of dusk in the wintertime (like dying, when the dying is over and only the stillness is left) was in the wheels of the wagon that stood at the top of the hill with a little fine snow drifting through the spokes, and in the windows of the church, and looking back, in the meadow they had left. But Anna was with him. That made it all the nicer for being that way. You would know it was Christmas night no matter where you were and if you had no idea of the date at all.

They were too tired to play that night. They left their things beneath the tree. They only looked at them or touched them. Outside, Christmas moonlight latticed the snow with shadows that grew out longer and longer from the dark roots of the trees. And when David went to bed, sleep covered him at once like an extra blanket drawn up.

A Tale of Three Stockings without Holes

RHODA GRASER

"Hanukkah is to enjoy, a celebration of lights," says Mama in front of whom we are standing like the three stooges. "So why the long faces?"

"We want to hang stockings like the Christmas crowd does," pipes up Betty. Weldy and me also believe this is only fair.

Betty nudges me to keep up the argument. "We heard what that Rabinovitch told you, you know, about how you shouldn't let us hang stockings on Hanukkah and if you did, which you shouldn't, you have to put potato peels and onions in them — so we won't want to do it anymore."

Now, Mama has a sweet disposition, and a big interest in seeing her children laughing instead of whining. She waves her hand like it's nothing. "Who would listen to that? Come, sit here on the couch with me and I'll tell you a good story," she coaxes.

"About what?" Weldy wants to know.

"Sit down, you'll hear."

We are by nature suspicious, but also filled with curiosity. Is it possible this story will include hanging stockings or decorating a tree? Everybody's talking about the Lipkins who don't live on King Street where everybody knows your business. Well, they have a tree decorated with blue and white ornaments and silvery tinsel around Christmas-time. They call it a Hanukkah bush. Mama already let us know Daddy said there was no such thing as a Hanukkah bush and would not like to see a Christmas tree pretending to be a Hanukkah decoration in our living room when he gets home from the country, so we better stick with her plans and never mind the Lipkins and their bush.

We snuggle into the couch around Mama and she begins her story.

"You know how long we've been celebrating Hanukkah? For over two thousand years. Imagine that!"

Weldy looks surprised. "Was you there, Mama?"

Mama tried not to laugh. "No, but I heard about it. It was a time when our people lived in the Land of Israel, and they had a big headache because they were ruled by a cruel Syrian king. At first he seemed like a friendly person, but then he wanted the people to worship idols in the Temple. When they refused he robbed and wrecked the Temple. I'll tell you, things were a mess. The people, when they saw this, got all upset and rebelled. Their leader, Judah the Macabee, also known as the Hammer, had only a small band of fighters, but they defeated the bad king and his army, and chased them right out of Judea. When the people went to clean up the Temple they looked all over for the sacred oil to light the Menorah again. Finally they spotted a small jug, which was sealed so they knew it was pure, but, problems, problems — there was only enough to keep the Menorah flame going for one day. Guess what? A miracle happened and it burned for eight days. And now we celebrate the miracle by lighting Hanukkah candles for eight days. That's the story."

Betty looks sideways at Weldy and me. "Not bad. What else?"

"Well," says Mama, "you play a game with dreidlach tops, and whoever wins get a penny."

"What else?" I want to know.

Mama sighs. "Wait and see. On the eighth day, maybe a miracle."

Each night Mama lights one more candle on the Menorah, and every day Betty comes home from school with all these stories about how the other kids are bragging that they're going out in the woods to chop down their Christmas trees and what they expect Santa Claus to bring them. She'd pretend she didn't care, but when she got home she never stopped talking about it.

Mama says, "Enough already," but then Betty just sits down and crosses her arms over her chest real tight and pouts. To tell you the truth, I never saw her do that before. Usually I'm the one trying Mama's patience. "You've got a lot to say, Missy" is how she'd put it to me, and Weldy would just kick the summer kitchen door or something like that, so she'd know he was mad.

By the eighth night of Hanukkah, Daddy is back home and gone to the synagogue for services. Mama lights all the eight candles on the Menorah, and the dining room looks bright and beautiful. We're standing there looking at her and waiting for the miracle about which we didn't forget. We also have a stocking or two ready without any holes in them, just in case.

"Everybody around the corner on Brunswick Street is putting up their trees," I tell Mama. "I went with Butty Satter to look in the windows. Pretty soon it's going to be Christmas."

"That's nice," smiles Mama and checks the Hanukkah candles. "Only don't go snooping in other people's windows. It's bad manners."

"What happened to that Hanukkah miracle? That's what I want to know." Weldy looks like he's practicing kicking foot, back and forth.

Mama looks at his foot and stops smiling. "You know how at Christmastime all the children are supposed to be good and not nag, or kick, if they want presents? Well the same applies to Hanukkah!"

This is not good news — we've been nagging all week. Weldy stops moving his foot back and forth right away. "Is it too late for that to help?" I want to know.

Mama puts her hand on her chin and looks at the ceiling. "Mmm, I don't think so — of course you shouldn't wait any longer or the candles might burn out — that could be a problem. Maybe we should all go in the living room," she says, like the idea just came to her.

Well, there hanging on the mantle are our stockings, one each, with big bulges in them. They're stuffed with oranges and striped candy canes. Betty and me each have a little doll in ours, and hair ribbons, and Weldy has a tiny car. We're jumping up and down and kissing Mama, who is all smiles.

The Mysterious Mummer

BERT BATSTONE

There should have been nothing mysterious about the incident, but there was. The story as told by eight-year-old Jimmy and his three pals was simple and would have remained so, except for what occurred in the days and years to come.

Jimmy and his three friends had done what many children did in Newfoundland villages: dressed-up as mummers at Christmastime. It was a clear moonlight night, and snow and frost held the whole village in a winter grip. Dressed in their motley costumes, they had gone from house to house and had been well received along with others doing the same.

It was nearly time to go home, but they wanted to test their disguises on some of their friends who lived on the other side of the cove. To get to the other side necessitated crossing a bridge which spanned a fast flowing brook. Where the bridge crossed, the banks were steep and about ten feet high. The bridge was wide, and a waist-high rail prevented anyone from stepping over the edge.

Snow had drifted along the banks beside the river and sloped down to the narrow border of ice which had frozen along the edge. In the centre, the brook ran fast and clear. The black water reflected the moonlight as the four boys came to the bridge. Jimmy, the most adventurous of the group, decided where others walked was not enough challenge for him. He attempted to walk on the rail. Whether he tripped in his costume or stepped on a piece of ice no one knew, but he had made only a step when he lost his footing and fell. He tumbled unhurt down the soft snow of the banks and came to rest on the narrow strip of ice bordering the brook. He lay there unhurt but not daring to move, lest he slip out into the brook and be swept away. The three boys looked in horror at their friend lying below. They kept calling and asking if he were hurt. Jimmy kept shouting, "Help, I'm slipping."

There should have been others around, but at that time there was no one in sight to hear their cries for help. They were afraid to leave Jimmy and were not sure where to go or what to do. Lying on the ice below, Jimmy, with the least effort, found himself slipping toward the open water, which would certainly sweep him away to a tragic end.

Just when the boys were most desperate about what to do, a lone mummer appeared beside Jimmy. They did not see from where he came, but he was there, reaching out and pulling the frightened boy to safety. It was almost as if he had come from under the bridge or just out of the thin air. He pulled the boy to safety and, throwing him across his shoulder, scrambled quickly up the snowy bank and deposited him with his friends.

The boys had enough mummering for the night and decided to head for home. In their relief they did not pay much attention to the rescuer. They would eventually find out who he was. They looked back as they hurried away, and he was standing beside the bridge. He waved to them, and they waved back. When they looked again, he was gone.

The boys, in telling the story to their parents, found they could not remember much about the mysterious mummer. They had not really noticed any mask he wore. He was tall, and they knew he was strong to be able to carry Jimmy up the steep bank. The only detail they recalled was that he wore a dark cloak.

The mystery deepened the next day when Jimmy's father went to see where his son had fallen. There were the marks the boy had made as he tumbled off the bridge. He could even see the place where he clung to the strip of ice along the shore. But that was all. There were no marks or footprints in the snow of anyone else having gone down or come up from the brook. In fact, the only prints were those Jimmy had made falling down. His father dismissed the rescue to the vivid imagination of the boys, and Jimmy forgot his experience in the Christmas activity which followed. He did not try walking on the rail again. Several times, however, Jimmy's father thought to himself, "I saw how he went down, but not how he got back."

Mummering as a Christmas pastime is strictly a Newfoundland tradition. Up to the beginning of World War II, it was practiced quite extensively, though since that time it has lost some of its popularity. There may be some comparison to the North American masquerading at Halloween, but the practice is much more extensive and involved. It was the practice, beginning on Christmas night and for the full twelve nights of Christmas, to "dress up," as it was called. During the Christmas season, few nights were missed that crowds of adults and older children did not "dress up" and go around to as many homes as time would allow. Everyone vied with the other in creating the most imaginative costumes that would not only delight the observers but hide the identity of the wearer. It was a blow to one's dignity to be recognized. Conversation was carried on in a voice which didn't betray the speaker. Many people were quite adept at such disguises. Practically no home was barred to the mummers. It was part of Christmas, and without them Christmas would not really be Christmas. Only the old or the infirm did not "dress up" at least once during the season. The larger the group, the more fun was had. It was not, however, unusual to find one lone mummer making his way from house to house. The loner required a more subtle disguise because the attention of the whole household was centred on him or her, as the case may be.

There is some confusion about the origins of this practice. At least one writer has put forth a long, complicated theory which suggests there may have been some American influence behind it. The Newfoundland of the nineteenth and early twentieth centuries was not in any way influenced by any part of the North American continent beside which it was located. All Newfoundland practices were influenced by

English or Irish customs and, to a lesser degree, by Scottish tradition. If there was any influence from the western side of the Atlantic, it came from the import of rum and molasses from the West Indies, the latter being the raw material out of which local alcohol was made. More pertinent data suggests that in the time of Cromwell, 1599-1658, the celebration of Christmas was forbidden. This was reinforced by the teachings of such Cromwellian Puritans as John Milton (1608-1674) and Richard Baxter (1615-1691), each of whom held office in Cromwell's government. Traditions die hard, and people wanted to celebrate Christmas, and so it was often done in disguise, lest an observer of such festivities should notify the authorities.

In the next century and with the birth of Wesleyanism, Puritanism received renewed impetus. Out of this milieu came those who found their way to Newfoundland in the eighteenth and nineteenth centuries. The majority of the planters who came to settle in the numerous bays and coves of Newfoundland fell back on many of the practices which had long since died out in the country from which they had come. Shut off from civilization as they were most of the time, and particularly in winter, with little access to tools of civilization, they resorted to types of entertainment they could cheaply and easily initiate themselves. Thus mummering at Christmas, a passing and at one time necessary element in their history, came to be full blown during the traditional twelve days.

The people had to make their own fun, and mummering was fun. It was never practiced as extensively in Roman Catholic communities, although Roman Catholics, who were mainly of Irish descent, picked up the idea from the Protestant English. Good, wholesome fun was no respecter of religious boundaries.

Jimmy and his friends were keeping alive an old tradition, the basis of which had been laid by their ancestors several generations before in a land they had never known and would probably never see.

Winter gave place to summer, and mummering was forgotten.

When again the Christmas bells rang out and ice and snow were heavy on the land, everyone geared themselves for another season of mummering. In spite of many inquiries, no one had learned the identity of Jimmy's rescuer.

One night on the Christmas following Jimmy's experience, he was at home with the rest of the family, enjoying the groups of mummers which came and went. It was toward the end of the evening when a lone mummer knocked on his door. Jimmy, always the one to open the door with a flourish and said "Come in," was suddenly taken back to a year before and his experience under the bridge. There at the door was the one who had rescued him. Not knowing why he should feel scared, Jimmy showed him in.

"It's him," shouted Jimmy. "This is the one who saved me from falling into the brook. He was wearing the same outfit."

"Maybe it's the outfit," said his mother, "but it could be another person."

By this time the mummer had come into the light of the kitchen-living room where the rest of the family were. On his head he wore a cone-shaped felt hat. Fastened at the neck, the cape he wore came down to his knees. It could have been made from a grey woollen cloth. Under the cape was a dark green blouse with balloon sleeves which ended underneath the straps of black leather gloves. His trousers were tight fitting and with a silver-coloured buckle just below the knee. Black woollen socks and ankle-high boots completed the outfit, except for a skin-tight mask which covered his face. Twinkling blue eyes looked out through holes in the mask.

Jimmy kept insisting it was the mummer who pulled him from the brook. The mummer made no sign he even acknowledged the inference. As with most the mummers, the conversation consisted of small talk: how far he had come, was this his last call, whether anyone would know him if he didn't have on a mask. All the time each member of the family was guessing who it might be. One suggested he may not be from their village at all. He was offered a drink of homemade wine, which he politely refused. He didn't sit down but wandered slowly around the room, looking at the pictures on the walls and photographs on the mantel. He made an inquiry here and there in a voice soft and mellow which appeared to be his own natural voice.

"Are you speaking in your own voice?" Jimmy's father asked, to which he replied, "It's the only voice I have, and the one I always use."

"Were you the one who pulled my boy out of the brook last Christmas?" he asked. "Little boys should not walk on icy rails," he replied.

When the family suggested he should call it a night, take off his mask and have lunch with them, he again refused and insisted he must be on his way.

Jimmy's father saw him to the door and bade him goodnight, to which he responded, "I will see you next Christmas." He disappeared around the corner of the house and was gone.

After he was gone, they recalled every clue which might reveal his identity, but they were completely at a loss. While there was something strangely mysterious about him, they all felt a warm sense of rapport with him. If there was a mystery, they were sure it was good. If he was Jimmy's rescuer, there was only one hint, and that was his reference to falling off the rail. Jimmy had no doubt at all that he was the one.

The next day the family asked among neighbours and friends if the lone mummer had come to their house. While there had been single mummers, there was no one matching the description of their visitor. With the passing of Christmas, the mysterious mummer was forgotten, or was he? Jimmy's father found it hard to forget, "I will see you next Christmas."

The seasons rolled on in their inevitable cycle, and the "I will see you next Christmas," became more immediate to Jimmy's family as Christmas approached. They had talked to neighbours and friends about their experience. They were now sure, considering no one else had seen the mysterious mummer, that he was a visitor from some other time or space. The neighbours response was unanimous. "It is the devil."

The Newfoundland villager, after generations of prejudice and superstition, was innately inclined to view anything he did not understand as evil. There were intimations that Jimmy and his family were in league, in some way, with this mysterious visitor, at the ultimate expense of the rest of the village. All sorts of allegations were hurled their way, and every innocent activity was looked on with suspicion. The family, however, was convinced that any influence from the mummer would be for good.

When Christmas did come again, Jimmy's father waited expectantly for their visitor. Five nights, ten nights of Christmas went by. They were beginning to feel a little silly, waiting for someone who may not even exist. Each day the neighbours hurled jokes at the family: "Did the devil come last night?"

Finally it was nearly the end of the twelfth night. Most of the groups had done the rounds of the village. Some chose not to include Jimmy's home on their itinerary. The family was beginning to hope he would not come and continue what was becoming something of a nightmare for them. They were almost to the point of believing someone was playing a mean trick on them. Even though they had a sense of dread because of the neighbours, they were a little disappointed that they might not see him again. One night Jimmy had gone and stood at the end of the bridge across the brook where he had first met the stranger. He wondered if there was something about the bridge which might bring him back.

Just when the family was sure Christmas was over, there was a timid knock on their door. They didn't have to open the door to know it was him. The same outfit — grey cape, hat, buckles at the knees; the same twinkling blue eyes through the mask. The same quiet voice; the same sense of warmth in his presence, like the visit of an old friend.

As before, he did not sit down but politely refused the offer of a chair. As before, he walked around and examined the pictures on the walls and was intensely interested in the family pictures.

"Who are you, and why do you come to us?" asked Jimmy's father. "I feel you don't want to harm us, and I know you are the one who saved Jimmy's life; but are you from heaven or hell?"

"What is heaven or hell, my friend," replied the mummer, "but states which men invent or create? Your preachers say God can send you to heaven or hell. Whatever life there is to be is but an extension of what you are here and now, untrammelled indeed by the limitations you now have; but what you are now you yet will be. Men find what they seek. The intensity of that search doesn't end with death, for it is the spirit which lives. Death does not change the spirit. God does not send men anywhere, he just allows them to continue the search."

The family may not have understood what the mummer had said, for in one statement he had said more than in all his previous visits.

"Are you a spirit or are you real?" Jimmy's father went on.

"Is love real?" the mummer asked. "Can you touch and handle kindness and truth? Is not the evil that men think real, and yet it is of the spirit. It is the flesh which is fleeting, my friend; only the spirit is real."

"Why do you come only at Christmas?" they asked, almost in unison.

"If you were to practice the spirit you demonstrate at Christmas, much good could come to you," the mummer went on.

"Will you come again?" Jimmy asked.

"I may not," the mummer replied, "for now in your village there are those who have chosen to think evil. There are those who search for the hell you asked about. If they find it, I cannot be part of it."

With that remark the mummer left, but over his shoulder as he went he said, as if he were not sure what to say, "Until we meet again." And then he was gone.

When Jimmy and his family tried to relay to the neighbours what their visitor had said, they were laughed at. "Maybe the mummer was Jesus Christ," they said. "Perhaps he wanted to go mummering on his birthday," they scorned. "If he comes next year, we are all going to have a go at him. We will find out where he comes from," they chorused.

As Christmas faded, the mummer, if not forgotten, came less to dominate the conversation of the villagers. It seemed, however, that wherever Jimmy and his family went, the subject was bound to come up. Some listened with more respect than others. The local minister of the church simply refused to be brought into the discussion, although he talked at some length to the family. He assured them that any person, real or imagined, who spoke as he did could mean no harm.

It was with some trepidation that the family faced the third Christmas since the visitor had appeared. Several people had intimated they would be waiting. What they planned to do was not clear, but one way or another they were going to find out who or what he was.

When Christmas finally came, fewer groups were doing their nocturnal rounds. Whether out of fear of the mysterious mummer or the group who threatened to lie in wait for him, no one was sure. Night after night, a group of six or seven men waited in the cold shadows around Jimmy's house. The family inside were aware they were there, even though they could not see them. While they hoped he would come, they feared any violence which might result. When people get caught up in a cause, they are sometimes blind to reality.

It was the last night of Christmas, and more groups than usual were out. None of them came to Jimmy's door. The men in the shadows were tired and cold. Some of them were having second thoughts about this escapade. If it were the devil, as most of them suggested, they were not sure they wanted to tangle with him. Some thought it was but an innocent prank; but one way or the other they were going to find out.

The night was almost gone, and nearly all the mummering groups had gone home. Some of the men wanted to give up the wait, but others prevailed on them for a few more minutes. Suddenly, as if out of nowhere, he was there at Jimmy's door. There was no mistake: the pointed hat, the grey cape. He had just raised his hand to knock on the door when the men rushed him. There was a brief scuffle, and then they realized they were only scuffling with each other. The mummer had disappeared as mysteriously as he had come.

When Jimmy's father came out to investigate the noise outside his house, he was met by a group of men who stood looking sheepishly at each other. In response to his request for an explanation, they responded that they only wanted to help. Jimmy's father felt the better part of valour would be not to tell the men what he thought of them. He left them and went into the house. Muttering to each other, the men went their separate ways. They had accomplished nothing, except now they were convinced of the mystery surrounding the visitor. They were now left with their private fear. Some of them wondered if in some lonely hour or place the visitor might not return to exact vengeance for their attack.

When Jimmy came out of doors the next morning, there to one side was a crumpled felt hat. He picked it up and brushed off the snow. He pushed it into shape, for he knew it was the hat the mummer had worn.

Christmas after Christmas came and went, but the mysterious mummer never came again. Jimmy grew to be a man, got married and had a family of his own. He kept the old felt hat and hung it always in a cherished place. To a select few he would tell the story behind the hat. A new generation of mummers grew up and went from door to door. Some of them had heard the story of the lone mummer, but for the most part it was forgotten. It became one of those legends which was told just for the sake of the telling.

By the time Jimmy became an old man, most of the people who lived in his village on that first cold, moonlit night had gone. It may be he was the only one left who could remember. Every time he looked at the hat, no different than when he had picked it up, he remembered again. He wondered how things would have been if the mummer had been left alone.

It was cold and moonlit on the twelfth night of Christmas. The brook ran free under a new bridge, but snow covered the banks, and a narrow border of ice had formed along the shore. It was a night not unlike that night when our story began. Mummers singly and in groups made the rounds from house to house. No one came to Jimmy's house, for Jimmy was near death. That night all his family had gathered in his room. The old hat hung on the wall, where he could see it from his bed. He had left it in the care of his eldest son.

When the last mummer had gone home, the old man breathed his last. The family looked up from the bed to where the hat had hung for many years. It was gone. After all these years, the mysterious mummer had come again. No one saw him, but those who had heard the story knew he had rescued Jimmy for the last time.

Four O'Clock, New Year's Morning, New River Beach

ELISABETH HARVOR

You hear him cry in the
dark. The air smells of floor wax,
cold duck fat, the tree
shedding its needles down into the
room whose bay window looks out
on the winter ocean. You even think you can hear,
above the roof's peak, how the new
snow is steadily falling
on the ice crust of the old year.

You feel for your kimono,
to the right of a hulk of sleeping
shoulder, the dark hull of a husband
going down in a sleep-floe. You
cross the floor to the cold window;
see a snowfall of soot falling
between your mother-in-law's house
and the boathouse, the only white flakes
flying into the cone of light

shining down on the ice-glazed path to the beach.
Shivering, you yawn down at the snowed-on lawn
as you wrap one half of your kimono over the

other half, like a thought of something sombre
you long ago promised yourself you'd remember.

Out of the Bay of Fundy night
it comes back to you: the vow to be less bitter, happier,
a different person. You pad through
the white cottagey gloom of the cold hallway;

old summer clothes spy on you — a once-brave
bathing suit, now salt-faded and puckered,
a scarecrow-short raincoat, smelling of rubber
and the beach. Now you're close enough to hear
him start to coo in response to your sleepy
progress of creaks. He is small
and audacious, and so you imagine
you can imagine what he is imagining: that
the two of you are in league, cahoots,

two lovers in love with the night.
In answer, your breasts start to
prick with new milk, making small
moons of damp on the kimono's pale silk. When you
duck into his low loft, he waves his legs,
he's so happy to see you. You lift him up,
hitch him onto a hip, take him to the window
to see the way the soot-snow
is falling in front of the

snow-snow
steadily, steadily.
He's so sleep-flushed! His hair is
damp grass still warm from his pillow,

his leggings have been
knit out of curdled white string,
his nightgown's a dwarf's surplice — roses
washed till they look like clover,
made littler, reduced
by time and detergent
are falling
through
the new year's fogged
sleeping dimness.

The Eaton's Beauty

DAVID WEALE

When I walked into the room, I noticed her immediately. Dressed in a crimson velvet dress, she was seated regally in a white wicker chair, her long dark hair falling over her shoulders, front and back. She was beautiful, with large serene brown eyes and a captivating smile on her smallish mouth. I also noticed that she wasn't wearing any shoes. When my host, who was standing next to me, saw me staring with such apparent interest, she asked if I would like to hold her. "I certainly would," I replied, and walked over and picked her up.

"She's over seventy years old," she informed me — and with that the story began.

When Ella Chappell, née Thompson, of York was a little girl growing up in North River, she and her sister Olive each received from an invalid aunt a Christmas present which was so far beyond their expectations they could scarcely believe their good fortune. Like many other girls at that time, they had spent hours poring over the toy section of the Eaton's catalogue. "It was our prayer book," was how Ella put it. And of all the wonderful items they perused in that catalogue there was none more alluring than the "Eaton's Beauty," a doll attired in a fancy lace-frilled dress with a wide ribbon which ran diagonally across her front. She had moveable joints, and eyes with log lashes which opened magically when she was picked up, and closed when she was laid down.

But the "Eaton's Beauty" cost $1.98, an amount equivalent to several days wages in that farming society of the 1920s. Being members of a large family, it was utterly unthinkable that they might ever actually receive such an extravagant present, and so they imagined, but dared not hope; dreamed, but dared not wish.

Another woman from that same generation told me that she always wanted an Eaton's Beauty but never got one. One year, instead of giving her what she wanted, her mother redressed an old doll in new clothes. "I was not impressed," she added ruefully. Ella and Olive Thompson were more fortunate, and on that memorable Christmas over seventy years ago, the unthinkable happened. When the wrapping came off the presents, there were two dolls, one for each of them. "My soul, we were excited," exclaimed Ella, "because $1.98 then would be like $200 today. At that time, you know, eggs were ten cents a dozen, and a yeast cake was four cents."

The two dolls were almost identical. The only difference between them was that one had brown eyes — like Ella — and the other blue — like Olive. It seemed a perfect coincidence.

The little girls named their dolls — both of them — after their Aunt Lizzie, the patroness responsible for their good fortune. Olive got her word in first and named her doll Elizabeth Mary. Ella, with a stroke of childish ingenuity, settled for Mary Elizabeth. And in talking with Ella I got the clear impression that, in this ritual of naming, the two girls, the two dolls, and their beloved aunt were joined together in a pact of indissoluble affection which has remained, undiminished, over the years. "I always thought so much of my aunt," added Ella, "that when I gave birth to my only daughter she was called Elizabeth Ann — after Aunt Lizzie."

When the girls were older, and the dolls began to show the wear and tear of being present at so many tea parties, and of having their hair combed so often, their mother placed them in a trunk where they remained for over thirty years. They might have stayed there even longer if it had not been for a trip Ella took to Toronto to visit Olive who had married and moved there years before. "I saw this sign up on a store, *Doll Hospital*," recalled Ella, "and I thought about those dolls in the trunk. I said to Olive, 'I think we'd better send the dolls up to the hospital and get their eyes fixed, and get new wigs.'"

And that's exactly what they did. The $1.98 dolls each received a $100 treatment, which restored them to their original condition. "I was so excited," said Ella, "I was just in my second childhood when my sister came back from Toronto and brought those dolls."

A few years later, Ella was shopping at Norton's in Charlottetown, and spied a small, white wicker chair with a teddy bear seated in it. Immediately she thought of her doll. She asked the clerk if the chair was for sale and was informed that it was. The price was $65. "My word," she thought, "I'd hardly pay $65 for my own chair, but if it's for the doll then that's all right." She took out her purse and paid the money, and now the doll sits in that very chair, in her living room in York, a daily reminder of dear Aunt Lizzie, her sister Olive, and her own Christmas bliss of long ago.

And so I picked up the doll, and was surprised by the amazement I felt when those big brown eyes opened wide. I tilted her back and lifted her up several times, just for the pleasure of it. And caught myself smiling back.

The Homeward Trail

CHARLES G.D. ROBERTS

In the lumber camp, far back upon the lonely headquarters of the Quah-Davic, there was the stir of something unusual afoot. It was Christmas Eve, and every kerosene lamp, lantern, and candle that the camp could boast, was blazing. The little square windows gleamed softly through the dust and cobwebs of unwashen years. For all the cold that snapped and bit through the stillness of the forest night, the door of the camp was thrown wide open, and from it a long sheet of light spread out across the trodden and chip-littered snow. Around the doorway crowded the rough-shirted woodsmen, loafing and smoking after their prodigious dinner of boiled pork, boiled beans, and steaming-hot molasses cake. The big box-stove behind them, which heated the camp, was wearing itself to a dull red glow; and the air that rushed out with the light from the open door was heavy with the smell of wet woollens, wet larrigans, and wet leather. Many of the men were wearing nothing on their feet but their heavy, home-knit socks of country yarn; but in these they did not hesitate to come out upon the dry snow, rather than trouble themselves to resume their massive foot-gear.

Before the door, in the spread of the light, stood a pair of sturdy, rough-coated grey horses, hitched to a strong box sled, or "pung." The bottom of the pung was covered thick with straw, and over the broad, low seat were blankets, with one heavy bearskin robe. Into the space behind the seat a gaunt, big-shouldered man was stowing a haunch of frozen moose-meat. A lanky, tow-haired boy of fifteen on the left-hand side of the seat. The horses stood patient, but with drooping heads, aggrieved at being taken from the stable at this unwonted hour. In the pale blue, kindly, woods-wise eyes of both the man and the boy shone the light of happy anticipation. They seemed too occupied and excited to make much response to the good-natured banter of their comrades, but grinned contentedly as they hastened their preparations for departure. The man was Steve Williams, best axeman and stream driver in the camp; the boy, young Steve, his eldest son, who was serving as "cookee," or assistant to the camp cook. The two were setting out on a long night drive through the forest to spend Christmas with their family on the edge of the lonely little settlement of Brine's Brook.

When all was ready, the big-shouldered woodsman slipped into the seat beside his son, pulled the blankets and the bearskins all about him, and picked up the reins from the square dashboard. A sharp *tchk* started the horses, and, amid a chorus of shouts, — good nights and Merry Christmases, and well-worn rustic pleasantries, — the loaded pung slid forward from the light into the great, ghost-white gloom beyond. The sled-bells jangled; the steel runners crunched and sang frostily; and the cheerful camp, the only centre of human life within a radius of more than twenty miles, sank back behind the voyagers. There was the sound of a door slamming, and the bright streak across the snow was blotted out. The travellers were alone on the trail, with the solemn ranks of trees and the icy-pointed stars.

They were well prepared, these two happy Christmas adventurers, to face the rigours of the December night. Under their heavy blanket-coats were many thicknesses of homespun flannel. Inside their high-laced, capacious "shoe-packs" were several pairs of yarn socks. Their hands were covered by double-knit homemade mittens. Their heads were protected by wadded caps of muskrat fur, with flaps that pulled down well over the ears. The cold, which iced their eyelashes, turned the tips of their up-turned coat-collars and the edges of their mufflers to board, and made the old trees snap startlingly, had no terrors at all for their hardy frames. Once well under way, and the camp quite out of sight, they fell to chatting happily of the surprise they would give the home folks, who did not expect them home for Christmas. They calculated, if they had "anyways good luck," to get home to the little isolated backwoods farmhouse between four and five in the morning, about when grandfather would be getting up by candlelight to start the kitchen fire for mother, and then go out and fodder the cattle. They'd be home in time to wake the three younger children (young Steve was the eldest of a family of four), and to add certain little carved products of the woodsman's whittling — ingenious wooden toys, and tiny elaborate boxes, filled with choicest globulets of spruce gum — to the few poor Christmas gifts which the resourceful and busy little mother had managed to get together against the festival. As they talked these things over, slowly and with frugal speech, after the fashion of their class, suddenly was borne in upon them a sense of the loneliness of the home folks' Christmas if they should fail to come. Under the spell of this feeling, a kind of inverted homesickness, their talk died into silence. They sat thinking, and listening to the hoarse jangle of their bells.

In such a night as this, few of the wild kindreds were astir in the forest. The bears, raccoons, woodchucks, and chipmunks were snugly "holed up," and sleeping away the great white cold. The deer and moose were in their well-trodden "yards," for the snow was deep. The travellers knew that there were plenty of woodmice astir, — that if there had been light enough they would have seen their delicate trails wandering everywhere among the trees. But the jangling of the sled-bells was enough to keep all shy beasts at a distance. Only the porcupine was quite undaunted by the strange sounds. One came out into the middle of the road, and stood there seemingly to dispute passage. The boy, in whom primal instincts were still dominant, was for getting out and killing the insolent little bristler. But the father turned the team aside, and gracefully yielded the road, saying:

"Let him be, son! The woods is hisn as much as ourn. An' I respect him, fer he ain't skeered of nothin' that goes on legs!"

A hour later, when the boy was getting very drowsy from watching the ceaseless procession of dark fir-trees, his father nudged him, and whispered, "Look!" The boy, wide awake on the instant, peered into the gloom, and presently his trained young eyes made out a shadowy, slouching form that flitted without a sound from tree to tree.

"Lucivee?" he asked, breathless with interest, laying his mittened hand on his little rifle under the blankets.

"Yes, lucivee! Lynx!" answered the father.

"Let me take a shot at him," said the boy, removing the mitten from his right hand, and bringing out his weapon.

"Oh, what's the good o' killin' the beast Christmastimes!" protested the father gently. And the boy laid down the gun.

"What does he think he's follerin' us fer?" he inquired, a moment later.

"The moose-meat, maybe!" replied the man. "He smells it likely, an' thinks we're goin' to give it to him for a Christmas present!"

At this suggestion the boy laughed out loud. His clear young voice rang through the frosty shadows, and the lynx surprised and offended, shrank back, and slunk away in another direction.

"Bloodthirsty varmints, them lucivees!" said the boy, who wanted a lynx-skin as a trophy. "Ain't it better to shoot 'em whenever one gits the chance?"

"Well," said the father, dubiously, "maybe so! But there's better times fer killin' than Christmastimes!"

A little farther ahead, the road to Brine's Brook turned off. Here the going was very heavy. The road was little travelled, and in places almost choked up by drifts. Most of the time the horses had to walk; and sometimes the man and boy had to get out and tramp a path ahead of the discouraged team.

"At this rate, dad, we ain't a-goin' to get home in time fer breakfast!" exclaimed the boy, despondently. To which the man replied, "Don't you fret, son! It'll be better goin' when we git over the rise. You git into the pung now an' take the reins, an' let me do the trampin'."

The boy, who was tired out, obeyed gladly. He gathered up the reins — and in two minutes was sound asleep. The man smiled, tucked the blankets snugly around the sleeping form, and trudged on tirelessly for a couple of hours, the horses floundering at his heels. Then the drifts ceased. The man kicked the snow from his trousers and shoe-packs, and climbed into the pung again. "We'll make it in time fer breakfast yet!" he murmured to himself confidently as the horses once more broke into a trot.

They were traversing now a high table-land, rather sparsely wooded and dotted here and there with towering rampikes. Suddenly from far behind came a long, wavering cry, high-pitched and peculiarly daunting. The horses, though they had probably never heard such a sound before, started apprehensively, and quickened their pace. The man reined them in firmly; but as he did so he frowned.

"I've hearn say the wolves was comin' back to these here parts," he muttered, "now that the deer's gittin' so plenty agin! But I didn't more'n half-believe it afore!"

Presently the grim sound came again. Then the man once more awoke the boy.

"Here's somethin' to interest you, lad," said he, as the latter put a mittened fist to sleepy eyes. "Hark to that there noise! Did you ever hear the like?"

The boy listened, paled slightly, and was instantly wide awake.

"Why, that's like what I've read about!" he exclaimed. "It must be wolves!"

"Nary a doubt of it!" assented his father, again reining the uneasy horses down to a steady gait. "They've followed the deer back, and now, seems like their a-follerin' us!"

The boy looked thoughtful for a moment, then said, carelessly:

"Oh, well, I reckon there's deer a-plenty for 'em, an' they're not likely to come too nigh us, lookin' fer trouble. I reckon they ain't much like them Roosian wolves we read about, eh, Dad?"

"I reckon," agreed the father. At the same time, it was with a certain satisfaction that he set his foot on his trusty axe, amid the straw in the bottom of the pung.

As the high, quavering voices drew nearer, the horses grew more and more alarmed; but the man soothed them with his voice, and sternly held them in, husbanding their strength lest there should be more heavy going farther ahead. At length, some three hundred yards behind them, they caught a glimpse of their pursuers, four swiftly running shapes.

"Only four!" cried the boy, scornfully, as he patted his little rifle. "I thought there was always more'n that in a pack!"

"You needn't grumble," said the man, with a grin. "It's gittin' home fer breakfast we're after, not fightin' wolves, son!"

The road was so much better now that the man gave the horses their head a little, and the pung flew over the singing snow. But in a few minutes the four wolves, though keeping a distance of a couple of hundred yards, were running abreast of them. The animals were evidently unacquainted with horses or men and shy about a close investigation. The sled-bells, too, were to them a very suspicious phenomenon. Deer, assuredly, were safer hunting; but they would, at least, keep this strange, new kind of quarry in sight for a while, to see what might turn up.

For the next half-hour there was no change in the situation. From time to time, where the woods thickened, the wolves would draw nearer to the pung, and the boy, with shining eyes, would lift his rifle. But presently they would sheer off again, and the boy grew more and more scornful. Then came the winter dawn, a creeping, bitter grey, and for a few minutes the forest was an unreal place, full of ghosts and cold with a cold to pierce the soul. Then, a growing, spreading, pervading glory of pink and lilac and transparent gold. As the light streamed through the trees, the wolves got a clearer view of their quarry and perceiving in it a something distinctly dangerous, they dropped the chase and faded back into the thickets. The man looked at the boy's disappointed face and said, smilingly:

"I reckon they was extry-ordinary civil, seein' us home that way through the woods!"

A few moments later the woods were left behind, and the travellers came out among the snowy stump-fields. There below them, half-way down the hill, was home, bathed in the sparkling sun. Smoke was pouring cheerfully from the chimney, and there in the yard was Grandfather, bringing in a pail of milk from the barn.

"Mother'll have breakfast jest about ready!" cried the man, his rough face tender and aglow.

"But I wisht I could've brought her a nice wolf-skin for Christmas!" exclaimed the boy, sighing softly as he laid down the little rifle.

The Chalice

LISA MOORE

I met Florence O'Reilly on the street corner, a week before the Christmas of 1983. I was eighteen and attending Nova Scotia College of Art and Design and Florence was seventy-odd and begging for change. I gave her what was in my pocket, but Florence gripped my wrist.

My Archie died last night, she said. She began to cry, an almost silent, palsied weeping. The wind shifted and the smell of wine and body odour, a densely layered complicated stink, made my stomach twist. Florence's white hair was cakey with grease, there was an old and puckered scar on her temple. Her eyes were blue and though she was drunk, undrunkenly clear.

I was on my way home from life-drawing class, my fingers still black with charcoal. The model that evening had orange curly hair to her wrist: her shin was the starry, immaculate white only redheads seem to have. She was flawless. I blackened the paper, as black as black could be, and lifted the curves of her body out of the charcoal background with an eraser. When I finished, the drawing was so good it startled me.

All afternoon only the sound of charcoal on paper could be heard throughout the studio, the water pipes sighing, the rattle of the window panes.

When the model stepped out of the spotlights to put on her robe, winter darkness seemed to creep from the corners of the room. I felt a peculiar tingling through my body — a foreign flush that overwhelmed me, almost making me sick. I felt, briefly, as though I were possessed.

I decided I'd give the drawing to my boyfriend, Harold. Everything I did was for him. I was embarrassed about what I thought of as my condition; I was brain-addled; love had immobilized me. I'd left a long-limbed man on a futon sticky from lovemaking to go to class. I'd left a joint and a fat book, *The Will to Power*, which I was trying to read in order to impress him. Nietzche was like the nitrate drops the doctor had recently used to freeze my plantar wart. Freezing and burning at once, elemental, demented. Why did Nietzche want to strip God out of the universe so unceremoniously? Why did he have to be such a bad-ass? "Man's smallness and accidental occurrence in the flux of becoming and passing away." It seemed to me, snuggled in the first love as I was, curmudgeonly to carp about our insignificance. The snow was driving hard when I walked up Granville, almost horizontal in the ripping wind. The streets were lit up with swaying ropes of Christmas lights; a muted red and green glow burned through the gathering fur of snow that covered each tiny bulb.

I hardly saw Florence, though she was gripping my arm. I was still thinking about beauty; how unassailable it is. Impervious to will. And ephemeral. The model's beauty couldn't last. And that was part of it. I felt glad there was something like that in the world — something supremely unfair, something that could incite a lust as glittery as the charcoal.

My Archie was a good man, Florence was saying. He died on the pillow beside me last night. I listened to the death rattles. Have you ever heard death rattles, dear? His lips bubbled up with spit and the sound, dear, was like the devil come to get him. Please dear, will you come inside just to make sure he isn't in the bedroom still?

Once inside the boarding house, Florence became cheerful. There was a splotchy mirror in the hallway, Merry Xmas sprayed in artificial snow. A wooden crêche was set up on the hall table, pink cellophane straw in the manger, but the baby Jesus was missing.

Archie was a bank robber, dear, Florence said over her shoulder. He spent most of his life in jail. Just got out a few months ago at the age of seventy-eight. You'll be rewarded dear, I can guarantee you. Archie had a fortune and that's coming to me. A lot of money dear. I'll be sure you get a little something.

She found the key to her rooms in a change purse with a picture of the Pope on the side, and when the door opened, I gagged. Wine and filthy clothes, garbage and cat shit, but something else too, which I thought must be the smell of death. I opened what I hoped was her bathroom door and threw up over and over again in the toilet. Then I came out into the kitchen and saw she had already boiled the kettle.

You're not one of them lesbians are you, dear? I want you to stay the night with me. I'm afraid to go to sleep alone. She poured the water over a teabag and stirred, clinking the spoon. Then she cocked her head and raised a finger to silence me. She was rapt and I turned to see what she was looking at, but there was nothing.

She whispered, Do you hear something, dear? She reached her hand out and shouted, I'm right here, Archie.

She went into the bedroom, I heard her whisper. It's only a little girl, Archie, come to help me. Settle down, Arch. Don't trouble yourself. I followed her into the room. I half expected to see Archie's body, but instead there were, lined against the baseboards, perhaps fifty kewpie dolls with feather headbands in dusty cellophane packages.

Florence turned down the sheets and lifted her dress over her aged head and stood before me naked. My second nude of the day.

I was in the Halifax explosion dear, she said. In the darkness I saw hundreds of white scars all over her aged body, glowing dimly like a constellation. She leaned toward me, putting her hand on my shoulder.

Archie robbed a church there, he stole a chalice. Her chin crinkled and she began to cry again, a trembling taking over her whole body.

It was the last thing he did, dear. That's why he's gone to hell. She put on a housecoat and went back into the kitchen. I realized it was the third day in a row I had thrown up, and I knew suddenly I was pregnant. I had known, in some way, standing on Granville Street in the squall while the world was blowing past.

The men came and took him dear, she said. The Greek called the men and they came. Strapped him into a stretcher, dear, and they carried him down the stairs and out into the snow.

I decided to stay with Florence until she was asleep. Later, I would go home and find that Harold had left without a word, and I would not be surprised or even disappointed. Sitting on the chair in Florence's kitchen, I felt incandescent with purpose. Florence sipped from the teacup and passed it toward me.

Noisy Afternoon – Silent Night

RONALD F. HAWKINS

When discussing disability pensions with Leslie Williams, he told me this story about how he received his wound during the Second World War. Leslie is a red-haired, quiet fellow with a strong build and a determination to match. . . . He increasingly struggled for control as he projected his thoughts back into the fighting in Holland. After a while it was clear that he was reliving his role and the experiences of his infantry section as they came to grips with the enemy.

At the first of the war I was in the Reserve Army, and we were stationed at Camp Utopia, New Brunswick. One time when we came home on leave, in 1943, I met Herb Falkner, the bartender at the Woodstock Legion. He asked several of us to join the Legion and we did. So I became a member of the Legion before the boys came home and well before the end of the war, and therefore I have longer membership in the Legion than many others.

Then when I joined the active force army and went overseas, my father paid my dues for me until I came home. I used to chum with six fellows, and we regularly had a meeting at the Legion up over Richardson's Drug Store every Saturday night. As the gang got married or died, the gang split up, and now I am the only one left.

After I arrived overseas, I was sent to the North Shore New Brunswick Regiment as a reinforcement because they had a lot of casualties. I joined the regiment at the dykelands on the edge of Holland, and soon we moved into Nijmegen. That town was all on fire and appeared to be gutted from shell fire.

Next we moved up into the winter front on the German border. In fact, we were out in a salient two or three times, and that salient jutted out into Germany. That is the only part of Germany that Canadian troops were in at that time. We were out there over Christmas and beyond into January. That was before the big drive was organized to cross the Rhine.

Then when the big attack started to cross the Rhine River and advance deep into Germany, we advanced through Kleve, Kalaperoch, Kapellen and on to the Rhine River. There was one particular attack that I was in that I will never forget. It was the hardest fight we ever were in. It was called the Kapellen drive. That town was ahead of us, out about one thousand yards across open country, fields, and lines of bushes.

A whole brigade attacked two days before, and they couldn't take the town and had to fall back. They were stopped cold and had backed off and were digging trenches in the fields in daylight. Those other battalions couldn't take it and fell back and started digging in right in front of us, trying to get cover.

Then the Eighth Brigade, that was us, was ordered forward, and we advanced, that is, the Queens Own, the Chaudière, and the North Shore New Brunswick Regiment. At the start, the shelling got unmerciful. Before we even got up to the houses on the outskirts, we had to advance across a big open field. The shells came in thick and fast.

The forward two companies kept going, and we came in behind, organized and moving steadily ahead. We came to the end of the street, which was very muddy, and I saw a terrible sight, I saw a woman and a young girl come running towards us down that street. I was the Bren gunner at the head of the section, and there was heavy firing every-where.

Suddenly that young woman fell headlong face down in the mud, and the young girl with her dropped just as suddenly in the muddy street. Both had been shot down, both were very dead. I had never seen a woman killed in action before. It was a terrible shock. I had seen many dead enemy soldiers and some of our own dead but never had I seen a woman killed.

That was deliberate killing. I don't know who they were or where they came from, but I guessed that they were running for cover. There was so much fire that it was difficult to tell what hit those women. The rain and fog made it very hard to see very far.

We had reconnaissance vehicles with us, and one came up with two men in it. It was an armoured vehicle for scouting forward, and it went right on past us up the street. These two women looked all right lying there, not torn or blown up, but their faces were right down in that deep mud.

The shelling and machine gunning was murderous. The Jerries were trying to break up our attack. We ran along and entered the edge of another field. German tanks were dug in farther up in the town. We knew that the fight for Kapellen was going to be vicious. Shellfire and direct fire from those tanks were playing havoc with the forward companies, and we dug in along the edge of the field.

Those other companies which had dug in out in the middle of the field were pinned down and being hammered to pieces. We took cover there for two or three hours while the company commander sent back for tank support for us. An armoured regiment was soon moving up through us, and I believe they were Quebec tanks. They might have been the Sherbrooke Fusiliers.

Those tanks moved up in a swing around the flank, taking some casualties as they moved in. In the next hour they lost a lot of tanks. Anyway, before long we received orders to move up and advance into the town. We spread out and advanced through the two companies ahead of us. We encountered heavy machine gun fire. I lost a buddy, he just dropped right down on the ground beside me. I didn't get a scratch.

I couldn't stop. I was the section Bren gunner. Finally we had captured several houses and took cover in one of them.

Suddenly, we heard a terrible rumble. It was a German tank breaking cover and taking off. It was leaving to get a better position. We sure heard it but we didn't see it, but we saw the tracks soon afterward.

Then we started fighting house to house, and we kept fighting from one house to another, clearing each street right up until dark. Kapellen was a hard fight for everyone. We lost many men there. As we moved farther into town, the other companies came in behind us to support us, so that after a while all four of our rifle companies were fighting together. We spread out, and each company was directed to take a specific part of town.

Major Ross from Woodstock was the only home-town officer I know of who was there. There was also a Lieutenant Charles Murphy from McAdam with us. My own company commander was Major Corbett. Soon we again got word to advance to the end of our street, and we did under constant shellfire. At the end of the street, machine gun fire came at us from several places.

We quickly ducked into a house, and then we heard a shell coming. We ducked down onto the floor against the wall, and that shell hit the roof. The whole upper story of that building came crashing down, but none of us in our section was hurt. We pulled out of the house and went to another house, and we kept ducking from house to house until we came to a crossroads.

There we again came under direct machine gun fire, which continued for a long time. Then one of the other companies came up on a flank and drove that Jerry machine gunner back. I kept up return fire with my Bren gun, firing short bursts at every place that I thought enemy fire was coming from.

Finally the enemy fire stopped, and the other companies advanced up to outflank the Jerry positions.

Anyway, towards night we got out of that house and into another one and then into a bomb crater. We thought that we were clear of enemy fire, so one fellow stood up, and immediately he got it from a sniper, right in the back. Then we set up for defensive fire for the night. That fellow who was hit in the back by the sniper was from Vancouver.

He asked me to write to his wife and tell her that he wasn't hurt, his name was Paussik, a Russian-Canadian or something. He was a tall six-footer from British Columbia. I saw a rifle lying there, and I assumed it was his. We always stuck the rifle up in the mud, sometimes putting a helmet on it to mark the place of a wounded comrade. So I picked the rifle up and drove the muzzle into the mud so it would stand up. Paussik was laying there on a stretcher.

However, a fellow from Newfoundland owned that rifle, and he found it with the muzzle driven into the mud. Oh, he was mad. He gave me hell, called me everything. I tried to explain, but he wouldn't listen. I had to clean that rifle for him. He wouldn't take another one from one of the wounded. He wanted his own rifle. It was some job getting all of that mud out of the barrel. The barrel was packed full for about four inches. I told him that I was awful sorry.

Then the tanks moved in, and together we held through the night. We collected the morning dead and tended the wounded while we tried to take turns resting. In the morning, the next two miles was another tough fight. But we were thrilled and proud that we held and beat the Jerries back. We went into a house to take cover from the shellfire, and a shell hit the roof, and that whole roof of red brick tile came down with a heavy crash.

We scrambled down into the basement where it was more safe. During a lull, we came out again, and near the door we saw some German women. They were watching a large group of prisoners walk by. They must have been a whole company of German prisoners. They must have been boyfriends or husbands of those women. The Germans were panzer grenadiers.

By the look on the women's faces, I think they believed that we were going to shoot the prisoners. Of course, we would never do anything like that. Those prisoners were sent back to the rear with only two guards. They didn't want to fight anymore, and they just walked along as if they were glad their war was over.

We stayed in Kapellen for a number of days, perhaps two weeks. In that period we received reinforcements to replace the casualties, and also we received mail and supplies. We were getting new men and supplies to get ready to cross the Rhine River. That was our next objective. The Brigade sent out a regiment, the North Shore, across first, and British troops operated the boats to ferry us over.

D Company of the Chaudière led the attack on our left, and did they ever holler and shout, making a terrific noise. It was a moonlit night and we crossed about two a.m. With five or six in a boat, the British quickly put us across the river. They were well organized and no mistakes were made.

The British made a flanking attack, and that helped us tremendously. Those British troops moved ahead rapidly, and we advanced a little at a time until all of us reached the Reichewald Forest. About noon the advance slowed and soon was stopped by heavy fighting ahead.

I saw a German under a haystack. He came out and gave up. He was immaculate in a newly pressed uniform, and everything on him was perfect. He was an RSM (regimental sergeant major) and it seemed obvious that he was dressed prepared to surrender. Our boys were covered with mud, and several of them came over to inspect the German dandy. In that shell-torn and muddy place, he sure looked odd.

Just ahead of our company, our colonel was holding an Order Group to plan the next phase. All of the company commanders were there. Suddenly a shell landed near them and the colonel and four or five senior officers were killed. That was a terrible blow to our battalion.

Again we moved forward, using the ditches for cover, one soldier running ahead at a time. When we had to cross a road, one would run over while the others would fire to cover him. Every move had to be between shell bursts. I had the heavy Bren gun, and I stooped low to keep down in the ditch. That way I couldn't see too well, and I got ahead of my section. When I looked I was surprised to see my section way back along the ditch. I was concentrating on keeping behind cover.

Three young Germans appeared with their hands up; they were paratroopers. To get a better chance to give covering fire, I ran ahead towards some trees. The Germans saw me, and two Spandau machine-guns opened up on me. I could see the bullets, hitting the cobblestones of the street only three or four feet from me, but missing as I ran.

Then the German gunner corrected his aim and hit me in the legs. I ran about three steps and fell. I hit the hard road and rolled over and over until I reached the ditch. I was hit in the left leg and grazed along my right leg. In a minute or so I got my Bren gun going and returned the fire. I tried to hit that German machine gunner.

One of our fellows ran up and dropped down beside me. I was trying to dress my wounds and stop the bleeding. That fellow asked me if I could dress myself and I answered, "Yes, I'm pretty well all fixed up." Then a fellow named Wiseman from Cape Breton came along. I knew that he was a darned good man. He had been in action since D-Day. Then a stretcher bearer came along looking for wounded.

My number two on the Bren came up, but he wouldn't take the gun. It really was his job and duty. Anyway, a new man named Duke came up and took the machine gun. My number two was a fellow from Lakeville. In fact, he was a poor number two on the Bren. He just didn't want no part of it, so Duke took the gun and turned out to be a mighty good Bren gunner. One time when the Duke fellow got pinned down, he put his helmet on a rifle and stuck it up for a target, the sniper fired at it, and Duke saw where he was. Then Duke poured the Bren fire onto him and got him.

Well, that street crossing was my Waterloo. That was in the town of Millegen. More stretcher bearers came up, and then I waved them down to stop. They were travelling in a vehicle equipped to carry two stretchers. I hollered, "Hey! You're right up front. There are German machine gunners just ahead, you'll get hit." If I hadn't stopped them they would have gone right into the German positions.

Then one of them asked, "Are you hit?" I said, "Yes, in the legs." They picked me up out of the ditch and put me into the vehicle. They put me up on top, thee were three other wounded there, and they also picked them up, two on top and two below. Then they turned in the mud and away we went, back to the aid station, where the doctor was. Our own unit doctor looked my wounds over and dressed them properly.

Next we were taken by a big ambulance back to the bank of the Rhine River. There all wounded were transferred to large amphibious boats like trucks for the river crossing. They were called "alligators." Two fellows picked me up on the stretcher. One was an English soldier and one was a little German prisoner of war.

We were moving down to the alligator when a shell came over quite a ways away. The German dropped his end of the stretcher and dived for a hole. I hollered, "Come back here you SOB," but the English soldier said, "Never mind, Canada, he can't help it, he has been through an awful shelling and his nerves are all shot." He came back, and they lifted me aboard the alligator and we crossed, and I was transferred to a field ambulance for the trip back to a proper hospital. The first hospital was in tents.

In a short while I was transferred to the Nijmegen Hospital. After one night in that hospital, I was taken back to Belgium. It was a big job to move the wounded. Dozens were coming in at once, and the roads were clogged with tanks and trucks and all kinds of vehicles moving both ways. In the forward dressing stations and field ambulance stations, there was no space to put the stretcher cases.

A lot of walking wounded were just sitting or standing around. All were treated according to the severity of their wound or injury and tagged accordingly. I spent one night in an army quonset hut in Belgium, and the next morning I was taken to an airplane and loaded. We landed in southern England and then on up to a hospital in Scotland, where I stayed for two months. After that I went on to a convalescent hospital.

One little story I remember is about a Christmas carol. Another fellow and I were taking our turn in a forward trench, point duty, while the unit waited in the dark night. It was Christmas Eve. We hadn't even remembered what day it was. The platoon was taking turns with two men at a time up forward, two hours on and four hours off.

The night was cold, and our many thoughts were about keeping warm. The night was clear, a crisp starlit sky overhead. A shell came in quite close, and we ducked down behind the bank. The mud didn't matter, you could not keep clean, warm, or dry anyway.

Then there was a lull in the firing. From back in our lines about two or three hundred yards, suddenly we heard a bugle. That was no ordinary bugler. He was a musician, not some guy who had learned to make the calls on a bugle. Strong, clear, and steady, beautiful notes came across that December air. Everyone was miserable, and that sound was unbelievably pleasant.

It was no ordinary bugle call. It was a melody, a musician's Christmas message to the front. Whoever it was played the Christmas hymn "Silent Night" with precision for about three or four minutes. There was absolute silence along the front. We looked at each other and then up at that starlit sky. That is one time that I wished that the shelling would stop and give us a break.

On a night like that, that horn could be heard for a very long distance. The magic spell was broken suddenly by the howling of incoming shells. For quite a few minutes, the Germans shelled our rear area. The flash of Christmas spirit was gone. Now, years later, whenever I hear "Silent Night" at Christmastime, I always think of that December night up near the Rhine River.

The Christmas Orange

DAVID WEALE

Perhaps the greatest difference between Christmas today and Christmas "them times" is that "them times," people were poor. Not that there aren't any poor today, but back then everyone was poor — or almost everyone. It wasn't a grinding end-of-the-rope kind of poverty. Most everyone had food enough to eat and warm clothes to wear. The woodshed was filled with wood, the cellar with potatoes and carrots, and the pickle barrel with herring or pork. In many ways it was an era of plenty, so you might say that rural Islanders weren't poor, they just didn't have much money.

What strikes me forcibly when I speak to old people is that the scarcity of money made it possible to receive very great pleasure from simple, inexpensive things. I know, for example, that for many children an orange, a simple orange, was a Christmas miracle. It was the perfect golden ball of legend and fairy tale which appeared, as if by magic, on December 25. In that drab world of gray and brown, it shone mightily like a small sun.

The orange was a kind of incarnation of Christmas itself, the very spirit and embodiment of the Christmas season. For many Islanders the most vivid, evocative memory of that blessed time is the memory of an orange in the toe of their stocking. One woman from a large family in Morell said that at her home you were fortunate if you received a whole orange for yourself. She recalled some lean years when she received half an orange, and was happy for it.

For children who ate oatmeal porridge for breakfast virtually every day of their lives and had molasses on bread most days in their school lunch; for children who looked at fried potatoes almost every evening for supper and considered turnip scrapings a special evening snack; for these children an orange was a marvel, something almost too wonderful and prized to be eaten — an exotic, sensuous wonder.

One woman confessed that she kept her orange for a week after Christmas, kept it in a drawer. Several times a day she would go to her hiding place and take out the orange just to fondle it, and smell it, and to anticipate joyously the pleasure which was to come. Eventually, it had to be eaten: deliberately, unhurriedly, ceremoniously, and gratefully. Piece by piece, and finally the peeling — it was all eaten, and it was all good.

But soon it was gone. All that remained was the hope there would be another Christmas and, if God would be good, another orange.

Cougar

MARK JARMAN

Motor to the mega mall and the mall moves me to a minor rage. I get in a fight with two women in the mall parking lot, a mother-daughter tag team. Then in the woods a sleek cougar nearly takes my head off, but I said ix-nay.

The story was, I was going to chop us a free Christmas tree, but feeling base and mortal and morbid and pretty fine I collected every damn pill in the trailer, including Flintstones and Aspirin and iron and old tiny Infant Tylenol bottles. What the hell, I'll try anything once. In my pockets I had a dog's breakfast of pills and I felt like a dog, felt lower than a snake's belly.

Things had gone wonky. No jobs in the woods, our old mill sold to foreigners, and foreigners shut it down tight. They don't live here. New softwood agreement too, and Asia gone down the tubes, so we're going right with them, they sneeze and we blow our nose. A letter falls into my black mailbox: they talk of markets, infrastructure, capital costs, mergers, new realities. I imagine them fine-tuning this letter in a meeting over Danish and mineral water. Do they actually know any more than we do?

My tiddly little house is for sale, but it's never going to sell because every nice little house is for sale there. I pawned the Husqvarna and moved down island. Everyone laid off. We're global now.

No money for presents. Wet weather: sore elbow, trick knee, bad back, feel I'm hobbling, falling apart, and my K car is acting up since it got rear-ended and the physio making me wear a stupid collar on my neck. A mild buffet of arthritis and angst in my bones, and my K car is not OK, the Reliant is less than reliant.

I was not, it seemed, lying on a sunny beach, I was not going to Disneyland after creaming the opposition, I was not leaning into a forest of microphones.

It's hard to explain suicidal tendencies. No one detail gets you, but little things add up, little things eat at you. No one uses signal lights and every busker is convinced he can play harmonica. These things kill me.

Drear faces, substantially altered by winter, marked by weakness, marked by woe, shadowed, teeth crooked and dun that were straight and white last summer, whole childhoods perverted, lost, gone down with Asia, and you wake up to learn the world is no longer your bright laboratory.

Regarding my mega mall parking lot argument: an old woman and daughter, both smug and slatternly in some japscrap car, stole my parking spot, even as I backed into it. I began to feel I don't recognize this good old world anymore and I am sick of being a *recipient*. Sick of rolling snake-eyes when I want the dice to come up boxcars. Once this world was sweet as the low rumble of sixteen poolballs dropping as one; now I'm a bozo arguing over a stupid parking spot.

The same night I motored past a Christmas tree lot. All those strung lights and exiled, pointy-headed trees leaning around a little trailer used to cheer me up, but instead of good cheer, all I could think of was the tiny newspaper clipping that said the singer of the Tacoma garage band, the Wailers, died in a fire in the trailer on a Christmas tree lot just like this one I drove by. The Wailers were a wild band I really liked back when, same time as the Sonics, both power pop punks from 1963 or so. I drove by, rain drumming, my car and head like an empty tin of British biscuits. The Wailers had some great tunes on Etiquette

Records: "Out of Our Tree," "Hang Up," "You Aren't Using Your Head," "Bad Trip." Maybe they covered "Louie Louie." Have to dig out my old vinyl.

Have to do *something* when Christmas starts to seem like a humongous tax, an annual root canal, to seem alien and overly familiar. To light out, I decided, to the dark woods, into the bush, into a valley to think about things.

Weird weather in the firs on the edge of a continent, wind over the dead ships and lost harbours, stop and go storms jumping off the ocean, wind punching through treetops and stopping abruptly. Strange lulls, torn green branches on the forest floor and crashing sea vibrating rock miles away.

Don't like the weather here, they say, just wait ten minutes. They have said these same words to me every place I've lived or visited.

I tracked through the false infinity of ferns and firs and oak and owls, hiking and humming, *If you go into the woods today, you're in for a big surprise*. I hiked up over rocks, then down a rocky draw, into a bit of jog moving downhill. Sometimes it's easier to run than hold back.

It was jogging along and WHAM! Like being hit between shoulder blades by speeding bicycle.

Mayday! Mayday! some automatic voice in me thought. AAOOGA! *Bogey at three o'clock*. A small thrilled monster with saliva and bad breath riding my neck, and we rolled in a tense frenzy. Noises against me, a cat's mouth and breathing inside its throat, a rush of wind in some pipeline above, bass notes fumbling as we rolled in rocks and moss and sword ferns, and I thought, illogically of course, my face smashed in the rocks and moss, I will kill myself when I'm damn well ready to go and perhaps because of global factors beyond my control, but just this instant some sad-ass cut-rate panther with a wild face and bad table manners is not going to cut me down out of the blue without so much as a hello sailor.

I didn't know it then, but the cat tore me up a bit, tore my scalp and ear, shoulder, back, but it could have been worse. The cat fell off with my neckbrace collar in its teeth. Maybe the physio's collar helped. The little cougar shook the white collar, then turned back to gaze at me, the real thing, pink meat in pink skin. The cat's fur was out like it was going for a punk look, a trendy looking dude or dudette, ears twitching and rotating like radar, Oriental face, mouth twisted, white chin, dark where the whiskers poked out, and some good looking teeth with drool falling out, which adds greatly to anyone's street cred.

My drool dried up severely.

Luckily my Christmas cougar was a skinny, paltry thing, not full grown, and I believe a female, not a big stud tomcat, and not knowing how to really hunt proficiently, or I'd be dead meat and not telling this yarn, I'd be remains with some dirt and leaves raked over me by the cat.

Remains. I suddenly knew, despite my pockets filled with pills, that I did not want to be unidentified human remains, bones scattered around the woods, bits partly buried by animals in a secret funeral, wallet found years later with two-dollar bills in it like that hiker I read about in the mountains.

I was not going to kill myself. My cockeyed world tilted, turned. I wish I could say I became magically happy, but I was not happy. More like mule-headed.

Remains: my neighbour, a university lady, hires me for odd jobs. I have helped her bury pigs. She dresses the pigs in flannel shirts, denim, sunglasses. We buried one pig in a pretty prom dress and white gloves.

I dig the holes for the university lady and she pays me. She studies the dressed pigs after they rot in the shallow graves, see what insects and beetles are present after one day, three days, a fortnight, year. Police check with the university lady when they need to know how long a body has been in the woods.

The university lady seems to enjoy her work. I don't like to be there when we dig up what I have come to think of as Arnold from the fine old TV show *Green Acres*. I didn't want to become Arnold, even though I thought I came into the woods to become Arnold.

***

The tan cougar feinted, put its head forward and trotted at me again, skinny but an impressive piece of work, muscles and moving parts leaping at you like you're a big gingersnap it's going to break in two. What my dad called a puma or a panther. In the highway ditches now the government uses expensive panther pee to scare deer away from the road, away from the voters.

Rare to see a cat in the bush, no matter how often you go in, and I've been in the bush a lot. They're good at hiding and are more active after dark. This is rare. This one came out of hiding to try me on for size, and I knew I wanted to get out and tell someone about this impressive little creature wielding muscle and razors if I could still get out, get out of the woods before dark drops, dark so early now in December.

The young cat eyed me, ears pinned back, small lower jaw dropped in a snarl, springing at my shoulders. I felt naked even with my folding saw and hardware-store gloves and heavy coat and boots. I ducked and turned but still got knocked over from the cat's force. I think my grandfather's heavy old mackinaw helped deflect her dark claws. How does such a skinny creature generate such amazing force? It was like being boarded by Eric Lindros.

In pure panic I got my old workboots up and kicked the small cougar, but not before she sliced me on the shins. I had a blurred close-up of curved canines, black gums, and white chin, her noise and cylindrical weight driving in at me and turning back, and I went crazy, shrieking like a fishmonger the entire time, using my boots, kicking her several good ones in the pale muscled gut and soft snout, her low centre of gravity and loose skin, her nose bleeding, head down. She tried to get one paw up around me like a drunk, both of us rolling around and scrapping, and then in the hurly-burly this moaning cat shit on me — no kidding, let go like a semi-automatic semi-liquid weapon.

I jumped about three yards trying to get away from that, found a handy hunk of fir and winged it and got her in the face with the wood, and she didn't like that. I cut her smooth broad nose, and she paused to peer at this prey that can throw things and was recently sprayed in runny cat scat.

What a world: slide into the woods feeling sensitive and Hamlet-like melancholy, feeling a fine fellow, albeit an anti-social suicide who'd like to blow up the mall, and does Mother Nature smile on you and proffer blackberries and real cream? No, Mother Nature says here is what I think of your finicky brooding.

Maybe at the mega mall I should have shit on them, like the cat did.

You can't *back* into a parking spot, the daughter sneered.

Yeah, you can't back in, they chorused with their arms folded: stealing a spot and then feeling on the side of right. I had pulled forward to allows the parked car to leave and then I started backing in. They zigzagged in, stealing from me and then blaming me for having a reverse gear! I sputtered in inarticulate rage and wanted dearly to smack their heads together like coconuts but didn't because I was raised right, unlike some others I could mention.

In the bush I had to walk backwards a mile or two and think about things while stepping very carefully in tripwire blackberry canes and salal, bloody hard uphill and down and stinking of cougar shit. An altered sense of time. I walked backwards trying to look large and swearing at the little puma, though it is hard to sound tough while retreating constantly.

The hungry animal followed me step for step, calmly placing her hind paw exactly where the front paw had stepped, stalking me in expired leaves and trees trying to live in rock and rucked landscape, skinny cat making yowling panther noises. It doesn't jump but stalks me step for step, following me like a machine, eyes in fearsome concentration, both of us thinking, and I waved a folding saw and waved a worthless stick like a B-movie pirate, a branch of punky oak that was about to fall to pieces, but the cat didn't know that. I walked backwards, waved a stick, and went back in time.

Decades back, my dad told me of a big tom that weighed as much as he did, a big cat that would lope along beside fleeing livestock and calmly flatten any goat or calf or sheep it wanted; one blow and it's down dead. A big tom can leap twenty or thirty feet from a perch, and it can snap your neck.

I knew that a woman died defending her kids from a cougar in the Interior, and a few years back a cat killed a child up the coast. When I was driving north from California to BC some years back, a woman in Northern California, a famous Olympic runner, was training in the woods, running fast, and was jumped from behind and killed, and I was driving through the redwoods and heard about it and was amazed but didn't know it would be visited on me later.

I knew this cat could kill me, and that impressed me, made things clear, and I knew that mall scene with the twin harpies was not important, even though I wanted to bend their windshield wipers into pretzels. It clears your mind wonderfully to walk backwards in the backwoods and wonder will you die from four sabre teeth or five claws attached to paws the size of country pancakes.

I walked backwards, went into my past, and recalled all the old jobs I'd had: truck driver, digging wells, digging clams by lantern light, spark-watching, whistle punk, faller for a dollar, bucker for a buck, busboy in Duncan, dry land sort and chainsaw maestro, choker, joker, smoker, timber cruiser, a snoozer, a scaler, feeding the green chain, working in a box factory, riding the milk train, and riding an orange forklift with a big batter on the back. Smoke meant money, but now all the jobs are gone up in smoke, love's labour lost. I walked backwards and thought of burying pigs in the woods. It's legal, but still there is something illicit about the act of burying a body in the woods.

I thought of the singer for the Wailers dying in the burning trailer and the space heater that killed him. Did his Christmas tree catch fire too?

I have too many friends dead of mundane things. Widow-maker branches blown down on their head or a chainsaw into an artery, or touching the wrong wire, or porch-climber wine in your hand, or just some greasy creations you eat once too often.

They jack-knifed their logging truck, or they drove a four-by-four backwards off a cliff in the snow, thinking they're just turning around, two guys and two women. The whole truck drops backwards with them it it, good aimed up, when the driver was just trying to turn it around, trying to get them back home. Imagine their surprise, the terrible dashboard light on their faces.

I walked backwards, cursing at the cougar and remembering all the battered buses and muddy trucks, the company crummies with your black lunchbox and sugary coffee and long muddy drives into the tees, driving logging roads to the show and driving out the same way, hours and hours, the tiny taverns by the bay much later at last light, trees by the parking lot, water a silver curve at the picture windows, wind rushing the glass, and drinking feels good and logical. It's dark and you should be heading home, *true*, but not right away. There are pickled eggs and perfect clubhouse sandwiches and one more round, oyster shells piled outside, beer cases and kegs piled inside, enough draft to float a coal ship, float a peeler, start a fight in the parking lot, the crews and friends and enemies and gilt-edged girlfriends and ex-girlfriends who never thought you were like this, what does anyone really know of anyone, and your friends die too young, play harmonica well, and drive innocently just one foot too far over the cliff in the snow, the jilted joking faces and farces, the smiling hours I thought were disposable, the smiling hours I thought would never run out.

One young woman from the four-by-four crawled out at the base of the giant cliff, crawled for miles looking for me to help her, and I'd had a few, I saw her crawling like a turtle in the headlights and stopped, thinking, What in Christly tarnation are these crazy schoolkids up to now? and then we found out what had happened and the whole town in shock.

I was driving my '68 Cougar; that was a very nice car but I had to sell it some time ago to a child who I knew would crash it on Kangaroo Road, wreck my good '68 Cougar. I saw him drive away and envisioned his head busting right through the windshield and my nice green car wrapped around a tree up by the reservoir.

How you miss that job you cursed and the guys that ragged on you;

you miss the car that broke down, the life that never was but seems sweet now in retrospect.

The cougar's face is a mask. When kittens their eyes are blue, but later they turn yellow. Her dark eyes are almost crossed — strange, hypnotic eyes, circles in a triangle, her eyes round and slitted and triangular at the same time, a weird geometry, her dark eyes fierce and relaxed, like a good fighter, a boxer's broad nose, fur scrunched up on her nose like a tiny rug piled up.

It stared at me and scrunched its nose, mouth pulled back, four good curving teeth, two up, two down, a perfect clamp. Teeth bared, that cougar walked me back over muck and rock and hill and dale to adrenalin and feeling; that cougar walked me back to sensation, blood, good bread, IPA, choice, the pull of home, to draw breath. I moved my brain in the woods.

Out of the pitch and pine and turpentine the puma walked me back to life. The cat quit following me when it saw the rusty K car, and it melted away in two seconds, gone like a ghost, no regret on its face. Perhaps a slight wince, didn't approve of the dull car.

Clothes cut up, and lacerations starting to hurt more, after the fact, like in hockey, when you don't notice some welts until later. Covered in blood, stinking and shaking after I stopped and sat and thought about my date, my escort, how close I'd been.

Stupid car starts. In reasonably reliant Reliant I drove into town, past a Christmas tree lot, and I thought again of the burnt guy from the Wailers, but it was all right: I'll have some grog or eggnog in memory of him and his old fuzz-tone band. I believe he'd appreciate that more than any moping or mooning about death and gases and fire.

Stars and constellations floating like shirts in the December sky, Saturn's rings and Jupiter's moons moving right over her white shining trailer.

Her porch and door lit yellows; tiny blue and red lights glowing on two shrubs. I limped through the silky colours, saw her reading on the couch.

Her kitchen was warm and toasty; soup smelling good on the stove, her whole trailer creaking when you walk. It creaks like a ship, creaks like me. The soup sits on a flame, and flames killed the singer for the Wailers, but soup will heat up my guts, restore me. Soup equals life at this moment. Poor cat starving; it didn't eat me. I hope it has an okay Christmas, finds a few fat rabbits or a little blacktail or a Chihuahua, wrapped in a sweater like a burrito.

Did you get a tree?

Uh. Not quite. Guess I forgot the tree.

How can you forget? Were you out drinking again? What happened to your pants: you look . . . is that blood? You get in a fight or run into some wild woman?

Well yeah. I did just that. Both. A real hellcat she was.

I thought of the cougar's face. It thought it had me dead to rights but there was also a kind of glum resignation and hooded resentment there in its face. A lost nation. Both of us missed a connection, lost a world. I tried to tell her this in the kitchen.

She knew something was up. She knew I was telling her something, and she went quiet because she's smart and she waits for me to cut the crap.

I have no real job and no irons in the fire and no cash on the barrel-head and there are no mills hiring and no king salmon run past our window. No one in Bedford Falls brings me baskets of money, and the only job I can wrangle is burying pigs for the university lady, but I am back in the world, and I am going to have some good steaming chowder and after that a good beer, and maybe a crossword puzzle in ink, as I am careful and reckless. And maybe some screaming Buffalo wings — suicide wings we used to call them — and maybe clams in a metal bucket and another beer and maybe a bath with some salt for my multiple slashes from the cat, and her big soft bed with the creaking filigree headboard rattling Morse code to the wall.

I was out of the woods. I was not remains, not eating hospital food. In terms of rolling dice, I now felt I was throwing boxcars.

Have yourself a very Merry Christmas, spoke a red bakelite radio on the oilcloth. Decided I liked that radio.

Damn right, Merry Christmas to you, I said back. That soup ready? It smells great.

Please, she said, testing the waters.

I said the magic word and was rewarded, and I thought, my house up island ever sells I'll look for a '67 or '68 Cougar, a sharp looking car, light green paint job, pretty glittery paint, and I'll put good tires on it, get a grip, *control*.

I see myself perched behind a clean dark windshield, my brain steering the car, and every red and green wire in my world working. Reflected in my shining chrome are bright planets and dark woods flashing past us like the briefest of seasons.

The Radio

ELSIE CHARLES BASQUE

I was about eight years old when radio first came to Hectanooga. Oliver and Nellie Saulnier had just arrived from the States with this new invention.

A box-like contraption sat on a table. A large disc-shaped gadget about three feet in diameter hung on the wall. This was the speaker. If the audience consisted of several people, wires were adjusted, knobs were turned, and voila! voices, music boomed out of the wall. If only one or two persons wanted to enjoy this phenomenon, then earphones were easily accessible. What a marvellous invention!

It was sometime in November when Papa and I went to see, hear, explore this wondrous discovery.

We sat in the holiest of holies . . . the living room or parlour as it was commonly called, way back then. Only the priest on his yearly visit was allowed in there, but now . . . this new miracle introduced us not only to the world, but to the parlour as well.

I was so enthralled. Voices, music seemed to be coming out of the wall. There was a lot of static, but in my child mind, that was the way it was supposed to be.

Suddenly, sleigh bells were heard, at first from a distance, then, closer and closer. Santa's voice boomed loud and clear: "Ho Ho Ho! Merry Christmas, everybody."

I climbed on Papa's knee, speechless and spellbound. I had heard Santa's voice! I really and truly heard Santa Claus's voice! He was calling boys and girls by name. I was too excited to know if he had called my name or not. Unbelievable! As I remember, it only lasted a few minutes, but what a few minutes it was.

On our way home later on, Papa carrying a lantern in one hand, and mine carefully tucked in his other hand, he talked about the miracle we had just witnessed.

"Voices spoken as far away as New York! Heard as plainly as if they were in the very same room. This new invention will be improved upon. Some day we'll hear people from all over the world talking to us," Papa prophesied.

Nick Boudreau, who owned the only store in Hectanooga, was probably the first to invest in this new media. A large console model sat in the middle of the store. On "Fight Nights," the whole neighbourhood gathered to listen to such greats as Jack Dempsey, Joe Louis, and Max Schmelling among others.

Our world was getting smaller.

Sarasota

RICHARD CUMYN

Chafe had never been able to put away Christmas with the determination required to keep one clear eye on the New Year while lights, tinsel, and baubles returned to their boxes. A rustling curtain or an errant spruce needle could set him festive again, and so he retreated while Patricia got out her step ladder. Nana Mouskouri sang two versions of "Ave Maria." Patricia had a good voice, though untrained, and she crooned along in accompaniment. Chafe emerged when it was time to haul the tree out to the curb.

After work on Christmas Eve, they had driven to the U-Cut farm near Clayton. She chose the tree. He told her that she had an artist's eye for symmetry. They brought it home secured on the roof of the car with yards of yellow rope tied in intricate knots.

They drank brandy and eggnog while they decorated. Between them they managed to break all four of the antique glass baubles Chafe had inherited from his parents. Perturbed, Patricia disappeared into the kitchen. Chafe squinted to blur the colours of the tree, and the room began to sway like an amusement park. She returned with a needle and thread and a bowl of cranberries and popcorn.

"This is glorious. This is Christmas," he said, pulling her down to him, spilling some of the bowl.

"No," she said, "*this* first."

***

In the morning they were both sick to their stomachs. Chafe roused around noon and stole to the basement where he had hidden Patricia's gifts. He took the wrapped presents and the white plastic bag full of stocking stuffers, and went back upstairs. She was sitting pale on the couch. Beside her on the floor was her underwear still rolled inside her pantyhose. The lights of the tree were on. He told her not to look as he filled her stocking. She assured him that turning her head or any other part of her body at that moment was impossible.

"I thought we agreed not to do Christmas stockings anymore." Chafe ignored her, whistling blithely "Good King Wenceslas" as he slid bath oil and scented powder, lacy black underwear, a red and white wooden spinner designed to resemble a hypnotist's aid, a crossword book, socks, and the latest *Vogue* into the bulging boot of felt, which his mother had sewn, stitching "Patricia" in flowing script across the top. Of course then she had to push herself off the couch and fret around the house to find stuffers for him: a handful of unshelled walnuts, a candy cane off a bough, a small wrapped package transferred from under the tree, an unopened bar of soap lifted from the bathroom medicine cabinet.

He pulled each impromptu thing out with delight, exclaiming over it, slowing the process to a crawl. He conjured a mandarin orange from the toe of his stocking and peeled, sectioned, and consumed it before her very eyes. The fruit, bought just the day before in the crammed, frantic grocery store, was now a wonder in his hands.

"How can you eat that?" she said.

"It's magic, I'm transformed, I love you," he said.

"We missed a whole side of the tree."

"It's the most beautiful tree ever."

"You're becoming tiresome."

"I can't help it."

"You're not an eight-year-old, Chafe, and I'm not your mother. Everything you do does not delight me."

Then she made her way carefully, queasily, to the laundry room toilet.

They were hungry by the time his parents arrived for Christmas dinner. As the light faded, the thin colours of the day seemed to coalesce around the table. Patricia had bought tablecloth fabric especially for this meal, a deep wine red with metallic thread tracing a leaf pattern throughout. Against this were gold-coloured napkins. It had taken her weeks to find the right marriage of color and texture. Two green candles in plain pewter holders stood in the middle of the table.

His mother gasped when she saw the table. “Chafe, you never told me she was so talented.”

Chafe’s father said, “Something smells mighty good,” Patricia’s cue to disappear and tend to the bird.

“I’ll help,” said Chafe’s mother, rising to follow.

“Margaret, sit down and have a sherry,” said his father. “Give the girl some breathing room.”

“You try wrestling a turkey that size all alone, mister. Let me tell you. I know.”

But as Chafe had already gone to help his wife, his mother settled into an armchair, accepting a Dubonnet as consolation. She scanned the tree beside her.

“I don’t see the Victorian balls we gave them,” she said.

“He can put whatever decorations he wants on his Christmas tree. He’s a man now.”

“I had so hoped we could get through this without incident,” she said.

Chafe felt his father’s monologue coming all through the meal. Patricia was offering seconds of candied yams and mashed potatoes while Chafe stood brandishing the bone-handled carving knife.

“Still plenty of dark meat. Dad?”

"Oh, no, I couldn't. I'm still feeling the effects of last week's poker. Did we eat! Hell of a night, Chafe. Your old man cashed out big."

"No kidding. More wine?" said Chafe as he poured.

"I think I know two things for certain: no matter how much I try to lose, I almost always win; and nothing I win ever satisfies me."

"Which begs my perpetual question, Noah. Why continue to play?" asked Margaret.

"Let me revise. No matter how much I win at poker, I am never satisfied. And I am never really happy unless I am losing."

"I can understand that," said Patricia.

"Oh, then please, explain it to me, dear. This is one dark corner of masculinity I have never fathomed."

"If you lose, no one resents you."

"Precisely. Clever girl. A very perceptive soul-mate you have here, my boy." Patricia blushed but leaned in closer. He had her under his spell. "It's exactly that. When you are down on your luck, you know that your friends are rooting for you, in their straight-faced manner. There's no feeling like it. Furthermore, losing implies a change of luck. Therein lies the real source of all joy, you see. The change, that point at which one turns the corner and watches the wheel swing up, the smile return, that is *the* sought-after moment. To win endlessly is to lose hope, to tarnish, to begin to feel the others' eyes on your back. But to let a bloke lose it all only to slowly gain it back, well, therein lies the power."

Chafe watched his father's face, richly lit by the candlelight. More of his life had now been spent living away from this man than with him. Having been too young to enlist, his father became an undying student of that just-missed war. His friends were all veterans accustomed to long stretches away from domesticity. When they came home from combat, many sought the frontiers, the sea or the northern wilderness.

"We lived most of the year in tent camps, where we ate, slept, fought, drank when we could, shot bears, all the while mapping a battle plan against the rock, sizing up its riches. Gold, silver, nickel, cadmium, uranium.

"When it rained we played bridge, crib, poker, all day and night, under kerosene lamps while the airtight stove blazed against the downpour. That's when we thought about home, about women, hot baths, home cooking, family. It either kept a man sane or got him shipped out."

Chafe pictured his father, a lean young man wearing loose-fitting wool trousers tucked into rubber boots, a heavy leather belt cinching layers of shirts with button-down pockets. In his fist, like an extension of his arm, the handle of an axe held at the blade head.

"Surely this was what it was to be a man, out in the air, the unbroken vista before me, spruce and tobacco like a cologne on my skin. All my life I've tried to recreate that feeling.

"I know you've never understood that about me, Margaret. But this young woman, this lovely woman, our son's wife — no, don't look at me that way — she, she can empathize."

"You'd do well to ignore him, Patricia."

"There was no room to be cynical, you see," he said, addressing Patricia but looking straight at Margaret. "What we were doing, whether it was looking for gold traces in the clear streams or cutting gridlines or running surveys, was vital. No one was going to take that away from us. Not from these men who had endured so much for their country.

"I recall one man, Jock Hovey, saying to me, 'When you get back down there to civilization and your sweetheart, Noah, you think about what you've been fighting for up here. By opening up this frontier, mining all the riches of this great land, you've been holding the line against laziness and ungodliness. Look what's ahead of you. Of all times recorded, this will be the best time to be a man.'"

Chafe's father emptied his wine glass. His eyes were damp.

"Dad, do you remember we'd drive north sometimes on a Saturday and tramp around the abandoned mines?"

Noah laughed. "You couldn't take the heat."

Chafe would follow his father, flies biting and branches slashing across his faces, his throat parched.

"Nothing like up North, boy," his father would say. "Look at that, schist, magnetite, pyrrhotite." He would break apart a hunk of weathered rock with the blunt side of his axe, and Chafe would look up for a clue.

It was as if his father could see the rivers of molten rock, the folding, the faulting, syncline and anticline, all held in its clean face.

On road trips he would halt the car and scale cuts of salmon-coloured granite, his rock hammer stuck in his belt, traffic flashing by as Chafe and his mother sat waiting for him.

"A man carves his signature into the landscape. A man sets a structure against chaos. A man wills, and by doing so changes the very nature of space. Any more of this plonk?" he said, twirling the stem of his wine glass.

"The only thing I remember about all that, Patricia, is Noah calling out the car window, in a voice loud enough to crack glass, 'Where do the men go?' which means," she added for Patricia's benefit, although Chafe could see that his wife understood perfectly, "where do the men go to drink in this woebegone town? Where is the smoke-filled long-house, the boathouse, the sweat lodge? Where can I go to get away from the wife?"

"You lacked women friends, Margaret, that's all."

"I lacked a husband."

As she lay in bed that night, Patricia told Chafe she was afraid that he was going to turn into his father, but also that he would not.

Chafe bought a bouquet of carnations, pastel interspersed with white, and on the advice of the florist kept them in water overnight in the coolest corner of the basement. When he went down to get them in the morning, the cement walls were draped in perfume. He wanted to keep the flowers himself for their redolence of spring. Instead, he replaced the plastic wrap they had come in, dried the ends of the stems on a paper towel, attached the card, and got into the car.

His parents' high-crowned dirt road had not been sanded after the night's ice storm. He kept the car in the middle and prayed he didn't meet an oncoming vehicle. An empty white Ford Tempo was nose down in the ditch in front of the Jenkins', their only neighbours for a kilometer in either direction. Chafe slowed to look and, seeing no one in the car, continued. The approach to the house was on the down slope and he had to be careful to avoid skidding past the entrance.

His mother answered the door. "Happy New Year," he said, offering the flowers. She brought the bouquet to her nose.

She was dressed in a black and white plaid sports jacket, over a white blouse clasped at the neck, trim black slacks and low-heeled shoes. A suitcase stood just inside the entrance.

"You're going somewhere?"

"Carnations are a very smart choice," she said. "They keep for ages. Let me just put them in water. Can I make you a cup of coffee?"

"I didn't really plan to stay." He followed her into the kitchen where he handed her the packet of preservative that came with the flowers.

"Your father is out on an errand. He shouldn't be too long, I should think, if you want to wait for him."

"Where are you off to?"

"Some people just don't know how to drive in this weather. He's driving a young woman home. Did you see her car on the way in? Why someone would drive a white car in winter is beyond me. The tow truck will scoot on past it, I'm sure. Let me make you a cup of instant, Chafe."

"I've got to be on my way."

"But it would . . . I think he would be so pleased to see you here when he got back."

"We had made plans for the day."

"You must thank Patricia for the flowers. They're lovely."

"Actually, I picked them out."

"But here is her name on the card, signed by you, quite obviously — I do that all the time myself, signing Noah's name to cards and such, it's so much easier than trying to track him down."

"Will you tell me what's going on?"

"You don't think I meant, 'Thank your wife for picking out the flowers,' do you? I am fully aware of the capabilities of young husbands nowadays."

"Who is Dad driving home?"

"She reminded me of one of those girls from Personnel. They call it Human Resources now, don't they? You know the type who comes around with the card for so-and-so who is having her baby or getting married or retiring. By the time it gets to you the card is always crammed full with signatures and now, with this pretty and pleasant and efficient person hanging over you, you have to come up with something new to say."

"Can't you work this out?"

"Oh, I always *work it out*. I've shaken this marriage back into place so many times, Chafe, I don't care to remember."

"What should I say to him?"

"Why don't you remind him of his little speech. 'I'm never really happy unless I'm losing.' Tell him to chew on that one for awhile."

"At least tell me where you're going."

"I'll be at the Strathmore. Don't worry, Chafe, I'm not leaving for good. After two nights even the best hotel room begins to smell."

As he helped his mother across the slippery driveway to her car, Chafe saw Mr. Jenkins spreading salt by his mailbox across the road. His eldest son, daughter-in-law and two grandsons lived with him and his wife. The son was soon going to take over the construction business entirely. Jenkins was an amateur bird cataloguer for the Audubon Society, both here and in Florida, where he and his wife of fifty-five years wintered near Sarasota.

Chafe said the name of the place aloud. Sarasota. It felt effervescent in his mouth, carbonated, like sarsaparilla, but with more of a pop. He said it again as he waved goodbye to his mother, backing the car tentatively down the driveway.

He flicked the wind chimes over the porch and went inside to wait for his father to come home. He wanted to hear more about the North.

White as a Sheet

HERMÉNÉGILDE CHIASSON

This morning a layer of light snow covers the yard in front of the house in which I have just slept as only a child can sleep. Everything is white. I gaze out at all this whiteness for hours on end. Overnight, the snow has clothed the world in its immaculate sheet. I want it to stay this way, no scratches or marks, no footprints marring the surface. A surface as flawless as a sheet of paper.

Perhaps this is the extension of another life, when I was Mallarmé or Edgar Allan Poe, but if so, I don't remember it. It's easy to step outside yourself this way. Poe's voyage to the North Pole, where, according to Ricardou, the page's blankness blending into the snow's whiteness constitutes one of the first instances of the Modern Novel.

People who come to the house put me in a bad mood because they ruin everything, they leave futile and illusory marks when they make themselves a path through the snow. When I tell my mother this, she tries to mollify my obsessiveness by telling me that there is no way to prevent such a desecration. People have to come and go. Sooner or later they have to make their marks. A door has to be either open or closed. Duchamp again, with his silence. He, too, must have loved snow.

I learn my lesson and take my medicine with as much patience as I am capable of. Maybe, without my being aware of it and in a completely painless way, I have at last learned the terrible law of creation and destruction that dwells in the artist like two of the faces of Shiva. The fact that we must destroy in order to create, that creation is a fire that must burn on the outside or else it will consume us on the inside.

I haven't had breakfast yet. I'm still watching the snow. Its amazing spectacle has become a revelation. This snow is questioning me. Hypnotizing me. Subconsciously, perhaps, I realize that the white surfaces are hiding something from me, something much greater and much more astonishing than I thought. I cannot resign myself to the idea that snow is nothing more than a weight upon the earth. I know that later there will be colours, words, stages, or screens.

But for now, I listen. It's warm, a childhood warmth full of smells and odours, a warmth that excludes adults, who have already stopped noticing some things and are busy forgetting everything else. I am watching the snow, I have no wish to turn away from it, to turn indoors where I will go back to being blind. I am the keeper of the snow, of its whiteness, and I keep watch to see who will dare to break this moment and who, without knowing it, will put an end to this ecstatic vision.

Much later. I am in the Gaité-Montparnasse metro station, looking up the address of a shop that sells nothing but paper. Years have gone by, and I am once again what I always ought to have been. I go to this shop often. I spend hours in it, looking at sheets of paper, at their different textures, touching them. I never buy anything. Possession, I have learned, kills beauty. I believe it is better to leave beauty to its own fate and console myself with the fact that these objects exist, to be happy leaving them in their proper place, and to be alive and sharing their presence.

Just when I am about to give in to temptation, I rush out onto the sidewalk without making a purchase. This no doubt calls for an adjustment to my priorities, but I still prefer to draw on newsprint, even though I know that in the end my work will disintegrate, like confetti. Like snow. But what right do I have to inflict my doubts and errors onto a sheet of paper that is already, by virtue of its whiteness, a perfect work of art? I know what others would do in my place, probably on the very sheet that I was contemplating inside, but at least it won't be me who has to live with the weight of such pretension.

These papers are very dear to me. I don't want my work to derive its interest from the fact that it has been printed on expensive paper. And yet it must be so. I must move on without giving in too much to this obsession with the whiteness of yesteryear's snow. To see the world as a work, its surface as an illusion, a mask, a trick of the eye. I take up a piece of chalk, it doesn't matter which one, and I make a mark, it doesn't matter what. I have a vague idea of what is going to appear, of what must surge forth, but I take a stab at improvisation. Suddenly, the deception interferes with what I'm trying to do, and I see that I have to work with the surface rather than against it. Another dimension thrusts itself up through the paper, the canvas, the screen, or the film.

A neighbour is walking with heavy steps across the field towards our house. There is something he needs to know. Without even being aware of the damage he is causing, he crosses the white yard, his footprints making craters and causing the earth to tremble at each step, his shadow falling on the snow like a hole in light. He advances, an unbeliever and an apostate, towards the porch and asks for some useless information as trivial and offensive as his presence, as unimportant as his words, as banal as his life. I vow to forget everything he has said. Nothing will remain of him except the memory of steam rising from his heavy woollen coat, his gaze as it sweeps across space, revealing his enormous transgression, the fragile claims of outraged beauty.

The work progresses, and I am so surprised by what it turns out to be that I forget what I had originally intended. I have buried the paper's pristine beauty under layers of signs and doubts and imprecations. The paper has disappeared, become something else. The snow has melted, opened up wounds through which I can see mud taking over the surface, expelling the whiteness. It's the end of autumn, or maybe the beginning of another spring. The man leaves.

He is a salesman, unwelcome company. He limps. His horse is tired. He leads it by a leather strap, and it follows him through the village, giving off light like an aura. The man shouts angrily at it, their slow steps seeding the snow, in the gaze of a child who preserves the entire scene in his feverish, fragmentary memory.

from Composing Winter

LYNN DAVIES

At night, the snow angels gossip
under the bird feeders where they've seen
other winged things gather by day.

They cannot go far, for they belong to the bodies
of the children who made them. They have no real names.
It's "hey angel" or "what happened to your wing?"

What an angel remembers of creation:
snow-sound and the weight of shadow after
the child rises. "Weren't you made beside me?"

We think they melt to animate the snowdrops.
But a child sees a snowy owl drift over a field
and thinks, oh! my angel, it flies away after all.

A Serpent's Tooth

STAN DRAGLAND

Can't tell a story to save my life and I feel one coming on. I know what I ought to do. I should take the Fool's advice to suffering Lear. "O, my heart, my heart!" Lear cries. He has banished the only daughter who loves him and now he's under the fangs of the other two, those bitches. Foolish old Lear. Takes one to know one? Maybe so; anyhow, I've never loved the old man as much as I do now. "Cry to it, nuncle," says the Fool of Lear's poor heart, "as the cockney did to the eels when she put 'em i'th' paste live. She rapped 'em o'th' coxcomb with a stick, and cried 'Down wantons, down!'" Yes, and I love the Fool, tears streaming down his cheeks while he improvises all those superior japes. And what did I say about my bum storytelling? This story got sidetracked before it got started. Never get to the punch line at this rate.

Anyway, I'm down there and — "Down where?" Down in her basement. "Whose basement?" Shit. My X. I'm down in my X's basement, and I see all these short pieces of board piled up. Left by the people she bought the house from. Did I say this is just before Christmas? "You did not." Well, it's a little over a week before Christmas, and my shopping isn't all done and I'm looking at those boards and I'm thinking axe. She needs an axe. Actually, a hatchet. If she were to chop each of those boards into kindling, they'd go twice or maybe three times as far. I'm living in the wrong time. I could have been a pretty fair settler, a good husbandman, back in the days when the husband was mostly supposed to figure out the very best ways to provide.

So I bought a hatchet at Canadian Tire, Kenmount Road. From the half-dozen choices, I picked one with a good sharp blade, not too heavy. A nice balance to it, a curved, rubber-covered steel handle, $19.95 before tax. Brought it home, wrapped it, laid it on the bedroom floor with the other presents in their little family groups. This was into the week before Christmas. Every night for the next few days, that isoceles package would catch my eye, and I'd run over my shopping for it and my wrapping of it. Why? I wasn't reliving the buying and wrapping of anything else. I wasn't writing out the little tags again, to so-and-so with love from Stan, or from Stan and Rachel. But that axe. A Christmas axe. The settlers were a practical people. They had to be. I once read that most of them owned just two books: the Bible and *Pilgrim's Progress*. Can that be true? Must have been the Protestant settlers. Anyway, they wouldn't have had much time to read, not the ones with a shot at getting ahead, not with wood to gather all through the winter when the going was easiest. An axe was like gold to the settlers.

But I'm not a settler. Things have come unsettled recently, yes, but the real pioneering is all done. Now we have luxuries. We buy too many Christmas presents for each other out of sheer marital momentum. My heart, my heart! An axe, though. No other present on my bedroom floor is so identifiable by its shape. To me, at least, who bought it and wrapped it up. There I go again. So I told Rachel about the axe and she smiled. There was no irony in that smile, nothing remotely like mockery, but it was enough. I unwrapped the axe and fished the receipt out of my wallet and returned it to Canadian Tire. After Christmas I went down to Hiscock Rentals, where I got the hose clamp for the dryer vent that took me down to that basement in the first place, and bought myself the perfectly good seven-buck wood-handled hatchet I had spied there. I need kindling, too. And now I'm addressing myself, for consolation, in the words of Eeyore, the very model of a self-involved pessimist: "Pathetic, that's what it is, pathetic." More Shakespeare might have made it less pathetic, but it's too late for that, because this story is done. So that's how I just barely kept myself from playing the fool again and giving my X an axe for Xmas.

Sky's Poem for Christmas

MILTON ACORN

As from milky vapour, dust of atoms jostling like hornets,
a nebula swigs great swatches of itself into a new sun
raw with light, ravener to its parent mists, messenger
to far astronomers thirsty for the word, the word
that'll unlock them: I've never lost a faith
or wrenched my roots of eyes from the heart . . .
Each doom to joy and torment's nourished
within an old love, becomes a new focus
pulsing radiation, disrupting
the foggy smut of death about it;
while I still step to the blood's rhythm,
the soul's reason in those old stories
of kings and white-hot new stars, wonderful babes
like Jupiter's yowl making that Island cave boom like an organ,
born to laugh a challenging at the old cruel gods.

Surely at least once when a new star bursts thru heaven
three old men forsook the stern fantasies
of mummy-clothes they'd wrapped around the world,
and surely they found at least one babe
who held great bear time by its short tail . . .

For the birth by birth the many-coloured creatures of Earth
break ranks and dance apart calling their names and numbers
to reassemble with shoutings and elbow-digs
in formations first seen by the mind's eye of a child.

Christmas I became that ho-ho-ho of a saint
to wind on a balky piebald disbelieving burro
along the Wise men's trail thru a desert of grown-up people
like cactus with its growth stalled in tormented poses:
til housed and run around by squirrels I found the boy Sky
with eyes hazel windows into outré dimensions
now looking out on wonder, now looking in
at wonder. . . . I came not with gifts but
for a present of the universe made strange, tumbling
with odd fuzzy animals, blue of high heaven
siphoned down to tank up my brain,
for meteors he caught and sent sizzling past my ears:
and for myself made quaint, totemic
like a thick oak wobbling, walking
grotesquely on its roots over patches of dark and sunlight.

What Possessed Him

MICHAEL CRUMMEY

Hayward sat on the bed in the dark to catch his breath, to ease the ache in his chest after climbing the stairs. Through the window he could see the illuminated star on the steeple of the Anglican church two blocks away, the dark glow of light through stained glass on either side of the doors.

He heard his wife's voice. "Your shoes," she was saying. She was speaking from the foot of the stair. "Your shoes are on the stand. In the closet."

"I know where the shoes are," he shouted back, not angry, but louder than he needed to be heard.

He stared at the church in the distance, across the newly empty lot graded level under snow. He still expected to look out on the Catholic school from here: the long line of classroom windows, the Blessed Virgin on a pedestal at the entrance, her hands held out in perpetual benediction. The view frightened him now, made him feel displaced in his life. It was like a disfigurement of his own face, like seeing himself missing an eye.

He'd sat in the backyard for days that fall, watching the building come down. Not enough children in town to fill the classes of two institutions, the students amalgamated at the public school. A few Catholic parents protested briefly, but there was no arguing with the reality of the situation. The roof came off first, followed by the white shingles, the rotten tar paper. The boards underneath darkened by age, by insidious water damage. The building, like a creature suffering through vivisection, stripped back a layer at a time to salvage windows, steel girders from the auditorium.

The day after they'd seen the specialist in Grand Falls, Etta came outside to stand beside him a while. An afternoon too cold to be sitting in the yard without a hat, she told him. "You'll catch your death," she said.

Hayward was sitting in a lawn chair, his shoes buried in leaves fallen from the single birch tree in the yard. Mid-November, the snow late this year. "I've already caught that," he said.

Etta put her hand to her mouth then, staring at the mutilated school, a film of tears blurring the clear blue of her eyes.

Across the street, a crane was lifting the statue of the Virgin Mary onto a flatbed truck. A saw started up somewhere out of view, ripping into the naked frame of the school. He could feel the noise shaking through the ground, travelling up through his spine.

She said, "You have to tell the children, Hayward."

"Etta."

"They have a right to know."

He nodded. "Let them have one more Christmas," he'd said.

The "children" were both nearing the age of fifty.

The first was born when Hayward was twenty-three and not more than a year married, still earning the underground trade. He'd sat up all night in the hospital waiting room, smoking cigarettes and looking to the swinging doors that led to the wards. Somewhere back there, Etta was in labour. More than that, he wasn't told.

Near nine the next morning, he was led back to the room where she lay exhausted and teary, exhilarated in an otherworldly way that made him feel like a child witnessing naked adult emotion for the first time. He waited at the bedside until she dropped asleep, then asked to be taken to the nursery. He stood outside of the large window while the nurse held his son in her arms on the other side of the glass. Tiny fists. Head spiralling on the spine, mouth open, as if the child was trying to get free of a bad dream. The nurse's name was Maggie Dawe. She nodded to Hayward after a minute and set the infant back in his crib.

He went to the Royal Stores for more cigarettes after leaving the hospital, then drove out the back roads to the dam where he parked near the water. He sat there two hours then, lighting each smoke off the butt of the last. Coins of sunlight in motion on the water's dark conveyer belt, his hands shaking as he brought the cigarette to his mouth. The eyelids of his infant boy so translucent he'd thought he could see the colour of the eyes beneath them. He felt transported and desperate somehow, as full of secret submarine life as the lake.

The thought of becoming a father hadn't occupied him much in the months leading up to this moment, and he was unprepared to feel it as something so implacably permanent, so irrevocable. A lump in his throat, so he could just inhale the smoke, those first hours when he experienced the love of his son only as a grinding, inexorable terror moving through him.

Sitting in the doctor's office that November afternoon as the X-rays and ultrasounds went up on the light board, something related to that old fear came back to him, the taste of it in his mouth. The specialist was a small fastidious man from New Delhi whose silver hair, in contrast to the darkness of his skin, seemed to cast light, as if it was connected to a battery. He and Hayward had difficulty with each other's accents and Etta was called upon to act as an interpreter.

"He said taking the lung out may not help," she told Hayward, "but it's the only chance you have."

Edgeless spots of darkness, like potato rot, blighting the phosphorescence of healthy tissue.

"And no more cigarettes," she added quietly.

"Bit late for that I expect," Hayward said. He was thinking of the boys, of having to tell them. For the first time in years, both sons were coming home for the holidays with their families, Warrick flying down from Labrador City where he worked the open-pit iron ore mines, Glen coming all the way from Alberta.

He said, "It'll have to wait till after Christmas."

"Hayward," Etta said.

He looked across at the doctor, "I can still have a scatter snort if I wants one, can I?" he asked.

The doctor shrugged helplessly and turned to Etta.

"Can he have a drink now and then, he wants to know."

The doctor shrugged again. "Drinks are not being the problem, Mr. Hayward. The lung is the problem. There is removing," he said. He pointed up at the series of images, the diffuse glow of them like light through stained glass. "And then there is hoping for the best."

Hayward nodded. "After Christmas," he said.

When he made his way back downstairs, Etta was at the tree. It was weighted down with lights, garlands, a cascade of tinsel. She held half a dozen construction paper ornaments made by the boys in grade school that she'd preserved for decades, placing them carefully on the branches. They had called from the airport in Gander an hour before. They were driving rented cars the rest of the way home. Hayward thought of them on the road, two men travelling the empty Black Rock highway, pushing for the place they'd first come to the light. Snow and dark waves of spruce crowding the pavement.

Warrick was only eighteen months old when Etta discovered she was pregnant a second time. The house they were living in was a company duplex heated by a wood stove in the kitchen. Behind cupboards and in closets, there was sometimes an inch of daylight showing where the walls failed to meet the floor. The baby slept with them for warmth, and on the coldest nights of the winter, when they woke to him crying to be fed, Hayward went out to stoke the fire, to run water in the bathroom and kitchen to keep the pipes from freezing solid. He remembers coming back to lie beside the child and his wife, the silky hair at the crown of the baby's head tucked close under his chin, the heat between them like something generated purely by emotion. He told Etta it seemed unfair to have more children, that he couldn't imagine loving another the way he did the first.

Etta clucked her tongue. "You have no idea how love works," she said.

He had taken offence to that, thought it was just like a woman to assume a man's incompetence in matters of the heart. Though he simply tipped his head side to side to indicate his disagreement, a motion she couldn't have registered in the dark.

Etta turned from the Christmas tree to look at him standing at the foot of the stairs with his shoes in his hand. He'd begun noticing lately how astonishingly tiny a figure she was, hips invisible under the dress. Frightening to think of the boys inside that body, the fight she must have had to shove them free. The bald wilfulness of it.

She had been right about him, of course. He'd had no idea how love works, what he would feel the first time he held Glen in his arms.

"Are you going to put those on?" Etta asked him.

He looked down at the shoes a moment, blinking away the first infuriating sting of tears. "They'll be hours yet getting here," he said.

"I suppose they will." Etta waited with her hands folded in front of her.

There was a new awkwardness between them now, unlike anything they'd known since those first few nights going to bed after they married. A constant sense of something about to be said that kept them on edge.

Hayward said, "Why don't we take a little drive somewhere?"

There was nowhere, exactly, to drive to. They skirted the perimeter of the town, moving slowly along streets lined with boarded windows, the desolation interrupted occasionally by houses strung with coloured lights. They drove by the lots where bunkhouses and storehouses and core sheds once stood. It wasn't emptiness they encountered, not even absence. It was loss, an object lesson in the inevitability of grief. The car's engine so quiet they could hear the tires hissing over the frozen pavement.

Hayward turned out the back roads toward the dam, driving parallel for a while with the rail bed, the ties taken up and sold off as firewood when the company began shipping the ore in eighteen-wheelers during the eighties. The notoriously slow train had been the only way into town before the road went through, endless games of crib and flasks of alcohol circulating among passengers to pass the time. Long nights of drinking that led more than one man into the tiny bathroom, the toilet a seat over a drafty hole in the floor, to vomit onto the tracks passing beneath the car. Enos Hawkins had lost his false teeth that way sometime in the fifties, just shy of town. He walked miles along the rail bed each year he came out moose hunting, his rifle in the crook of his arm, hoping to find those teeth.

"Poor old Enos," Hayward said, as if they had been discussing him aloud.

After they crossed the dam, he parked at the edge of the lake without turning off the engine, headlights shining out over black water. Neither of them spoke. Etta leaned forward to turn on the radio, her face illuminated in the blue light from the dash. Long ropes of static uncoiling as she moved through the dial and then the tinny drone of Christmas carols.

"I came out here after Warrick was born," Hayward said to her then. "That morning." He turned to look at Etta.

"Out here?" she said.

He nodded his head. "Holly Jolly Christmas" was playing on the radio. He shrugged his shoulders helplessly, unsure exactly what possessed him to confess this now.

Etta waited a long time for him to go on. Then she said, "We should probably be getting back."

Hayward nodded again, relieved. "All right," he said. But when they drove into town, he turned up Main Street, away from the house, toward what had once been company property.

He had never said a word to any one about his time smoking cigarettes in the car at the dam after seeing Warrick, when he tried to hold down that inexplicable sense of panic. It was close to noon, the sun high, when the girl came across the dam in a white blouse and dark skirt. She was still school age and couldn't have been more than sixteen, he knew. He waved to her through the open window and she walked slowly over to the car.

"What are you doing out this way?" he asked her.

She leaned on the window frame and shrugged. "Just walking," she said.

"That's a long ways to just be walking."

She shrugged again, in a way that was both helpless and defiant. There was a sullenness about her that seemed new to him, something she was trying to pass off as maturity. As if being openly dissatisfied with her life was a mark of adulthood.

He motioned with his head. "I can drop you back to town if you like."

They knew each other only in passing. She was the daughter of Cecil Quinlin who worked in the mill, and Hayward sometimes saw them together at the Royal Stores or during events at the Legion. She was a pretty girl, and he joined Cecil in teasing her about boyfriends or her precociously developing bust line. He had never thought of her as anything much more than a child. In the car, she sat with her back against the door so she faced him, one leg up on the seat. "Can I have a cigarette?" she asked him.

He turned his head away from her to stare out at the water. A moment ago, he'd been relieved to see her, as if talking to someone might ease his anxiety. But he could feel the uneasiness and fear turning in him now, moving lower in the pit of his stomach, becoming something else altogether. It seemed suddenly illicit to him to be sitting out beyond town limits, with this girl. "You're too young to be smoking, aren't you?" he said.

She leaned forward to push the lighter in, then picked out the longest butt she could find in the ashtray and carefully straightened the crushed end. She had fine dark hair that blew about her face in the breeze through the open windows. When the lighter popped, she lit the butt and blew a long line of smoke across the seat. She slipped her shoes off and sat back, putting one foot up on the dashboard. She said, "What else do you think I'm too young for?"

He would have thought she was simply teasing him, a kind of retaliation for the innocent ribbing he'd subjected her to, if there wasn't such an offhand recklessness to her tone, her posture. If he wasn't feeling a profound recklessness of his own. She was wearing red nail polish, the sleeves of her blouse rolled to her elbows. It occurred to him he had no real idea who she was.

Etta said, "Where are we going now, Hayward?" There was a note of impatience in his wife's voice, but he didn't answer her. The car rumbled over the speed bumps at the border of company property, which was unlit and eerily, still, like a graveyard of shipwrecks. Headlights picking out details of ruined machinery, old warehouses on the verge of collapse. On a bare concrete foundation, two ball mills, like works of some massive timepiece, were slowly going to rust in the open air. Hayward drove past them towards a long, low machine-shop that for a time after the mine closed had been a cottage factory producing granite headstones and knickknacks, slate clocks cut in the shape of the Island of Newfoundland.

It had been so long since he thought of his time with the girl that he was surprised to recall so clearly now the urge he had to touch her, knowing he could if he chose to, even if he was wrong to think that was what she wanted. He had turned his head toward her with his mind made up, drunk on the simplicity of it. How quickly he'd be displaced, how the shape of life would change. Like dropping a bottle onto concrete.

He pulled the car to a stop in front of a high wire fence at the back of the machine shop. It circled a yard of broken stone half buried in snow, rows of monuments tipped on their sides, only the polished corners visible. He reached out to turn the radio off and pointed towards the far corner where the Virgin Mary stood facing them, her hands turned out toward the headlights.

"They couldn't find anyone to take her when the school came down," he said.

The girl had slipped her shoes off after lighting her cigarette, and he turned back to her with his mind made up. He was about to say her name. Angela? Anita? He couldn't remember now. She was wearing dark socks and he saw that the heel on the dash had a hole worn through, showing a quarter-sized circle of flesh. It seemed a hopelessly childish thing, that rent in the cotton fabric. Something unintentionally, almost comically, innocent. He pointed with his finger. "You've got a hole there, my love," he said.

It was his paternal tone that embarrassed her. She dropped her foot to the floor quickly, pushing her shoes on. "Jesus," the girl said. She turn away to stare out the window, then doused the cigarette butt in the ashtray. She said "I have to go." She wouldn't look at him.

"All right then," he said. He sat there after she pushed out the door, watching her walk back the way she'd come.

He'd come that close to throwing everything away before he and Etta had hardly made a start. He reached his hand across the seat to find hers in the dark. He said, "Everything that matters to me in this world came through you."

She squeezed his hand in her lap, but didn't look at him. "You're going to have to say something to the boys when they get here," she said. And he knew she was right about that as well.

They sat a long time in silence then, staring at the figure on the opposite side of the yard. The elaborate folds of stone cloth about her head and shoulders in the steady beam of the headlights looked cold, comfortless.

"I keep thinking she must be lonely out here by herself," Hayward said finally. "All Christmas like this."

A light snow had begun falling and the flakes sparked around the statue in the wind before he put the car in reverse and pulled away. Mary offering her wordless blessing in the darkness behind them as they went.

Winter Dog

ALISTAIR MACLEOD

I am writing this in December. In the period close to Christmas, and three days after the first snowfall in this region of southwestern Ontario. The snow came quietly in the night or in the early morning. When we went to bed near midnight, there was none at all. Then early in the morning we heard the children singing Christmas songs from their rooms across the hall. It was very dark and I rolled over to check the time. It was 4:30 a.m. One of them must have awakened and looked out the window to find the snow and then eagerly awakened the others. They are half crazed by the promise of Christmas, and the discovery of the snow is an unexpected giddy surprise. There was no snow promised for this area, not even yesterday.

"What are you doing?" I call, although it is obvious.

"Singing Christmas songs," they shout back with equal obviousness, "because it snowed."

"Try to be quiet," I say, "or you'll wake the baby."

"She's already awake," they say. "She's listening to our singing. She likes it. Can we go out and make a snowman?"

I roll from my bed and go to the window. The neighbouring houses are muffled in snow and silence and there are as yet no lights in any of them. The snow has stopped falling and its whitened quietness reflects the shadows of the night.

"This snow is no good for snowmen," I say. "It is too dry."

"How can snow be dry?" asks a young voice. Then an older one says, "Well, then can we go out and make the first track?"

They take my silence for consent and there are great sounds of rustling and giggling as they go downstairs to touch the light switches and rummage and jostle for coats and boots.

"What on earth is happening?" asks my wife from her bed. "What are they doing?"

"They are going outside to make the first tracks in the snow," I say. "It snowed quite heavily last night."

"What time is it?"

"Shortly after four-thirty."

"Oh."

We ourselves have been nervous and restless for the past weeks. We have been troubled by illness and uncertainty in those we love far away on Canada's east coast. We have already considered and rejected driving the fifteen hundred miles. Too far, too uncertain, too expensive, fickle weather, the complications of transporting Santa Claus.

Instead, we sleep uncertainly and toss in unbidden dreams. We jump when the phone rings after 10:00 p.m. and are then reassured by the distant voices.

"First of all, there is nothing wrong," they say. "Things are just the same."

Sometimes we make calls ourselves, even to the hospital in Halifax, and are surprised at the voices which answer.

"I just got here this afternoon from Newfoundland. I'm going to try to stay a week. He seems better today. He's sleeping now."

At other times we receive calls from farther west, from Edmonton and Calgary and Vancouver. People hoping to find objectivity in the most subjective of situations. Strung out in uncertainty across the time zones from British Columbia to Newfoundland.

Within our present city, people move and consider possibilities:

If he dies tonight we'll leave right away. Can you come?

We will have to drive as we'll never get air reservations at this time.

I'm not sure if my car is good enough. I'm always afraid of the mountains near Cabano.

If we were stranded in Rivière-du-Loup we would be worse off than being here. It would be too far for anyone to come and get us.

My car will go but I'm not so sure I can drive it all the way. My eyes are not so good anymore, especially at night in drifting snow.

Perhaps there'll be no drifting snow.

There's always drifting snow.

We'll take my car if you'll drive it. We'll have to drive straight through.

John phoned and said he'll give us his car if we want it or he'll drive — either his own car or someone else's.

He drinks too heavily, especially for long-distance driving, and at this time of year. He's been drinking ever since this news began.

He drinks because he cares. It's just the way he is.

Not everybody drinks.

Not everybody cares, and if he gives you his word, he'll never drink until he gets there. We all know that.

But so far nothing has happened. Things seem to remain the same.

Through the window and out on the white plane of the snow, the silent, laughing children now appear. They move in their muffled clothes like mummers on the whitest of stages. They dance and gesture noiselessly, flopping their arms in parodies of heavy, happy, earthbound birds. They have been warned by the eldest to be aware of the sleeping neighbours so they cavort only in pantomime, sometimes raising mittened hands to their mouths to suppress their joyous laughter. They dance and prance in the moonlight, tossing snow in one another's direction, tracing out various shapes and initials, forming lines which snake across the previously unmarked whiteness. All of it in silence, unknown and unseen and unheard to the neighbouring world. They seem unreal even to me, their father, standing at his darkened window. It is almost as if they have danced out of the world of folklore like happy elves who cavort and mimic and caper through the private hours of this whitened dark, only to vanish with the coming of the morning's light and leaving only the signs of their activities behind. I am tempted to check the recently vacated beds to confirm what perhaps I think I know.

Then out of the corner of my eye I see him. The golden collie-like dog. He appears almost as if from the wings of the stage or as a figure newly noticed in the lower corner of a winter painting. He sits quietly and watches the playful scene before him and then, as if responding to a silent invitation, bounds into its midst. The children chase him in frantic circles, falling and rolling as he doubles back and darts and dodges between their legs and through their outstretched arms. He seizes a mitt loosened from its owner's hand, and tosses it happily in the air and then snatches it back into his jaws an instant before it reaches the ground and seconds before the tumbling bodies fall on the emptiness of its expected destination. He races to the edge of the scene and lies facing them, holding the mitt tantalizingly between his paws, and then as they dash towards him, zigzagging through them as the Sunday football player might return the much sought-after ball. After he was gone through and eluded them all, he looks back over his shoulder and again, like an elated athlete, tosses the mitt high in what seems like an imaginary end zone. The he seizes it once more and lopes in a wide circle around his pursuers, eventually coming closer and closer to them until once more their stretching hands are able to actually touch his shoulders and back and haunches, although he continues always to wriggle free. He is touched but never captured, which is the nature of the game. Then he is gone. As suddenly as he came. I strain my eyes in the direction of the adjoining street, towards the house where I have often seen him, always within a yard enclosed by woven links of chain. I see the flash of his silhouette, outlined perhaps against the snow or the light cast by the street lamps or the moon. It arcs upwards and seems to hang for an instant high above the top of the fence and then it descends on the other side. He lands on his shoulder in a fluff of snow and with a half roll regains his feet and vanishes within the shadow of his owner's house.

"What are you looking at?" asks my wife.

"That golden collie-like dog from the other street was just playing with the children in the snow."

"But he's always in that fenced-in yard."

"I guess not always. He jumped the fence just now and went back in. I guess the owners and the rest of us think he's fenced in but he knows he's not. He probably comes out every night and leads an exciting life. I hope they don't see his tracks or they'll probably begin to chain him."

"What are the children doing?"

"They look tired now from chasing the dog. They'll probably soon be back in. I think I'll go downstairs and wait for them and make myself a cup of coffee."

"Okay."

I look once more towards the fenced-in yard, but the dog is nowhere to be seen.

I first saw such a dog when I was twelve and he came as a pup of about two months in a crate to the railroad station which was about eight miles from where we lived. Someone must have phoned or dropped in to say: "Your dog's at the station."

He had come to Cape Breton in response to a letter and a cheque which my father had sent to Morrisburg, Ontario. We had seen the ads for "cattle collie dogs" in the *Family Herald*, which was the farm newspaper of the time, and we were in need of a good young working dog.

His crate was clean and neat and there was still a supply of dog biscuits with him and a can in the corner to hold water. The baggage handlers had looked after him well on the trip east, and he appeared in good spirits. He had a white collar and chest and four rather large white paws and a small white blaze on his forehead. The rest of him was a fluffy, golden brown, although his eyebrows and the tips of his ears as well as the end of his tail were darker, tingeing almost to black. When he grew to his full size, the blackish shadings became really black, and although he had the long, heavy coat of a collie, it was in certain areas more grey than gold. He was also taller than the average collie and with a deeper chest. He seemed to be at least part German Shepherd.

It was winter when he came and we kept him in the house where he slept behind the stove in a box lined with an old coat. Our other dogs slept mostly in the stables or outside in the lees of woodpiles or under porches or curled up on the banking of the house. We seemed to care more for him because he was smaller and it was winter and he was somehow like a visitor; and also because more was expected of him and also perhaps because we had paid money for him and thought about his coming for some time — like a "planned" child. Sceptical neighbours and relatives who thought the idea of paying money for a dog was rather exotic or frivolous would ask: "Is that your Ontario dog" or "Do you think your Ontario dog will be any good?"

He turned out to be no good at all and no one knew why. Perhaps it was because of the suspected German Shepherd blood. But he could not "get the hang of it." Although we worked him and trained him as we had other dogs, he seemed always to bring panic instead of order and to make things worse instead of better. He became a "head dog," which meant that instead of working behind the cattle he lunged at their heads, impeding them from any forward motion and causing them to turn in endless, meaningless bewildered circles. On the few occasions when he did go behind them, he was "rough," which meant that instead of being a floating, nipping, suggestive presence, he actually bit them and caused them to gallop, which was another sin. Sometimes in the summer, the milk cows suffering from his misunderstood pursuit would jam pell mell into the stable, tossing their wide horns in fear, and with their great sides heaving and perspiring while down their legs and tails the wasted milk ran in rivulets mingling with the blood caused by his slashing wounds. He was, it was said, "worse than nothing."

Gradually everyone despaired, although he continued to grow grey and golden and was, as everyone agreed, a "beautiful-looking dog."

He was also tremendously strong and in the winter months I would hitch him to a sleigh which he pulled easily and willingly on almost any kind of surface. When he was harnessed, I used to put a collar around his neck and attach a light line to it so that I might have some minimum control over him, but it was hardly ever needed. He would pull home the Christmas tree or the bag of flour or the deer which was shot far back in the woods; and when we visited our winter snares, he would pull home the gunnysacks which contained the partridges and rabbits which we gathered. He would also pull us, especially on the flat windswept stretches of land beside the sea. There the snow was never really deep and the water that oozed from a series of freshwater springs and ponds contributed to a glaze of ice and crisply crusted snow which the sleigh runners seemed to sing over without ever breaking through. He would begin with an easy lope and then increase his swiftness until both he and the sleigh seemed to touch the surface at only irregular intervals. He would stretch out then with his ears flattened against his head and his shoulders bunching and contracting in the rhythm of his speed. Behind him on the sleigh, we would cling tenaciously to the wooden slats as the particles of ice and snow dislodged by his nails hurtled towards our faces. We would avert our heads and close our eyes and the wind stung so sharply that the difference between freezing and burning could not be known. He would do that until late in the afternoon when it was time to return home and begin our chores.

On the sunny winter Sunday that I am thinking of, I planned to visit my snares. There seemed no other children around that afternoon and the adults were expecting relatives. I harnessed the dog to the sleigh, opened the door of the house, and shouted that I was going to look at my snares. We began to climb the hill behind the house on our way to the woods when we looked back and out towards the sea. The "big ice," which was what we called the major pack of drift ice, was in solidly against the shore and stretched out beyond the range of vision. It had not been "in" yesterday, although for the past weeks we had seen it moving offshore, sometimes close and sometimes distant, depending on the winds and tides. The coming of the big ice marked the official beginning of the coldest part of winter. It was mostly drift ice from the Arctic and Labrador, although some of it was fresh-water ice from the estuary of the St. Lawrence. It drifted down with the dropping temperatures, bringing its own mysterious coldness and stretching for hundreds of miles in craters and pans, sometimes in grotesque shapes and sometimes in dazzling architectural forms. It was blue and white and sometimes grey and at other times a dazzling emerald green.

The dog and I changed our direction towards the sea to find what the ice might yield. Our land had always been beside the sea and we had always gone towards it to find newness and the extraordinary; and over the years we, as others along the coast, had found quite a lot, although never the pirate chests of gold which were supposed to abound or the reasons for the mysterious lights that our elders still spoke of and persisted in seeing. But kegs of rum had washed up, and sometimes bloated horses and various fishing paraphernalia and valuable timber and furniture from foundered ships. The door of my room was apparently the galley door from a ship called the *Judith Franklin* which was wrecked during the early winter in which my great-grandfather was building his house. My grandfather told of how they had heard the cries and seen the lights as the ship neared the rocks and of how they had run down in the dark and tossed lines to the people while tying themselves to trees on the shore. All were saved, including women clinging to small children. The next day the builders of the new house went down to the shore and salvaged what they could from the wreckage of the vanquished ship. A sort of symbolic marriage of the new and the old: doors and shelving, stairways, hatches, wooden chests and trunks and various glass figurines and lanterns which were miraculously never broken.

People came too. The dead as well as the living. Bodies of men swept overboard and reported lost at sea and the bodies of men still crouched within the shelter of their boat's broken bows. And sometimes in late winter, young sealers who had quit their vessels would walk across the ice and come to our doors. They were usually very young — some still in their teens — and had signed on for jobs they could not or no longer wished to handle. They were often disoriented and did not know where they were, only that they had seen land and had decided to walk towards it. They were often frostbitten and with little money and uncertain as to how they might get to Halifax. The dog and I walked towards the ice upon the sea.

Sometimes it was hard to "get on" the ice, which meant that at the point where the pack met the shore there might be open water or irregularities caused by the indentations of the coastline or the workings of the tides and currents, but for us on that day there was no difficulty at all. We were "on" easily and effortlessly and enthused in our new adventure. For the first mile there was nothing but the vastness of the white expanse. We came to a clear stretch where the ice was as smooth and unruffled as that of an indoor arena and I knelt on the sleigh while the dog loped easily along. Gradually the ice changed to an uneven terrain of pressure ridges and hummocks, making it impossible to ride farther; and then suddenly, upon rounding a hummock, I saw the perfect seal. At first I though it was alive, as did the dog who stopped so suddenly in his tracks that the sleigh almost collided with his legs. The hackles on the back of his neck rose and he growled in the dangerous way he was beginning to develop. But the seal was dead, yet facing us in a frozen perfection that was difficult to believe. There was a light powder of snow over its darker coat and a delicate rime of frost still formed the outline of its whiskers. Its eyes were wide open and it stared straight ahead towards the land. Even now in memory it seems more real than reality — as if it were transformed by frozen art into something more arresting than life itself. The way the sudden seal in the museum exhibit freezes your eyes with the touch of truth. Immediately I wanted to take it home.

It was frozen solidly in a base of ice so I began to look for something that might serve as a pry. I let the dog out of his harness and hung the sleigh and harness on top of the hummock to mark the place and began my search. Some distance away I found a pole about twelve feet long. It is always surprising to find such things on the ice field but they are, often amazingly, there almost in the same way that you might find a pole floating in the summer ocean. Unpredictable but possible. I took the pole back and began my work. The dog went off on explorations of his own.

Although it was firmly frozen, the task did not seem impossible and by inserting the end of the pole under first one side and then the other and working from the front to the back, it was possible to cause a gradual loosening. I remember thinking how very warm it was because I was working hard and perspiring heavily. When the dog came back he was uneasy, and I realized it was starting to snow a bit but I was almost done. He sniffed with disinterest at the seal and began to whine a bit, which was something he did not often do. Finally, after another quarter of a hour, I was able to roll my trophy onto the sleigh and with the dog in harness we set off. We had gone perhaps two hundred yards when the seal slid free. I took the dog and the sleigh back and once again managed to roll the seal on. This time I took the line from the dog's collar and tied the seal to the sleigh, reasoning that the dog would go home anyway and there would be no need to guide him. My fingers were numb as I tried to fasten the awkward knots and the dog began to whine and rear. When I gave the command he bolted forward and I clung at the back of the sleigh to the seal. The snow was heavier now and blowing in my face, but we were moving rapidly and when we came to the stretch of arena-like ice we skimmed across it almost like an iceboat, the profile of the frozen seal at the front of the sleigh like those figures at the prows of Viking ships. At the very end of the smooth stretch, we went through. From my position at the end of the sleigh I felt him drop almost before I saw him, and rolled backwards seconds before the sleigh and seal followed him into the blackness of the water. He went under once carried by his own momentum but surfaced almost immediately with his head up and his paws scrambling at the icy, jagged edge of the hole; but when the weight and momentum of the sleigh and its burden struck, he went down again, this time out of sight.

I realized we had struck a "seam" and that the stretch of smooth ice had been deceivingly and temporarily joined to the rougher ice near the shore and now was in the process of breaking away. I saw the widening line before me and jumped to the other side just as his head miraculously came up once more. I lay on my stomach and grabbed his collar in both my hands and then in a moment of panic did not know what to do. I could feel myself sliding towards him and the darkness of the water and was aware of the weight that pulled me forward and down. I was also aware of his razor-sharp claws flailing violently before my face and knew that I might lose my eyes. And I was aware that his own eyes were bulging from their sockets and that he might think I was trying to choke him and might lunge and slash my face with his teeth in desperation. I knew all of this but somehow did nothing about it; it seemed almost simpler to hang on and be drawn into the darkness of the gently slopping water, seeming to slop gently in spite of all the agitation. Then suddenly he was free, scrambling over my shoulder and dragging the sleigh behind him. The seal surfaced again, buoyed up perhaps by the physics of its frozen body or the nature of its fur. Still looking more genuine than it could have in life, its snout and head broke the open water and it seemed to look at us curiously for an instant before it vanished permanently beneath the ice. The loose and badly tied knots had apparently not held when the sleigh was in a near-vertical position and we were saved by the ineptitude of my own numbed fingers. We had been spared for a future time.

He lay gasping and choking for a moment, coughing up the icy salt water, and then almost immediately his coat began to freeze. I realized then how cold I was myself and that even in the moments I had been lying on the ice my cloths had begun to adhere to it. My earlier heated perspiration was now a cold rime upon my body and I imagined it outlining me there, beneath my clothes, in a sketch of frosty white. I got on the sleigh once more and crouched low as he began to race towards home. His coat was freezing fast, and he ran the individual ice-coated hairs began to clack together like rhythmical castanets attuned to the motion of his body. It was snowing quite heavily in our faces now and it seemed to be approaching dusk, although I doubted if it were so on the land which I could now no longer see. I realized all the obvious things I should have considered earlier. That if the snow was blowing in our faces, the wind was off the land, and if it was off the land, it was blowing the ice pack back out to sea. That was probably one reason why the seam had opened. And also that the ice had only been "in" one night and had not had a chance to "set." I realized other things as well. That it was the time of the late afternoon when the tide was falling. That no one knew where we were. That I had said we were going to look at snares, which was not where we had gone at all. And I remembered now that I had received no answer even to that misinformation, so perhaps I had not even been heard. And also if there was drifting snow like this on land, our tracks would by now have been obliterated.

We came to a rough section of ice: huge slabs on their sides and others piled one on top of the other as if they were in some strange form of storage. It was no longer possible to ride the sleigh but as I stood up I lifted it and hung on to it as a means of holding on to the dog. The line usually attached to his collar had sunk with the vanished seal. My knees were stiff when I stood up; and deprived of the windbreak effect which the dog had provided, I felt the snow driving full into my face, particularly my eyes. It did not merely impede my vision, the way distant snow flurries might, but actually entered my eyes, causing them to water and freeze nearly shut. I was aware of the weight of ice on my eyelashes and could see them as they gradually lowered and became heavier. I did not remember ice like this when I got on, although I did not find that terribly surprising. I pressed the soles of my numbed feet firmly down upon it to try and feel if it was moving out, but it was impossible to tell because there was no fixed point of reference. Almost the sensation one gets on a conveyor belt at airports or on escalators; although you are standing still you recognize motion, but should you shut your eyes and be deprived of sight, even that recognition may become ambiguously uncertain.

The dog began to whine and to walk around me in circles, binding my legs with the traces of the harness as I continued to grasp the sleigh. Finally I decided to let him go as there seemed no way to hold him and there was nothing else to do. I unhitched the traces and doubled them up as best I could and tucked them under the backpad of his harness so they would not drag behind him and become snagged on any obstacles. I did not take off my mitts to do so as I was afraid I would not be able to get them back on. He vanished into the snow almost immediately.

The sleigh had been a gift from an uncle, so I hung on to it and carried it with both hands before me like an ineffectual shield against the wind and snow. I lowered my head as much as I could and turned it sideways so the wind would beat against my head instead of directly into my face. Sometimes I would turn and walk backwards for a few steps. Although I knew it was not the wisest thing to do, it seemed at times the only way to breathe. And then I began to feel the water sloshing about my feet.

Sometimes when the tides or currents ran heavily and the ice began to separate, the water that was beneath it would well up and wash over it almost as if it were reflooding it. Sometimes you could see the hard ice clearly beneath the water but at other times a sort of floating slush was formed mingling with snow and "slob" ice which was not yet solid. It was thick and dense and soupy and it was impossible to see what lay beneath it. Experienced men on the ice sometimes carried a slender pole so they could test the consistency of the footing which might or might not lie before them, but I was obviously not one of them, although I had a momentary twinge for the pole I had used to dislodge the seal. Still, there was nothing to do but go forward.

When I went through, the first sensation was almost of relief and relaxation for the water initially made me feel much warmer than I had been on the surface. It was the most dangerous of false sensations for I knew my clothes were becoming heavier by the second. I clung to the sleigh somewhat as a raft and lunged forward with it in a kind of up-and-down swimming motion, hoping that it might strike some sort of solidity before my arms became so weighted and sodden that I could no longer lift them. I cried out then for the first time into the driving snow.

He came almost immediately, although I could see he was afraid and the slobbing slush was up to his knees. Still, he seemed to be on some kind of solid footing for he was not swimming. I splashed towards him and when almost there, desperately threw the sleigh before me and lunged for the edge of what seemed like his footing , but it only gave way as if my hands were closing on icy insubstantial porridge. He moved forward then, although I still could not tell if what supported him would be of any use to me. Finally I grasped the breast strap of his harness. He began to back up then, and as I said, he was tremendously strong. The harness began to slide forward on his shoulders but he continued to pull as I continued to grasp and then I could feel my elbows on what seemed like solid ice and I was able to hook them on the edge and draw myself, dripping and soaking, like another seal out of the black water and onto the whiteness of the slushy ice. Almost at once my clothes began to freeze. My elbows and knees began to creak when I bent them as if I were a robot from the realm of science fiction and then I could see myself clothed in transparent ice as if I had been coated with shellac or finished with clear varnish.

As the fall into the winter sea had at first seemed ironically warm, so now my garments of ice seemed a protection against the biting wind, but I knew it was a deceptive sensation and that I did not have much time before me. The dog faced into the wind and I followed him. This time he stayed in sight, and at times even turned back to wait for me. He was cautious but certain and gradually the slush disappeared, and although we were still in water, the ice was hard and clear beneath it. The frozen heaviness of my clothes began to weigh on me and I could feel myself, ironically, perspiring within my suit of icy armour. I was very tired, which I knew was another dangerous sensation. And then I saw the land. It was very close and a sudden surprise. Almost like coming upon a stalled and unexpected automobile in a highway's winter storm. It was only yards away, and although there was no longer any ice actually touching the shore, there were several pans of it floating in the region between. The dog jumped from one to the other and I followed him, still clutching the sleigh, and missing only the last pan which floated close to the rocky shore. The water came only to my waist and I was able to touch the bottom and splash noisily on land. We had been spared again for a future time and I was never to know whether he had reached the shore himself and come back or whether he had heard my call against the wind.

We began to run towards home and the land lightened and there were touches of evening sun. The wind still blew but no snow was falling. Yet when I looked back, the ice and the ocean were invisible in the swirling squalls. It was like looking at another far and distant country on the screen of a snowy television.

I became obsessed, now that I could afford the luxury, with not being found disobedient or considered a fool. The visitors' vehicles were still in the yard so I imagined most of the family to be in the parlour or living room, and I circled the house and entered through the kitchen, taking the dog with me. I was able to get upstairs unnoticed and get my clothes changed and when I came down I mingled with everybody and tried to appear as normal as I could. My own family was caught up with the visitors and only general comments came my way. The dog, who could not change his clothes, lay under the table with his head on his paws and he was also largely unnoticed. Later as the ice melted from his coat, a puddle formed around him, which I casually mopped up. Still later someone said, "I wonder where the dog has been, his coat is soaking wet." I was never to tell anyone of the afternoon's experience or that he had saved my life.

Two winters later I was sitting at a neighbour's kitchen table when I looked out the window and saw the dog as he was shot. He had followed my father and also me and had been sitting rather regally on a little hill beside the house and I suppose had presented an ideal target. But he had moved at just the right or wrong time and instead of killing him the high-powered bullet smashed into his shoulder. He jumped into the air and turned his snapping teeth upon the wound, trying to bite the cause of the pain he could not see. And then he turned towards home, unsteady but still strong on his three remaining legs. No doubt he felt, as we all do, that if he could get home he might be saved, but he did not make it, as we knew he could not, because of the amount of blood on the snow and the wavering pattern of his three-legged tracks. Yet he was, as I said, tremendously strong and he managed almost three-quarters of a mile. The house he sought must have been within his vision when he died for we could see it quite clearly when we came to his body by the roadside. His eyes were open and his tongue was clenched between his teeth and the little blood he had left dropped red and black on the winter snow. He was not to be saved for a future time anymore.

I learned later that my father had asked the neighbour to shoot him and that we had led him into a kind of ambush. Perhaps my father did so because the neighbour was younger and had a better gun or was a better shot. Perhaps because my father did not want to be involved. It was obvious he had not planned on things turning out so messy.

The dog had become increasingly powerful and protective, to the extent that people were afraid to come into the yard. And he had also bitten two of the neighbour's children and caused them to be frightened of passing our house on their journeys to and from school. And perhaps there was also the feeling in the community that he was getting more than his share of the breeding: that he travelled farther than other dogs on his nightly forays and that he fought off and injured the other smaller dogs who might compete with him for female favours. Perhaps there was fear that his dominance and undesirable characteristics did not bode well for future generations.

This has been the writing down of a memory triggered by the sight of a golden dog at play in the silent snow with my own excited children. After they came in and had their hot chocolate, the wind began to blow; and by the time I left for work, there was no evidence of their early-morning revels or any dog tracks leading to the chain-link fence. The "enclosed" dog looked impassively at me as I brushed the snow from the buried windshield. What does he know? he seemed to say.

The snow continues to drift and to persist as another uncertainty added to those we already have. Should we be forced to drive tonight, it will be a long, tough journey into the wind and the driving snow which is pounding across Ontario and Quebec and New Brunswick and against the granite coast of Nova Scotia. Should we be drawn by death, we might well meet our own. Still, it is only because I am alive that I can even consider such possibilities. Had I not been saved by the golden dog, I would not have these tight concerns or children playing in the snow or of course these memories. It is because of him that I have been able to come this far in time.

It is too bad that I could not have saved him as well and my feelings did him little good as I looked upon his bloodied body there beside the road. It was too late and out of my control and even if I had known the possibilities of the future it would not have been easy.

He was with us only for a while and brought his own changes, and yet he still persists. He persists in my memory and in my life and he persists physically as well. He is there in this winter storm. There in the golden-grey dogs with their black-tipped ears and tails, sleeping in the stables or in the lees of woodpiles or under porches or curled beside the houses which face towards the sea.

Christmas Fortunes

BERNICE MORGAN

Christmas, formerly thought of as an extra Sabbath day, is celebrated differently this year. In addition to the usual worship service, Meg suggests that the scholars have a concert. The children are happy to show off what they have learned, and on the appointed night jump up one by one to bellow out memory verses. Patience, however, recites a long, long poem about Venus which shocks Meg, causing her to have a quiet word with Lavinia after the concert.

For most of them it is the best Christmas they can remember, one without the foreboding they have felt other years. Emma and Jane are spoken of often. People wonder how they are making out in St. John's, tell each other that the girls are missing a good Christmas. Frank and Annie seem reconciled to their separation, and Peter Vincent seems more settled. The young man has started work on a house, although he has no prospects of marriage as far as anyone can tell. The men are all home, and there is a good supply of food laid by.

Only Lavinia is miserable. At Ned's house for a feast of fish and brewis on Christmas Eve, she cannot keep from watching Thomas Hutchings. Following every move he makes, she sees that he, in turn, is watching Fanny.

Fanny, in her usual haze, seems unaware of Thomas's scrutiny, or of his existence for that matter. Somewhere among the half-frozen bushes, she has found a tiny rose and pinned it into her hair. Dressed in her rainbow-coloured rags, she wafts from person to person, bent on her new pastime of reading fortunes. Where she has come by this idea no one knows. Lavinia watches the girl circle the room picking up hands, studying palms. Charlie dodges out of her reach, Willie and Rose giggle and pull their hands away. She moves on to Isaac Andrews, picks up his hand and drops it after only a glance, but Patience submits and listens enthralled to the long and complicated future Fanny predicts for her. When Fanny reaches Peter Vincent, Lavinia is surprised to see the usually sullen young man smile and hold his hand out. With their heads together, his almost white and hers dark as jet, they study Peter's palm.

"You will live with a beautiful princess in that tower you're buildin', you'll have lots of sons and grow to be a crabby old man with a long beard," Fanny tells him, her impish face full of laughter.

Thomas is sitting next to Peter, but before Fanny can reach for his hand, Sarah swoops down. "Stop that foolishness this minute, you pure gives me the shivers. Mary, can't you make that girl stop?"

Mary ignores the request and Sarah reinforces her objections. "I had a second cousin used to tell fortunes with cards when she was a girl your age — one night she seen the devil himself in the cards. She was strange forever after."

Seeing a smirk on her son's face, she turns on him. "Get that silly grin off your face, Peter Vincent. Make no mistake, tellin' the future is devil's work — the Bible says we know not the day nor the hour."

Lavinia has a mind to ask Sarah why she is forever foretelling the future if it's a sin, but Ned has already started off on a story about a sailor he knew who had second sight and thereby became enormously wealthy.

The story continues, the sailor is transformed into a pirate, then a prince; Josh dozes and small children fall asleep in their mothers' arms; the fire turns to red embers, and Mary announces this is the last pot of tea she'll brew this night. Sometime well into the story-telling, Lavinia notices that both Thomas and Fanny have vanished.

It is already Christmas morning when the story ends. People stand stiffly, pull on coats, wrap scarves about their heads, and stumble out into the clear, crisp air.

An Orange from Portugal

HUGH MACLENNAN

I suppose all of us, when we think of Christmas, recall Charles Dickens and our own childhood. So today, from an apartment in Montreal, looking across the street to a new neon sign, I think back to Dickens and Halifax and the world suddenly becomes smaller, shabbier, and more comfortable, and one more proof is registered that comfort is a state of mind, having little to do with the number of springs hidden inside your mattress or the upholstery in your car.

Charles Dickens should have lived in Halifax. If he had, that brown old town would have acquired a better reputation in Canada than it now enjoys, for all over the world people would have known what it was like. Halifax, especially a generation or two ago, was a town Dickens could have used.

There were dingy basement kitchens all over the town where rats were caught every day. The streets were full of teamsters, hard-looking men with lean jaws, most of them, and at the entrance to the old North Street Station cab drivers in long coats would mass behind a heavy anchor chain and terrify travelers with bloodcurdling howls as they bid for fares. Whenever there was a southeast wind, harbour bells moaned behind the wall of fog that cut the town off from the rest of the world. Queer faces peered at you suddenly from doorways set flush with the streets. When a regiment held a smoker in the old Masonic Hall you could see a line beginning to form in the early morning, waiting for the big moment at midnight when the doors would be thrown open to the town and any man could get a free drink who could reach the hogsheads.

For all these things Dickens would have loved Halifax, even for the pompous importers who stalked to church on Sunday mornings, swinging their canes and complaining that they never had a chance to hear a decent sermon. He would have loved it for the waifs and strays and beachcombers and discharged soldiers and sailors whom the respectable never seemed to notice, for all the numerous aspects of the town that made Halifax deplorable and marvellous.

If Dickens had been given a choice of a Canadian town in which to spend Christmas, that's where I think he would have gone, for his most obvious attitude toward Christmas was that it was necessary. Dickens was no scientist or organizer. Instead of liking The People, he simply liked people. And so, inevitably, he liked places where accidents were apt to happen. In Halifax accidents were happening all the time. Think of the way he writes about Christmas — a perfect Christmas for him was always a chapter of preposterous accidents. No, I don't think he would have chosen to spend his Christmas in Westmount or Toronto, for he'd be fairly sure that neither of those places needed it.

Today we know too much. Having become democratic by ideology, we are divided into groups which eye each other like dull strangers at a dull party, polite in public and nasty when each other's backs are turned. Today we are informed by those who know that if we tell children about Santa Claus we will probably turn them into neurotics. Today we believe in universal justice and in universal war to effect it, and because Santa Claus gives the rich more than he gives the poor, lots of us think it better that there should be no Santa Claus at all. Today we are technicians, and the more progressive among us see no reason why love and hope should not be organized in a department of the government, planned by a politician and administered by trained specialists. Today we have a super-colossal Santa Claus for The Customer: he sits in the window of a department store in a cheap red suit, stringy whiskers, and a mask which is a caricature of a face, and for a month before every Christmas he laughs continually with a vulgar roar. The sounds of his laughter come from a record player over and over, and the machine in his belly that produces the bodily contortions has a number in the patent office in Washington.

In the old days in Halifax, we never thought about the meaning of the word democracy; we were all mixed up together in a general deplorability. So the only service any picture of those days can render is to help prove how far we have advanced since then. The first story I have to tell has no importance and not even much of a point. It is simply the record of how one boy felt during a Christmas that now seems remote enough to belong to the era of Bob Cratchit. The second story is about the same. The war Christmases I remember in Halifax were not jolly ones. In a way they were half-tragic, but there may be some significance in the fact that they are literally the only ones I can still remember. It was a war nobody down there understood. We were simply a part of it, swept into it from the mid-Victorian age in which we were all living until 1914.

On Christmas Eve in 1915, a cold northeaster was blowing through the town with the smell of coming snow on the wind. All day our house was hushed for a reason I didn't understand, and I remember being sent out to play with some other boys in the middle of the afternoon. Supper was a silent meal. And then, immediately after we had finished, my father put on the greatcoat of his new uniform and went to the door, and I saw the long tails of the coat blowing out behind him in the flicker of a faulty arc light as he half-ran up to the corner. We heard bagpipes, and almost immediately a company of soldiers appeared swinging down Spring Garden Road from old Dalhousie. It was very cold as we struggled up to the corner after my father, and he affected not to notice us. Then the pipes went by playing "The Blue Bonnets," the lines of khaki men went past in the darkness, and my father fell in behind the last rank and faded off down the half-lit street, holding his head low against the wind to keep his flat military cap from blowing off, and my mother tried to hide her feelings by saying what a shame the cap didn't fit him properly. She told my sister and me how nice it was of the pipers to have turned out on such a cold day to see the men off, for pipe music was the only kind my father liked. It was all very informal. The men of that unit — almost entirely a local one — simply left their homes the way my father had done and joined the column, and the column marched down Spring Garden Road to the ship along the familiar route most of them had taken to church all their lives. An hour later we heard tugboat whistles, and then the foghorn of the transport, and we knew he was on his way. As my sister and I hung up our stockings on the mantelpiece, I wondered whether the vessel was no farther out than Thrum Cap or whether it had already reached Sambro.

It was a bleak night for children to hang up their stockings and wait for Santa Claus, but next morning we found gifts in them as usual, including a golden orange in each toe. It was strange to think that the very night my father had left the house, a strange old man, remembering my sister and me, had come into it. We thought it was a sign of good luck.

That was 1915, and some time during the following year a boy at school told me there was no Santa Claus and put his case so convincingly that I believed him.

Strictly speaking, this should have been the moment of my first step toward becoming a neurotic. Maybe it was, but there were so many other circumstances to compete with it, I don't know whether Santa Claus was responsible for what I'm like now or not. For about a week after discovering the great deception, I wondered how I could develop a line of conduct which would prevent my mother from finding out that I knew who filled our stockings on Christmas Eve. I hated to disappoint her in what I knew was a great pleasure. After a while I forgot all about it. Then, shortly before Christmas, a cable arrived saying that my father was on his way home. He hadn't been killed like the fathers of other boys at school; he was being invalided home as a result of excessive work as a surgeon in the hospital.

We had been living with my grandmother in Cape Breton, so my mother rented a house in Halifax sight unseen, we got down there in time to meet his ship when it came in, and then we all went to the new house. This is the part of my story which reminds me of Charles Dickens again. Five minutes after we entered the house it blew up. This was not the famous Halifax explosion; we had to wait another year for that. This was our own private explosion. It smashed half the windows in the other houses along the block. It shook the ground like an earthquake, and it was heard for a mile.

I have seen many queer accidents in Halifax, but none which gave the reporters more satisfaction than ours did. For a house to blow up suddenly in our district was unusual, so the press felt some explanation was due the public. Besides, it was nearly Christmas and local news was hard to find. The moment the first telephone call reached the newspaper offices to report the accident, they knew the cause. Gas has been leaking in our district for years and a few people had even complained about it. In our house, gas had apparently backed in from the city mains, filling partitions between the walls and lying stagnant in the basement. But this was the first time anyone could prove that gas had been leaking. The afternoon paper gave the story. DOCTOR HUNTS GAS LEAK WITH BURNING MATCH — FINDS IT!

When my father was able to talk, which he couldn't do for several days because the skin had burned off his hands and face, he denied the story about the match. According to modern theory this denial should have precipitated my second plunge toward neurosis, for I had distinctly seen him with the match in his hand, going down to the basement to look for the gas and complaining about how careless people were. However, those were ignorant times and I didn't realize I might get a neurosis. Instead of brooding and deciding to close my mind to reality from then on in order to preserve my belief in the veracity and faultlessness of my father, I wished to God he had been able to tell his story sooner and stick to it. After all, he was a first-class doctor, but what would prospective patients think if every time they heard his name they saw a picture of an absent-minded veteran looking for a gas leak in a dark basement with a lighted match?

It took two whole days for the newspaper account of our accident to settle. In the meantime the house was temporarily ruined, school children had denuded the chandelier in the living room of its prisms, and it was almost Christmas. My sister was still away at school, so my mother, my father, and I found ourselves in a single room in an old residential hotel on Barrington Street. I slept on a cot and they nursed their burns in a huge bed which opened out of the wall. The bed had a mirror on the bottom of it, and it was equipped with such a strong spring that it crashed into place in the wall whenever they got out of it. I still remember my father sitting up in it with one arm in a sling from the war, and his face and head in white bandages. He was philosophical about the situation, including the vagaries of the bed, for it was his Calvinistic way to permit himself to be comfortable only when things were going badly.

The hotel was crowded and our meals were brought to us by a boy called Chester, who lived in the basement near the kitchen. That was all I knew about Chester at first; he brought our meals, he went to school only occasionally, and his mother was ill in the basement. But as long as my memory lasts, that Christmas of 1916 will be Chester's Christmas.

He was a waif of a boy. I never knew his last name, and wherever he is now, I'm certain he doesn't remember me. But for a time I can say without being sentimental that I loved him.

He was white-faced and thin, with lank hair on top of a head that broke at right angles from a high narrow forehead. There were always holes in his black stockings, his handed-down pants were so badly cut that one leg was several inches longer than the other, and there was a patch on the right seat of a different colour from the rest of the cloth. But he was proud of his clothes; prouder than anyone I've ever seen over a pair of pants. He explained that they were his father's and his father had worn them at sea.

For Chester, nobody was worth considering seriously unless he was a seaman. Instead of feeling envious of the people who lived upstairs in the hotel, he seemed to feel sorry for them because they never went to sea. He would look at the old ladies with the kind of eyes that Dickens discovered in children's faces in London: huge eyes as trusting as bird dog's, but old, as though they had forgotten how to cry long ago.

I wondered a lot about Chester — what kind of a room they had in the basement, where they ate, what his mother was like. But I was never allowed in the basement. Once I walked behind the hotel to see if I could look through the windows, but they were only six or eight inches above the ground and they were covered with snow. I gathered that Chester liked it down there because it was warm, and once he was down, nobody ever bothered him.

The days went past, heavy and grey and cold. Soon it was the day before Christmas again, and I was still supposed to believe in Santa Claus. I found myself confronted by a double crisis.

I would have to hang up my stockings as usual, but how could my parents, who were still in bed, manage to fill it? And how would they feel when the next morning came and my stocking was still empty? This worry was overshadowed only by my concern for Chester.

On the afternoon of Christmas Eve he informed me that this year, for the first time in his life, Santa Claus was really going to remember him. "I never ett a real orange and you never did neether because you only get real oranges in Portugal. My old man says so. But Santy Claus is going to bring me one this year. That means the old man's still alive."

"Honest, Chester? How do you know?" Everyone in the hotel knew that his father, who was a quartermaster, was on a slow convoy to England.

"Mrs. Urquhart says so."

Everyone in the hotel also knew Mrs. Urquhart. She was a tiny old lady with a harsh voice who lived in the room opposite ours on the ground floor with her unmarried sister. Mrs. Urquhart wore a white lace cap and carried a cane. Both old ladies wore mourning, Mrs. Urquhart for two dead husbands, her sister for Queen Victoria. They were a trial to Chester because he had to carry hot tea upstairs for them every morning at seven.

“Mrs. Urquhart says if Santy Claus brings me real oranges it means he was talkin’ to the old man and the old man told him I wanted one. And if Santy Claus was talkin’ to the old man, it means the old man’s alive, don’t it?”

Much of this was beyond me until Chester explained further.

“Last time the old man was home I seed some oranges in a store window, but he wouldn’t get me one because if he buys stuff in stores he can’t go on being a seaman. To be a seaman you got to wash out your insides with rum every day and rum costs lots of money. Anyhow, store oranges ain’t real.”

“How do you know they aren’t?”

“My old man says so. He’s been in Portugal and he picks real ones off trees. That’s where they come from. Not from stores. Only my old man and the people who live in Portugal has ever ett real oranges.”

Someone called and Chester disappeared into the basement. A hour or so later, after we had eaten the supper he brought to us on a tray, my father told me to bring the wallet from the pocket of his uniform which was hanging in the cupboard. He gave me some small change and sent me to buy grapes for my mother at a corner fruit store. When I came back with the grapes I met Chester in the outer hall. His face was beaming and he was carrying a parcel wrapped in brown paper.

“Your old man gave me a two-dollar bill,” he said. “I got my old lady a Christmas present.”

I asked him if it was medicine.

“She don’t like medicine,” he said, “When she’s feelin’ bad she wants rum.”

When I got back to our room I didn’t tell my father what Chester had done with his two dollars. I hung up my stocking on the old-fashioned mantelpiece, the lights were put out, and I was told to go to sleep.

An old flickering arc light hung in the street almost directly in front of the hotel, and as I lay in the dark pretending to be asleep the ceiling seemed to be quivering, for the shutters fitted badly and the room could never be completely darkened. After a time I heard movement in the room, then saw a shadowy figure near the mantelpiece. I closed my eyes tight, heard the swish of tissue paper, then the sounds of someone getting back into bed. A foghorn, blowing in the harbour and heralding bad weather, was also audible.

After what seemed to me a long time I heard heavy breathing from the bed. I got up, crossed the room carefully, and felt the stocking in the dark. My fingers closed on a round object in its toe. Well, I thought, one orange would be better than none.

In those days hardly any children wore pyjamas, at least not in Nova Scotia. And so a minute later, when I was sneaking down the dimly lit hall of the hotel in a white nightgown, heading for the basement stairs with the orange in my hand, I was a fairly conspicuous object. Just as I was putting my hand to the knob of the basement door I heard a tapping sound and ducked under the main stairs that led to the second floor of the hotel. The tapping came near, stopped, and I knew somebody was standing still, listening, only a few feet away.

A crispy voice said, "You naughty boy, come out of there."

I waited a moment and then moved into the hall. Mrs. Urquhart was standing before me in her black dress and white cap, one hand on the handle of her cane.

"You ought to be ashamed of yourself, at this hour of the night. Go back to your room at once!"

As I went back up the hall I was afraid the noise had wakened my father. The big door creaked as I opened it and looked up at the quivering maze of shadows on the ceiling. Somebody on the bed was snoring and it seemed to be all right. I slipped into my cot and waited for several minutes, then got up again and replaced the orange in the toe of the stocking and carefully put the other gifts on top of it. As soon as I reached my cot again I fell asleep with the sudden fatigue of children.

The room was full of light when I woke up, not sunlight but the grey luminosity of filtered light reflected off snow. My parents were sitting up in bed, and Chester was standing inside the door with our breakfast.

My father was trying to smile under his bandages, and Chester had a grin so big it showed the gap in his front teeth. The moment I had been worrying about was finally here.

The first thing I must do was display enthusiasm for my parents' sake. I went to my stocking and emptied it on my cot while Chester watched me out of the corner of his eye. Last of all the orange rolled out.

"I bet it ain't real," Chester said.

My parents said nothing as he reached over and held it up to the light.

"No," he said. "It ain't real," and dropped it on the cot again. Then he put his hand into his pocket and with an effort managed to extract a medium-sized orange. "Look at mine," he said. "Look what it says right here."

On the skin of the orange, printed daintily with someone's pen, were the words, PRODUCE OF PORTUGAL.

"So my old man's been talkin' to Santy Claus, just like Mrs. Urquhart said."

There was never any further discussion in our family about whether Santa Claus was or was not real. Perhaps Mrs. Urquhart was the actual cause of my neurosis. I'm not a scientist, so I don't know.

The Authors

MILTON ACORN was born in Charlottetown in 1923 and lived on the island until 1951, at which time he moved to Montreal. Among his many poetry collections, *I've Tasted My Blood* (1969) is one of his best known, but it was *The Island Means Minago* (1975) that won the Governor General's Award. In 1981 he returned to Prince Edward Island, where he lived until his death five years later.

ELSIE CHARLES BASQUE was born in 1916. A teacher, elder, and advocate for native culture, she was the first Mi'kmaw in Nova Scotia to obtain a teaching license. She spent much of her life in Boston, and now resides in Saulnierville, Nova Scotia.

BERT BATSTONE, born in 1922, grew up in an isolated Newfoundland hamlet, where, he has said, "life in the village was virtually unchanged from what it had been more than one hundred years before." When he left Newfoundland, he earned degrees from Mount Allison and McGill universities. *The Mysterious Mummer and Other Newfoundland Stories* was published by Jesperson Press in 1984.

PAUL BOWDRING is a novelist, poet, editor, and teacher; he was born on Bell Island in Conception Bay, Newfoundland. He is the author of two novels, *The Roncesvalles Pass* (1989) and *The Night Season* (1997). He was also a long-time editor of *TickleAce*, a literary magazine. He lives in St. John's, Newfoundland.

HARRY BRUCE was born in Toronto and made his home in Nova Scotia from 1971 until his recent move to Moncton, New Brunswick. He is a celebrated essayist, editor, journalist, and writer, with a dozen books to his credit, including *An Illustrated History of Nova Scotia* (1997) and *Down Home: Notes of a Maritime Son* (1988). In 1997 he won the Evelyn Richardson Prize for Non-Fiction, nearly twenty years after it was first awarded to him.

CAROL BRUNEAU hails from Halifax. She is the author of two short story collections, *After Angel Mill* (1995) and *Depth Rapture* (1998). She is best known for her first novel, *Purple for Sky* (2000), which won the Thomas Head Raddall Atlantic Fiction Award and the Dartmouth Book Award in 2001.

ERNEST BUCKLER was born at Dalhousie West, Nova Scotia, in 1908. Best known for his novel, *The Mountain and the Valley* (1952), he also wrote short fiction, essays, and a memoir. His work of verse and prose, *Whirligig* (1977), won the Stephen Leacock Award. He was also awarded several honorary degrees for his contribution to literature. He died in 1984.

HERMÉNÉGILDE CHIASSON holds a PhD from the Sorbonne and a master's degree in Fine Arts from the State University of New York. He is a writer, multidisciplinary artist, film director, and advocate for Acadian culture. Three of his books have been nominated for the Governor General's Award; he won this award for *Conversations* (1999). In 2003, he was appointed Lieutenant-Governor of New Brunswick. He lives in Grand Barachois and Fredericton, New Brunswick.

JOAN CLARK was born in Liverpool, Nova Scotia. She writes novels, short fiction, and novels for young adults. She has won numerous awards, including the Marian Engel Award, the Canadian Authors' Association Literary Award, the Mr. Christie Award, and the Jeffrey Bilson Award. Her most recent novel is *Latitudes of Melt* (2000). She lives in St. John's, Newfoundland.

MICHAEL CRUMMEY was born in Buchans, Newfoundland. His debut novel, *River Thieves* (2001), was nominated for the Giller Prize and won the Winterset Award, the Thomas Head Raddall Atlantic Fiction Award, and the Atlantic Booksellers' Choice Award. He also won acclaim for *Flesh and Blood* (1998), a book of short fiction. His most recent collection of poetry is *Salvage* (2002). He lives in St. John's, Newfoundland.

RICHARD CUMYN was born in Ottawa and has lived in Halifax for many years. He has written a novella, *The View from Tamischeira* (2003), as well as four short story collections, of which *The Obstacle Course* (2002) is his most recent. He is also Fiction Editor of *The Antigonish Review*.

HERB CURTIS was raised near Blackville, on the Miramachi, and now lives in Fredericton, New Brunswick. His collection of short fiction, *Luther Corhern's Salmon Camp Chronicles* (1999), was nominated for the Stephen Leacock Award. *The Last Tasmanian* (1991, 2001), one of four novels, garnered the Thomas Head Raddall Atlantic Fiction Award and was a regional finalist for the Commonwealth Writers' Prize.

LYNN DAVIES grew up in Moncton, New Brunswick, and spent sixteen years in Nova Scotia before returning to her home province. Her first collection of poetry, *The Bridge That Carries the Road* (1999), was nominated for the Governor General's Award. She also writes children's stories. She lives in McLeod Hill, New Brunswick, near Fredericton.

STAN DRAGLAND was born in Alberta. He taught at the University of Western Ontario, and after taking early retirement, he moved to St. John's, Newfoundland. He was a founding editor of *Brick, A Journal of Reviews*, and he also co-founded Brick Books, a poetry press, with Don McKay. He has published fiction, poetry, and literary criticism.

RHODA GRASER writes fiction and non-fiction. She was born in Fredericton and lived there during the Depression and World War II. A number of her stories were published in *The New Brunswick Reader* in 2000. She lives in Toronto.

WILFRED GRENFELL was born in Parkgate, England, in 1865. He studied medicine and later volunteered to go to Newfoundland and Labrador, where he quickly gained great respect among the people. He established a mission, an orphanage, and a school at St. Anthony, Labrador. His tale *Adrift on an Ice Pan* (1908, 1992) is an account of how he was stranded overnight on the ice. He died in 1941.

ELISABETH HARVOR, a poet, short story writer, and novelist, grew up in New Brunswick's Kennebecasis Valley. One of her three short story collections, *Let Me Be the One* (1996), was a finalist for the Governor General's Award. She won the Gerald Lampert Memorial Award for her first book of poetry, *Fortress of Chairs* (1992). In 2000, she published her first novel, *Excessive Joy Injures the Heart*.

RONALD F. HAWKINS was born in Woodstock, New Brunswick, in 1923. He enlisted in the Carleton Light Infantry when he was only fourteen. By the time he was discharged from the army in 1946, he had seen action in North Africa and throughout Europe. He wrote several books about the war, including *We Will Remember Them* (1995). He died in 2002.

MARK ANTHONY JARMAN teaches fiction at the University of New Brunswick in Fredericton. A graduate of the Iowa Writers' Workshop, he has had stories shortlisted for such awards as the Journey Prize, the Pushcart Prize Anthology, and the O. Henry Prize. He has published a novel, *Salvage King, Ya!* (1998), and short fiction, of which *19 Knives* (2000) is his most recent collection. He has also published a work of non-fiction, *Ireland's Eye* (2002).

WAYNE JOHNSTON was born in Goulds, Newfoundland. He has written five novels, of which *The Navigator of New York* (2002) is the latest. His previous novel, *The Colony of Unrequited Dreams* (1998), was nominated for the most prestigious fiction awards in Canada; it won the Thomas Raddall Atlantic Fiction Prize and the Canadian Authors' Association Award for Fiction. His memoir, *Baltimore's Mansion* (1999), was awarded the Charles Taylor Prize for Literary Non-Fiction.

GRACE LADD was born in Yarmouth, Nova Scotia, in 1864. She spent many years travelling around the world with her husband, Frederick Arthur Ladd, a Nova Scotian sea captain. Their children, Forrest and Kathryn, were raised on board ship. Her letters to her family offer a rich account of a life aboard sailing ships and steamers during the Victorian era.

HUGH MACLENNAN was born in Glace Bay, Nova Scotia in 1907. A novelist and essayist, he became a Rhodes Scholar at Oxford and later completed a PhD in classics at Princeton. He won the Governor General's Award more often than any other writer: three times for fiction and twice for non-fiction. His best-known novels are *Barometer Rising* (1941), *Two Solitudes* (1945), and *The Watch that Ends the Night* (1959). He died in 1990.

ALISTAIR MACLEOD was born in North Battleford, Saskatchewan, in 1936, and grew up in Cape Breton, Nova Scotia. He taught for many years at the University of Windsor. He is known for his short fiction – *As Birds Bring Forth the Sun* (1986) and *The Lost Salt Gift of Blood* (1976) – and his novel, *No Great Mischief* (1999). This novel won the International IMPAC Dublin Literary Award in 2001.

LUCY MAUD MONTGOMERY was born in Clifton (now New London), Prince Edward Island, in 1874. Her first novel, *Anne of Green Gables* (1908), was followed by more than twenty others. Long after her death in 1942, she remains one of Canada's most beloved writers.

LISA MOORE has written for radio and television; she has also written art criticism. She studied at the Nova Scotia School of Art and Design in Halifax, and now lives in St. John's, Newfoundland. Her first book of short fiction, *Degrees of Nakedness* (1995), was followed by a second, *Open* (2002), which was nominated for the Giller Prize.

BERNICE MORGAN was born in 1935 in pre-Confederation Newfoundland. She is best known for her two novels, *Random Passage* (1992) and *Waiting for Time* (1994). *Random Passage* was made into a mini-series for CBC television. Her most recent book is *The Topography of Love* (2000). She lives in St. John's, Newfoundland.

ALDEN NOWLAN was born in Windsor, Nova Scotia, in 1933. Though he was largely self-taught, he was a prolific writer who published poetry, plays, short stories, and novels. He received a Governor General's Award in 1967 for *Bread, Wine and Salt* (1967), and in the same year won a Guggenheim Fellowship. He became the writer-in-residence at the University of New Brunswick in 1969, a position he held until his death in 1983.

MARY PRATT was born in Fredericton in 1935. She received a Bachelor of Fine Arts degree from Mount Allison University in 1961. One of Canada's pre-eminent realist painters, she received the prestigious Molson Prize in 1997. She has written a book of personal reflections, *A Personal Calligraphy* (2000).

SIR CHARLES G.D. ROBERTS was born in Douglas, New Brunswick, in 1860. He attended the University of New Brunswick and later worked as a professor at King's College, situated at that time in Windsor, Nova Scotia. A pre-eminent member of the Confederation Poets, he was noted for his many poetry books and animal stories, as well as for more traditional fiction and non-fiction. He died in 1943.

DAVID ADAMS RICHARDS was born in 1950 in Newcastle, New Brunswick; by the time he was twenty-one he had written his first novel. He writes fiction, non-fiction, plays, screenplays, and poetry. He has won Governor General's Awards for both fiction and non-fiction. *Nights Below Station Street* (1988), *The Bay of Love and Sorrows* (1998), and *Mercy Among the Children* (2000) are among his best-known novels. His most recent novel is *River of the Brokenhearted* (2003).

DAVID WEALE, a professor of history at the University of Prince Edward Island, is a master storyteller. He has written six books, among them *An Island Christmas Reader* (1994) and *The True Meaning of Crumbfest* (1999). He has toured his stage shows, *A Long Way from the Road* (1998) and *Greenmount Boy* (2000), across the Island.

Acknowledgements

"Sky's Poem For Christmas," from *Dig Up My Heart* by Milton Acorn (1969), used by permission, McClelland & Stewart Ltd. *The Canadian Publishers*. "The Radio," by Elsie Charles Basque, from *The Mi'kmaq Anthology*, ed. Rita Joe and Lesley Choyce (Laurencetown Beach: Pottersfield Press, 1997), reprinted by permission. "The Mysterious Mummer," by Bert Batstone, from *The Mysterious Mummer and Other Newfoundland Stories* (St. John's: Jesperson Press, 1984), reprinted by permission. "Noseworthy (Est. 1929)," by Paul Bowdring, from *The Night Season* (St. John's: Killick Press, 1997), reprinted by permission. "Midnight Gossip," by Harry Bruce, © 2001, first appeared in *Saltscape* (Nov.-Dec. 2001); reprinted by permission of the author. "Silver Bells," first published in *Purple for Sky*, by Carol Bruneau (2000), reprinted by permission of Cormorant Books Inc., Toronto. "The Still of Christmas," from *The Mountain and the Valley,* by Ernest Buckler (1952, 1993), used by permission, McClelland & Stewart Ltd. *The Canadian Publishers*. "White as a Sheet," by Herménégilde Chiasson, translated by Wayne Grady, from *Available Light* (Douglas & McIntyre, 2002), reprinted by permission; originally published in 2000 as *Brunante* by XYZ éditeur; copyright © 2000 by XYZ éditeur and Herménégilde Chiasson, translation © 2002 by Wayne Grady. "Merry Christmas, Nancy Rose," extracted from *Latitudes of Melt* by Joan Clark, copyright © 2000 by Joan Clark, reprinted by permission of Alfred A. Knopf Canada. "What Possessed Him," extracted from *Flesh and Blood* by Michael Crummey, copyright © 1998 by Michael Crummey Ink, expanded Anchor edition 2003; reprinted by permission of Doubleday Canada. "Sarasota," by Richard Cumyn, from *I Am Not Most Places* (Vancouver: Beach Holme, 1996), reprinted by permission. "Thirsts of the Soul," by Herb Curtis, from *Luther Corhern's Salmon Camp Chronicles* (Fredericton: Goose Lane Editions, 1999), reprinted by permission. Excerpt from "Composing Winter," by Lynn Davies, © 2000, published by permission of the author. "Serpent's Tooth," by Stan Dragland, © 2003, published by permission of the author. "A Tale of Three Stockings without Holes," by Rhoda Graser, © 2000, first appeared in *The New Brunswick Reader* (Dec. 23, 2000); published by permission of the author. "How Santa Claus Came to Cape St. Anthony," by

Wilfred Grenfell, from *Christmas in Canada* (Toronto: J.M. Dent, 1959, 1972). "Four O'Clock, New Year's Morning, New River Beach," by Elizabeth Harvor, from *Fortress of Chairs* (Montreal: Signal Editions, Véhicule Press, 1992), reprinted by permission. "Noisy Afternoon — Silent Night," by Ronald F. Hawkins, from *We Will Remember Them* (Saint John: Imagesetting, 1995), reprinted by permission. "Cougar," by Mark Jarman, from *19 Knives* (Toronto: Anansi, 2000), reprinted by permission. "Draper Doyle's Debut," from *The Divine Ryans,* by Wayne Johnston (1990, 1998), used by permission, McClelland & Stewart Ltd. *The Canadian Publishers*. "An Orange from Portugal," by Hugh MacLennan, from *The Other Side of Hugh MacLennan* (Toronto: Macmillan, 1978), reprinted with permission of McGill University. "Winter Dog," from *As Birds Bring Forth the Sun and Other Stories,* by Alistair MacLeod (1986), used by permission, McClelland & Stewart Ltd. *The Canadian Publishers*. "The Chalice," by Lisa Moore, ©2002, first appeared in *The Globe and Mail* (Dec. 24, 2002); published by permission of the author. "Christmas Fortunes," by Bernice Morgan, from *Random Passage* (1992), published with the permission of Breakwater, St. John's, Newfoundland, copyright the author. "The Kneeling of the Cattle," by Alden Nowlan, from *Various Persons Named Kevin O'Brien* (Toronto: Clarke, Irwin, 1973), reprinted by permission of Claudine Nowlan. "Christmas Aboard the *Belmont*," by Grace F. Ladd, from *Quite a Curiosity: The Sea Letters of Grace F. Ladd*, ed. Louise Nicols (Halifax: Nimbus Publishing, 2003), reprinted by permission of Nimbus Publishing and of the Yarmouth County Museum Archives. "Katherine Brooke Comes to Green Gables" is excerpted from *Anne of Windy Poplars*, by L.M. Montgomery, with the permission of Ruth Macdonald and David Macdonald, trustees, who are the heirs of L.M. Montgomery; *L.M. Montgomery* is a trademark of Heirs of L.M. Montgomery Inc. *Anne of Green Gables*, characters, names, and related indicia are trademarks and/or Canadian official marks of the Anne of Green Gables Licensing Authority Inc., which is located in Charlottetown, Prince Edward Island. "The Far-Away Present," by Mary Pratt, from *A Personal Calligraphy* (Fredericton: Goose Lane, 2000), reprinted by permission. "The Tale of a Tree," by David Adams Richards, © 2000, originally appeared in *The Globe and Mail* (Dec. 23, 2000); reprinted by permission of the author. "The Homeward Trail," by Charles G.D. Roberts, from *The Watchers of the Trails* (Boston: L.C. Page, 1904). "The Eaton's Beauty," from *An Island Christmas Reader* (Charlottetown: Acorn Press, 1994), and "The Christmas Orange," from *Them Times*, (Charlottetown: Institute of Island Studies, 1992), by David Weale, reprinted by permission.